ELYSIUM

Also by Robert M. Bersi:

"Boys Unto Men"
"Jack and Jill: The Voyage"
"Jack and Jill"
"Silver Mountain"
"Armed and Abandoned"
"Mount Parnassus"
"Raising Margaret Ann"
"Shaping our Environment"
"Restructuring the Baccalaureate"
"A Short History of Philanthropy in America"

ELYSIUM

*A STATE OR PLACE OF PERFECT BLISS

ROBERT M. BERSI

Contents

"Grandfather, what is true love?" The little girl was looking up at the old man who had been scattering bread crumbs. The birds were crowding about their bench, cooing and pecking at the grass.

"My goodness," he said, continuing to crumble the dry crusts in his hand. "What a big question from such a small person."

"Does it hurt?"

"What have you been reading?" He was looking down at her now, smiling indulgently.

"Well, does it?" She persisted.

"No, no, not true love, never."

"Why?"

"Because it gives everything and asks nothing." They had risen now and were walking hand in hand towards an ice cream vendor.

"It sounds nice." She grasped the cone that he handed her. "Will I find it?"

"It must find you."

"I don't understand," she sighed, shrugging her shoulders as if tiring of the subject.

"You will, someday."

They paused to watch the swans swimming gracefully in pairs about the grand pond. It was a splendid day to be in Letniy Park. After a long winter, spring had finally come to Leningrad.

PROLOGUE

The old man stirred and made a sound. The woman sleeping fitfully in the armchair next to him wakened with a start and grasping the metal guard rail of his hospital bed rose quickly to her feet. Moving the I.V. tubes aside with her forearm she straightened the rumpled sheets, carefully tucking them over his bare shoulders. She leaned closer, peering at his face in the dawn light searching for signs of discomfort. His breathing seemed to have grown more labored. Gently touching the artery on his neck she strained to get a pulse. Much too feeble and erratic, she decided, and pressed the nurse call button. A few moments passed and she turned, exited the room, and headed for the nurses' station. They would be busy preparing to change shifts.

"Zoya!" A tall, balding man dressed in a tuxedo with a stethoscope dangling from his pocket caught her by the shoulders, avoiding a collision. "Where's the fire?" E. Francis Blair, M.D. and one of their dearest friends, looked down on her.

"Frank, my God." She was obviously startled. "Where did you come from? What are you doing here at this time of the morning?"

"I'm a cardiologist, remember. Been here since midnight. Back to back emergencies. Abandoned poor Kate on the dance floor, but she's used to it after all these years." He shrugged his shoulders. "I'm on my way down to the O.R. to change and scrub for a procedure. Thought I'd check on Jack. You've been here all night obviously."

Zoya nodded, brushing her hair back with one hand. "Frank, do you have a moment? Jack's breathing is..." He had already stepped past her into the room. Standing next to the bed he moved his stethoscope over the sleeping man's chest. Then rolling him on his side he listened through the back for half a moment, and gently resettled him. He took her by the elbow and moved to the doorway near the lighted hall.

"He came in when, three days ago?"

"Yes," she answered. "He was feeling so exhausted after the birthday party. So Jim Bradley admitted him for a few day's observation and tests."

He glanced at his wristwatch and frowned. "Well, I looked at his chart on the way in and they hadn't come up with anything specific as of last night when Brad made rounds. Were you here? Did you get a chance to speak with him?"

She nodded. "Like you said, nothing specific. He seemed concerned though."

"Where are the twins?"

"Angelique is driving up from Stanford. Max is at the airport meeting my mother. She's flying in from London today."

Blair reached for the phone near the nurses' station. "I'm paging Brad, Zoya. I think he'll want to get over here right away. Go back and stay with Jack. I'll speak with the floor nurse on my way out."

While she waited anxiously, she fussed over him. She could see that he was in pain and trying not to show it. He seemed to struggle for every breath. As she placed a damp washcloth on his forehead he motioned her closer and whispered into her ear. She kissed him on the cheek. Lowering the side rail, she sat on the bed and reclined, embracing him in her arms. Pressing her cheek to his she began to speak softly, rocking him ever so gently. Thus entwined, they slipped away. She, in dreamless exhaustion, and he, blissfully transported to when it all began.

ONE

Lillian Baxter Holt sat alone in the elegant dining room of New York City's Plaza Hotel. The wealthy and socially prominent matriarch of a venerable northeastern family, she was not accustomed to being kept waiting. She glanced at her watch, sighed, and motioned to a passing waiter.

"Madam?"

"Vodka martini, up." As the waiter turned to leave she noticed Jack Stark being led to her table. "Make that two." She added.

"Lillian, sorry I'm late." Jack took his seat and nodded to his escort.

"You're not. I'm early. I'm never early, Jack."

"Ah, Madam Chair, some members of the board have been at you..."

"Not some, all. They're a bit shocked and disappointed."

"I doubt that Lillian. After all, it has been more than seven years."

"So you're determined to leave us."

"It's a personal decision."

"Well you're right there, Jack. I'm taking it very personally. I was one of the new bunch just appointed to the board when Trent Budreau pushed you for the presidency. On paper you certainly didn't fit the ivy profile we were accustomed to. However, as Chair, Budreau made a convincing case that the college was headed for troubled times and that you possessed all the requisite skills to turn things around."

"And how did I do in your opinion?"

"Well, you turned us on our heads. Brockton blossomed into a university and things are humming. Hell, that doesn't even describe it; you hit one home run after the other, Jack. But my point is, we weren't convinced of that when we voted to bring you in. Truth be told, it was your new bride that brought the gravitas that tipped the scales for many of us."

"Yes I know. That was quite obvious to me from the very beginning."

"Not that we ever saw much of her." Lillian elevated her chin.

"Everyone knew Joelle was a world renowned concert violinist. You all celebrated it."

"Yes, yes, of course. But that globe hopping life she led. It must have been a challenge for you and the boy."

Jack looked away.

"Oh dear. Forgive me. I didn't mean to…"

"It's all right, Lillian. It's been more than a year. I've made my peace with it."

She sighed. "Yes, one tries… I know. But then there's the little girl. She must be…"

"Two, this August. Since the divorce she lives in Brussels with her mother and grandparents. Joelle plans to restrict her concerts to the capitals of Europe."

They were interrupted by the arrival of the vodka martinis.

"I don't drink at lunch, Lillian… and never martinis. You know that."

"Of course I do, Jack. But a lady simply does not order two at the same time for herself. But please, go on by all means."

He studied her for a moment. "Lillian, my departure surely can't come as a disappointment to many on the board. It serves everyone well. The university is in exceptionally good shape and, as such, it's an appropriate time for a CEO to make a move. Your public relations people have an abundance of things they can point to with pride."

"Yes, yes, all right." She drew herself up and struck the table with the flat of her hand. "But of all places Jack… Nevada? It's a goddam desert! You won't last six months."

Seven Years Later

Jack Stark stood, hands in his pockets, staring out the window at the Manhattan skyline. The spectacular view from the upper floor of the World Trade Center tower almost made up for the fact that he really hadn't wanted to make this third trip in as many weeks to New York City. The underwriters had insisted that protocol required the Chancellor of the Nevada state university system be physically present to sign the $200,000,000 higher education bond issue. The Nevada Governor and his entourage would be present. However, since the state's university system was a constitutional fourth branch of government, Chancellor Stark's signing was a legal imperative. Cameras flashed, recording the smiles and obligatory handshakes. Attending dignitaries received elegant commemorative Italian leather cases embossed with the state seal and their name in gold leaf. The underwriters pocketed $6,750,000 in fees.

As the champagne corks popped, Jack handed his case to an aide and distanced himself from the celebrants to a quiet corner of the room where he stood surveying the great city from the top of the world. It was his fifty-fifth birthday, and thanks to the distractions of the day, no one had noticed and that suited him. His tall, athletic good looks belied the stress and demands of his job, and as he peered out the window his mind was on earlier, easier days. He'd phoned his mother, Angelique, at precisely 3:47 A.M. California time, and thanked her for enduring the breach birth that brought him into the world. She'd been up, brewing coffee, waiting for his call. It had been an unbroken ritual for as long as they could remember. His father, Gus, had been deceased for nearly three years, but they always spoke of him as if he were still among them. Angelique and his father enjoyed a lifelong love that also profoundly influenced their son.

John 'Jack' Stark was born and reared to young manhood in a family filled with passion. His father, Gustavo 'Gus' Stark, eloped with Angelique Piazza, the daughter of a prominent Swiss Italian family. Whisking her from St. Louis to north central California caused such uproar that no one even thought to study the marriage license or tally the months until the birth of her son.

The Stark family did not share the distinguished position in the Swiss Italian community held by Angelique's father, Franco Piazza. Gus was the rough and tumble son of one of the city's most notorious professional gamblers. Angelo Stark was a brute, both in physical stature and demeanor, who insisted on referring to himself as merely a "Businessman".

His wife, Katerina, was little more than house-bound chattel and dutiful stewardess of his meek younger son, Virgil. Gus, the elder, was a virtual bond servant to the old man and his ventures. By fifteen Gus was six feet tall, hard as granite, street-wise, and determined to get out. One moonless night he kissed his stoic, tearless mother on the cheek, and grasping the bundle she had prepared for him, slipped away: his destination, U.S. Marine Corps Barracks, Parris Island, South Carolina. It would be twelve years before anyone heard from or saw him again.

Angelique would always willingly retell the story of her first sight of him. Home from her freshman year of college, she had succumbed to the pleadings of her younger brother to let him drive her new Ford Roadster to a neighborhood dance. She could even come with him to ensure its safe return. She recalls not bothering to wear her best dress.

Still in uniform, Gus was leaning slightly on a cane, a tall bronze god with piercing steel-grey eyes. A girlfriend whispered his name in Angelique's ear and giggled. Throughout her childhood she had heard her father, Franco, telling notorious Stark anecdotes at the family dinner table. Her eyes were still on him when he caught sight of her. She turned her head away quickly.

"He's coming this way," her friend gasped. Indeed, he had broken away from the small circle surrounding him and was making directly for them.

"Dance with me?" He was smiling. She sensed that it was more of a command than a request. She caught her breath.

"Angelique Piazza, isn't it? You probably don't remember me. Gus Stark. Our families were acquainted some years ago."

"Yes," she responded, "I ..."

"Good," he interrupted, and slipping his arm about her waist, moved into the stream of dancers. The cane was dangling from his left forearm.

"Doesn't it hurt?" she managed to ask as he whirled her about the floor.

"Yes," he said softly.

Approximately a year later, in far off California, a baby boy was born to Gus and Angie Stark. Franco and Caroline Piazza threw open their hearts and arms to their errant daughter and her new family. After a month-long visit to St. Louis, Gus Stark respectfully declined his wealthy father-in-law's job offer and returned to California. There, on a modest grape farm, in a beautiful valley, Jack grew up in a world he shared with Gus and Angelique. Hard work was respected, as were all who were a part of it. And the man who had seen the worst of this world, and the woman who loved him, sought to ground their son in durable values. Jack learned to humble himself to the culture and language of the men who worked beside him in the fields. Gus, the former U.S. Marine Corps Pacific Fleet light heavy weight champion, taught his son self-defense, honor, and to choose peace over conflict whenever possible.

They were a pair, Gus and Angie, passionately in love every day of their lives. Young Jack liked to watch them as they stood on the porch after dinner, looking out over the land. His mother would always lean into his father, stroking his shoulder, while his arm slipped around her waist and drew her closer to him. The boy could not help but believe that it must be this way everywhere, with everyone, always.

Jack was jolted from his thoughts by the voice of his legislative aide. "Chancellor, the Governor's party is leaving."

"Thanks, Brendon." Jack turned and walked quickly, intercepting the cluster of figures now moving toward the elevators.

"There he is," the Governor called out, extending both arms. "Nevada's economic ambassador." He draped one arm around Jack's shoulder and turned to the smiling New York bankers. "This guy is a one man chamber of commerce," he declared, tightening his grip on Jack. "Why, together we've double-teamed a hell of a batch of business to home." Jack could see that the champagne and the altitude had obviously kicked in. "Hell," the Governor went on as they stepped into the elevator. "He speaks four languages, including Russian." He looked up at Jack who played along by rattling off a few lines in the language. There was a burst of laughter as they rocketed downward. In the main foyer of the tower everyone again offered their congratulations along with farewell handshakes and began to disperse.

The senior member of the banking team, James Talbot, turned to Jack as they walked. "So, you do indeed speak Russian?"

"Yes," Jack responded, "It's a bit rusty. Not much opportunity in Nevada. Why?"

"Well, we're hosting a rather posh reception this evening for a group of businessmen from Moscow, very high level. If you have no other plans, perhaps you might wish to ..."

Jack broke in. "I appreciate the invitation, Jim, but I'm booked on a flight this evening to Chicago, then on to Reno two days later. Sorry."

"That's a shame. I know you'd enjoy this Russian delegation and you would certainly be free to work the crowd for Nevada." He paused. "And quite honestly, Chancellor, we would appreciate having someone with your credentials who understands the language and the culture on our team for the evening. Our corporate jets shuttle regularly to the west coast. We'd be happy to drop you off in Chicago and when you're finished with your business there, take you on to Nevada. I would even offer to compensate you for your time if you stay over this evening, but we both know that would be imprudent in light of the business we just transacted upstairs."

Jack laughed. "You don't know Nevada. But, personally, I agree. If I arrange to stay over let's simply say you'll owe me a favor."

"Then you'll join us?" He was obviously pleased.

"I will," Jack answered with a smile. "I hate commercial air travel these days."

"Very well, then. A limo will call for you this evening at seven. And as to that favor, Dr. Stark, no problem. I've seen the movie."

Jack spent the rest of the day on the phone or working at his desk in the hotel. As the limo picked him up that evening, he was still preoccupied with events unfolding in Carson City. When the Nevada legislature was in session one should never, never, wander far from home. That was his rule, and this trip was the third time he had broken it in a month. Not that there had been much of a choice considering the bonding timetable, but he'd kept his absences off the radar by spending more time in the air than on the ground in New York. He would red-eye from Nevada, attend the requisite meetings in Manhattan and return that evening in time to knock back a few drinks with the committee chairs of Ways and Means or Senate Finance. As the legislative session ground on, everyone in the game accepted thorough exhaustion as the price one paid to play. As long as you wore a fresh shirt and smelled good no one particularly noticed that you were an empty suit. This trip had been different. He had scheduled three full days out and now with this Russian thing it would be four. But at least he felt rested and this evening would be the nearest thing to recreation that he'd had in months, so what the hell, he mused.

The limo came to a stop at the curb, and as the driver opened his door Jack stepped out to find himself back at the World Trade Towers. A smartly dressed woman standing close by was holding a small discreet sign bearing his name. As he approached her and nodded his head, she smiled and tucked the sign into a slim leather briefcase. "Good evening, Dr. Stark. I'm June Peebles, Mr. Talbot's assistant. Please allow me to escort you up." Jack was soon to learn that 'up' was the Windows on the World room at the very tip of the north tower. As the elevator neared its destination, his escort informed him that the guests had already arrived and that Mr. Talbot was waiting for him in the outer lounge.

"Chancellor," James Talbot greeted Jack as the elevator doors opened. The two shook hands and began walking toward the sounds of a string quartet competing with the chatter of the crowd. "If you don't object to the charade," he said softly, "would you be open to not revealing your fluency in Russian for a while?"

Jack looked at Talbot and smiled. "Just grin, nod, and listen, right? Okay, James, but it's still going to cost you."

"God," Talbot groaned under his breath. "You Nevada guys are as tough as the Russians."

"Not even close, my man," Jack said breaking into a practiced smile as they entered the room. "Not by a mile."

Talbot kept Jack close to his side as they worked the room together. Jack nodded and smiled, all the while complimenting the guests of honor on their clumsy English.

The savvy investment banker introduced the Chancellor as being from Las Vegas which engendered predictable interest from the guests. Jack mingled, listening to the Russians' side conversations, making mental notes and enjoying again the sound of a language he had labored so hard to master half a lifetime ago. Finally, finding himself alone and hungry, he made his way to an extravagant buffet table, pausing in front of a huge silver bowl filled with black caviar. "Enough Beluga to please a prince," he said softly to himself in Russian.

"*Hochitsa, da?*" (Tempting isn't it?) The woman's voice startled him, and he turned quickly to see a classic beauty with long, wavy auburn hair and stunning green eyes smiling at him. She was dressed conservatively in black pants and a short red jacket over a white silk blouse. Caught by surprise, he extended his hand and introduced himself in perfect Russian.

"Ah," she responded politely. "*Ti italianski, da?*" (You are Italian, yes?)

"*Nyet,*" Jack shook his head emphatically. "*Ya Amerikanitz.*" And then again in English as if to make his point, "No, I'm an American."

"I'm so sorry." She was obviously embarrassed, and now speaking English. "You speak Russian with an Italian accent, I just assumed ..."

"That's all right," Jack reassured her. "My instructors considered it an asset. It's a long story." He reached for the caviar, spooned it onto a small plate and offered it to her.

Taking the plate she carefully placed it on the table. "Here, let me show you." She took three pieces of thin toast the size of silver dollars and carefully spread them with butter and then a layer of caviar.

"There." She handed him the plate. "Try it that way, Russian style."

Jack, not wanting to speak while chewing, nodded his head in approval. She smiled back and turned to leave.

"You are with the delegation, then?" he asked quickly.

She paused. "Yes and no."

He waited a moment and then laughed. "That's a very Russian response. You probably already know who I am."

"Of course," she responded politely and walked away in the direction of the delegates and their hosts, stopping briefly to speak with June Peebles. Talbot, with a microphone in his hand, was about to make some remarks.

A short time later as the evening was drawing to a close, June took Jack aside, explaining that things had gone exceptionally well according to her boss and that they were very much in his debt. She and Talbot would be in touch and that Jack could expect to arrive in Chicago no later than 2:00 PM, central time.

"I noticed you speaking with Zoya at the buffet table," June said, as they stepped outside and waited for the limo to pull up. "I'm glad you got a chance to meet her."

"So that's her name." Jack quipped, "She's Soviet all right, cryptic as well as charming."

"Not exactly." Peebles followed Jack into the back seat of the limo. "She's definitely Russian, but she works for us at the corporate office."

On the way across town Jack got the whole story. Zoya Chalkin traced her lineage through generations of distinguished Russian scholars, including her mother who still served as professor of engineering/economics and Dean at the Academy of Science founded by Tzar Alexander I. Zoya graduated from the prestigious English School in

Leningrad, immigrated to the United States and earned a B.A. in economics from CCNY, Phi Beta Kappa. Talbot's investment banking group recruited her into its employee/ MBA program. June obviously had become her mentor and revealed that last month Zoya proudly raised her right hand and became a U.S. citizen and that this week she would graduate with honors from Columbia University Graduate School of Business, all while working full time at the bank. June laughed. "She's Russian to the core, but since coming to America she's become quite the little capitalist."

The limo had pulled to a stop in front of Jack's hotel. "Wow, and she's what, twenty-five or twenty-six?"

"Twenty-five." Peebles sighed. "I should hate her, but she's such a brilliant, hard-working kid."

"I'm not surprised," Jack observed. "A thousand years of Russian culture powers that young lady's engine. There's an old Russian saying: '*Bez muki, nyet nauki*', loose translation, no pain, no gain." Jack prepared to step out of the limo. "Not to mention she's drop dead gorgeous. Thanks for the ride."

"Men!" June exclaimed, closing the door and waving as the limo pulled into traffic.

TWO

Jack sat watching Andy Anderson devour the last morsel of a thirty-two ounce porterhouse. The dinner crowd at the Chicago Chop House was waning, and Jack had long since pushed aside his own unfinished plate. He was now patiently sipping the last of a good zinfandel while amusedly reflecting on his old friend's timeless love affair with prime blood-red beef.

"What?" Anderson looked up.

"Nothing," Jack smiled. "I was just thinking that aside from tomorrow's game, it was worth the trip out just to watch you attack that steak."

"Yeah, well, tomorrow will be a hell of a contest. And it wasn't easy getting those seats, I'll tell you."

"Really, I figured the gate was always open for you NCAA big shots."

"Hell no, that would be compromising, man! I had to put out for those tickets myself.'"

Jack laughed. "Not like the old days, huh, when you were a linebacker for the Saints."

"Well," Anderson admitted, "I did have to reach out to a brother who was connected, but it still cost me."

"Okay, so I'll get dinner." Jack reached for his wallet.

"Put your hand down. It's covered."

Jack smiled. "Expense account, huh. How big is it these days?"

"Bigger than yours," Anderson smirked, and swaggered in his seat.

Jack countered dismissively with a wave of his hand. "In your dreams."

"You boys will have to settle that somewhere else," a woman's voice interrupted. The two men looked up to find their tall full figured blonde waitress towering over them, notepad in hand. "How about desert? The peach cobbler's a big hit tonight." She raised an eyebrow, awaiting their response.

"He'll have the pie," Jack said indicating Anderson who had just forked in the last of his steak "A la mode, with coffee, and I'll have a brandy from the well."

"You got it," she snapped, tucking the pad into her waist band.

"They never really grow up," she muttered to herself as she turned and ambled away.

Anderson grunted, "I heard that," and followed her with his eyes as she skillfully navigated her ample booty through the crowded dining room. His attention finally returned to the table. "What the hell are you grinning about?"

"You, " Jack answered, shaking his head. "You haven't changed… any size, any shade. Forty-eight years old, and still an unwed pussy hound."

"Well, I like the life," Anderson shot back.

The waitress returned empty handed. "I'm sorry big guy, but the cobbler went fast tonight… only a couple of pieces left and they're pretty beat up. I thought I'd better ask."

"No problem," Anderson smiled up at her. "Just bring the check." He pushed back his chair and rose. "We'll be having a drink in the lounge."

They had finished their second brandy and were preparing to leave when their waitress finally found them and placed the dinner check on the bar. Anderson brushed Jack's hand aside and dropped his credit card on the plate. "You didn't really think we'd stiff you with this, did you, darlin'?"

She smiled for the first time. "No, not you guys, but it happens." She spun around, treating the two men to a hip-snapping departure. "Be back in a jiff."

Moments later, she returned. Anderson quickly signed the check, stood, and pressed a fifty dollar bill into her palm. "You don't remember me, do you Shirley?" He sighed, shook his head and taking Jack by the arm, guided them both out the door.

As the taxi pulled away, Jack turned to Anderson. "You old ass-bandit; you never met that girl before in your life."

Anderson feigned wounded surprise. "What makes you think that, my man?"

"Because I overheard you ask the bartender for her name."

"Okay, but when I'm in town again, she'll remember me. You know, Stark, you were a hell of lot more fun when we were raising hell in California. I'm starting to worry about you."

"Yeah," Jack responded wistfully, "So am I." He continued to stare out the window. Together, at the largest university in the California state system, then Vice President for Student Life, Andy Anderson and Executive Vice President, Jack Stark had regularly teamed to confront daunting situations with a brash, unconventional management style that was risky, usually effective, and always fun.

"Christ, buddy," Anderson mused, "How long has it been now, a lot of years, right?"

"Fourteen, last May. I'll never forget that afternoon when Potter simply walked of the commencement platform while the band was still playing. You and I stayed on under the canopy and watched it rain shit on the crowd."

Anderson laughed, shaking his head. "Goddam Tau Eps and their fucking manure catapult."

"You knew?"

"Hell yes... the whole time they were building the damn thing. Truth be told, I never thought they'd pull it off. They got away clean though, the clever little bastards. No one ever found a trace of that huge catapult. I heard it crossed over into Mexico on a flatbed."

"Why didn't you blow the whistle?"

"What for?" Anderson shrugged. "Everyone deserves to make a pyric statement. And they did go out with a bang." He chuckled and stared ahead blankly, as if recalling the chaotic scene that sunny afternoon. "And Potter; didn't he run off with his mistress or something?"

Jack nodded. "Yeah, well, it turned out to be a bigger deal than that. I understand that they live on an island she owns somewhere off the coast of Italy." He paused and smiled. "President Potter Ames... we all underestimated the old fox."

Anderson grunted. "Yep, then we bailed... me for Indianapolis and you for New York. We're all somewhere else now; just part of the legend." He turned to look directly at Jack. "What's with all the nostalgia, man? It doesn't sound like you. I hear they love your ass out there in Nevada. Is there a problem or something new you're not telling me?"

"No, just the usual bullshit. The people who count appreciate what I do. The rest don't matter."

"So, do you ever hear from Joelle?" Anderson leaned forward to rap on the passenger screen.

"No, not since she split for Europe eight years ago."

The cab pulled to the curb. They stepped out and began walking.

"How about the little girl… she must be nine or ten by now?"

"Yeah, that's about right, and a real prodigy… just like her mother. I understand they perform together now… they're all the rage over there. I could never be a part of her world, Andy. I accepted that reality eight years ago, and turned away."

"Oh that's raw, man. After all, you're her father."

"Actually Andy, that's just the point. According to Joelle, I'm not."

Bonnie McFall stepped through the partially opened door.

"Excuse me for breaking in, Chancellor, but there's a call you may wish to take." She glanced at the man sitting cross legged across from Stark. Hal Bostwick M.D., President of the Nevada College of Medicine, gave her a look of distain and continued his conversation.

"It's from New York, sir." Bonnie persisted, walking to Stark's desk and handing him a slip of paper. She stood waiting, ignoring Bostwick, as Jack read the note. Bonnie had her standards, and she let her boss know on more than one occasion that, in her opinion, Bostwick was a pompous jerk with plenty of baggage. Jack would listen patiently. Bostwick had come to Nevada a decade earlier from a prestigious northeastern medical school. The circumstances surrounding his move west remained somewhat obscure. Nevertheless, he wore his ivy league degrees like scout merit badges for all to see and admire. A widower, he married shortly after his arrival into one of Nevada's most respected families. When Jack assumed the chancellorship he recalls being counseled to tread lightly when dealing with Bostwick.

"We're pretty much done here, aren't we, Hal?" Jack rose and Bostwick sighed and reluctantly followed suit.

"Maybe we could finish up at lunch sometime later in the week," Stark suggested as Bostwick moved towards the door that Bonnie was now holding open.

"The Chancellor is booked for the rest of the week," she snapped, and ushered him out. Jack waited until the door closed completely, and then reached for the flashing line.

"Yes, hello, this is Jack Stark."

"Jack, hello! June Peebles here. I told your secretary this could wait, but she insisted on putting me through. She's so sweet."

"Well June, she can be, yes she can." Jack smiled as he pushed back his chair and threw one leg on to the corner of his desk. "How long has it been now, nearly a month?" He glanced at his watch. "Hey, you're working late back there, even for you."

"I'm calling from home, Jack. Listen, you're a busy guy, so let me get right to the point. I'm sure you remember meeting Zoya at the reception. We talked about her on the drive back to the hotel."

"Of course, I remember. She and I only spoke for a few moments. She was charming, and the background you gave me was very impressive. Why? What's up?"

"What I'm going to tell you has to remain between us, Jack, or it's my neck. Are we clear on that?"

"Absolutely, June. You have my word. Please, go ahead." Jack picked up a pen and yellow pad.

"Jim Talbot met with me a couple of days ago, and during our meeting he let something slip. It appears that Zoya is on the short list for something called a Feingold Fellowship."

Jack dropped his foot to the floor and sat up. "Christ, June, that's great. You guys must be so proud of her."

"Sure we are, officially. The company line is that we're always pleased when our people get recognized in some way."

"Recognized? Hell, June, a Feingold Fellowship. This is a full ride through the Ph.D. degree at any one of a half dozen of the most distinguished universities in the world. As I understand it, you can't apply for it and there are no interviews. The Foundation has its own methods of identifying and evaluating candidates. As I recall, they give out only a limited number of awards a year."

"That's why I wanted to talk with you, Jack. You're in a position to appreciate how big a deal this really is for Zoya."

"Well, June, let me put it another way. It's about as big a goddamn deal as any young person with Zoya's potential could possibly hope for. So what's the problem?"

"Jack, excuse my language but the assholes at the bank are going to block it. Zoya will never know, but it's clear to me that the boys upstairs intend for this not to happen."

"For Christ's sake, why?"

"I don't have a clue. I'm not in that close, but that's the deal unless someone with real juice does something. All I could think of doing was to call you."

Jack thought for a moment, searching for the right words to sidestep her request. "Gosh, June, I'm not sure that I'm in a position to help."

"You know people."

"June, I can see that this is really important to you, but…" Jack couldn't believe his own words. "Maybe I could ask around. No promises, you understand. Meanwhile, if you would provide me with whatever background data you folks have on her, it might prove helpful. Overnight it to my office, attention Bonnie McFall."

"I'm on it, and thanks, Jack." She was gone.

"Bonnie," Jack called out.

The office door opened enough for her to peer in. "You've got a buzzer, sir." In his seven years as Chancellor, he'd never used it, but she persisted.

"Bonnie, see if you can locate Abe Glassman for me. You know all the places he hangs out. Just find him and let me make the call personally." She nodded and ducked out, leaving the door ajar. It was 6:15 and the office was deserted. They often worked late together when things were quiet. Neither of them had family responsibilities any longer. She was a widow with no children, and Jack arrived alone and had stoically remained so. Bonnie knew as did everyone, that the topic was out of bounds.

"I found him." Bonnie was waving a slip of paper at Jack. "He's in Lake Las Vegas at the Spa." Jack took the paper, looked at the number, sighed, and began to dial.

"You can go home now, if you want," he said. "This may take a while."

"I'll stick around if you don't mind." She settled into a chair. "My nose tells me something interesting is going on. You may need me."

Jack shrugged. There were few secrets between them. "Abe!" Jack raised his voice. Abe Glassman was hard of hearing but neither he nor anyone else would acknowledge it. Now in his mid-eighties, he'd lived a fascinating life: smuggling arms and raising countless millions to aid the fledgling state of Israel. Along the way he managed to amass a communications empire. He was one of a dying breed, and for reasons of his own, he'd settled in Las Vegas. Glassman took his first measure of the new Chancellor when Jack, six years earlier, had defied a number of Nevada University Trustees by authorizing a forty-nine year lease of a small unusable corner of the Las Vegas Campus for the construction of a non-profit assisted care facility honoring Glassman's deceased wife.

"Abe," Jack repeated. "It's Jack Stark. Are you free to talk?"

"Jack, nothing in this life is free. I should have to tell you that?" The old man was laughing. "I'm sitting on my ass in the mud bath. You got me, so go ahead and talk."

"You sound well," Jack said with sincerity. "That warms my heart, Abe."

"Mazel tov. So, what's on your mind, Jack?"

"Have you ever heard of the Feingold Foundation, by any chance?"

"If you mean Jacob Feingold's thing in New York, yeah. I used to be on the Board of Directors. But I finally told Jake, hell, I can't be flying back there for meetings all the time. It's too tough on me."

Jack could hardly believe his ears. "Abe, the foundation I'm talking about awards scholarship grants for high end graduate work."

"Yeah, that was one of their deals. But I didn't have anything to do with it. We hired guys like you to make those decisions. I was on the endowment investment committee. We had to give away a shit-load of money every year. Jake was always getting excited about one thing or another."

"Is he still around? Are the two of you still in touch?"

"We'd better be. I'm going to his great-grandson's Bar Mitzvah next week. Sarah and David are coming with me. But why all this interest?"

"It's a long story, Abe. Maybe I shouldn't trouble you with it now. I can fly down tomorrow."

"Jack, I'm sitting here soaking in the mud. I'm bored. Tell me now. If you still want to fly down tomorrow, be my guest. I could use the company."

Jack went over the entire scenario in detail. Abe was especially curious about what Jack had overheard the Russians discussing. He gave the old man a few details. "Those bankers better be careful," Abe counseled. "Don't share any serious shit with them, Jack. Stay out of it."

"Don't worry, Abe. Butter wouldn't melt in my mouth."

"Smart boy. Now, this girl, Zoya Chalkin. Why would these asshole bankers want to screw her out of such an opportunity? Is she Jewish?"

"Who knows? The Feingold Foundation likes her for one of the awards. Somebody way up in the bank wants her out of the competition, and according to my inside source, they're going to shut her out. Abe, the only difference between this kid and us is a few generations. Our people were immigrants as well, who worked their asses off to make a good life here. With my family it was the fascists. With yours, it was pogroms in the Ukraine." Jack paused for a moment to let what he had said sink in. "She's swimming with the sharks with those bankers back there, Abe. She's busted her ass for these people."

"You sound pretty passionate about this, Jack. Are you sure it's worth all the effort?"

"Good question. I almost let it pass, but the more I think about it the more pissed I get. Those arrogant fuckers get nearly seven million dollars out of our bond deal and still find time to step on this kid's chance of a lifetime."

"Listen, Jack, they're telling me I have to get out of this tub now."

"Oh Abe, I've banged your ear too much about this." Jack feared he'd unduly burdened the old man.

"No, not at all. It's a fascinating story, and I want to hear more about the Russians. Jack, before we ring off, how's your health?"

"Everything still works, Abe."

The old man laughed. "You're such a damn mensch, taking time for this kid. I'm glad you called. And don't worry about New York. We'll talk again."

Bonnie had crept out during their phone conversation. Jack suddenly realized that he was sitting in the dark, his office lit only by the glow of the street lights below. He rocked back in his chair. The next few weeks would be heavy lifting. The legislative session was in its final, frantic days. Campus commencements would begin shortly thereafter. And the Trustees' bimonthly meeting was only twelve days away. He reached for the phone and dialed his widowed mother at the ranch in California, but there was no answer. She was in the habit of retiring early since Gus had passed. He rose with a sigh and walked slowly into the hall and down the two flights of stairs to the empty parking lot.

THREE

"I don't want to hear his goddamn reasons! I don't give a rat's ass about his fucking reasons!" State Senator Buck Stockwell's flushed face was only inches from Jack's as the two sat alone in the Senator's Carson City office. The Director of Rural Medical/Clinical Services, Dr. W. Barnard Kapp, was the topic at hand and Stockwell's rage was directed toward the President of the College of Medicine, Hal Bostwick. Apparently, Bostwick had just informed Kapp of his decision to phase out RM/CS and that Kapp should prepare to be out of a job. Bostwick, true to form, had consulted no one about his decision. While in Carson City, Jack had simply looked in on the Senator during the last days of the legislative session to swap jokes and thank the all-powerful Nevadan for his help and support. Things had gone very well this session for the nine campus university system. Stockwell as chair of Senate Finance had been key to the largest higher education budget appropriation in state history. Now, because of Bostwick's ill-timed action a bonanza of funding could evaporate in a matter of days.

Jack, completely blindsided, knew the old rancher well enough to just listen and never drop his eyes. "Shit,

Chancellor," Stockwell went on, "Barney Kapp and I began working together thirty years ago to start up these programs for the rural counties. The College of Medicine was only a dream back then and look at what all you've got today. The man devoted his life to the needs of the state's rural counties, and now this piss-ant Harvard egghead goes and fires him off the ranch like some damn drunken cowhand."

Jack nodded his head, never losing eye contact. He was hearing every word and the torrent had to slow before he ventured a comment. The Senator not only commanded a huge delegation, he was one of the most revered figures in the state. He was also a good man, a fair man. The moment would come to reason with him, but not yet. Jack just listened. "It's not going to happen, I tell you," Stockwell concluded. "Not now. Not like this, goddamn it."

The two men sat for a moment in silence. "Senator," Jack began. "The way I see it there's a couple of issues here." The old man leaned forward as if to speak, and Jack raised his hand slightly. "Let me finish, Buck; I got the message." Stockwell settled back in his chair.

"First, President Bostwick never gave me a head's up about his reorganization plans. Technically, he has the authority to take internal actions, but he also has an obligation to consult with me and others. He never has and obviously feels it beneath him. Hell, he was President over there five years before I got here. He even applied for my job. I shouldn't have to tell you how he operates. And Buck, to be completely honest here, you've always been easy with him. The truth of the matter is, he enjoys making end runs around me here at the Capitol, and you and the Trustees always look the other way. Now those chickens have come home to roost. As of yesterday, he's not just my pain in the ass anymore."

The Senator was silent, his weathered face, expressionless, as he gazed back at Jack. "Keep talking."

"It's simple enough. In order for your man to stay, mine has to go."

"Christ, you get right to it; don't you, Jack?"

"Sometimes, but I play fair, Senator. Hal Bostwick is a self-absorbed asshole who married into the right family when he came to Nevada and, truth be told, a lot of people are a bit weary of his arrogance. Barney Kapp is a native Nevadan, who has devoted his life's work to this state. He's never been one to kiss Bostwick's ivy-league ass and now Barney's only crime is that he's a bit long in the tooth."

"Well hell." Stockwell looked away for the first time. "They could say the same thing about me."

"I won't touch that one, Senator." They both laughed and the tension in the room evaporated.

"So there's no other way to finesse this, Jack?"

"No, sir. The University Code doesn't permit me to unilaterally reverse any president's internal personnel decision unless directed by the trustees or a court of law, and nobody wants to go there. The presidents, on the other hand, report directly to me. I'll wager Bostwick is just waiting for me to come to him, hat in hand, and ask him to reconsider his decision."

"He'll turn you down." Stockwell leaned back in his chair, placed his hands behind his head, and stared at the ceiling. "He wants me to ask."

"Well, Senator, if you ask him as a personal favor, that might do it, but this is Nevada. And you know what they say: There are no secrets in Nevada."

A moment passed and Stockwell, his hands still behind his head, leaned forward, and looked directly at Jack. "I don't like that picture much."

Jack sat, saying nothing.

"Have you ever fired a campus president, Chancellor?"

"I wouldn't use that term, exactly, but yes."

"Where?"

"Here, in Nevada," Jack answered matter-of-factly.

"I never heard about it."

"You weren't supposed to, Buck."

For the first time the Senator looked puzzled. Jack elaborated. "You've got to understand guys like Bostwick. The ego on these people is enormous, plus they never picture such a thing happening to them any more than they're aware of their own flaws or their place in the real world. When you first confront them with the reality that they're finished, they're shocked to the core, a virtual deer in the headlights. When they catch their breath, they begin blustering about lawyers and political connections. Then, finally, they realize that there is really no escaping the inevitable. You can sweeten the pot with a bit of time or money. But the most important thing you can offer is preservation of their dignity. After all Buck, isn't that really what it's about in the end. That's what's so unforgivable about Bostwick's handling of Barney Kapp. It totally devalues Kapp and the merits of a dedicated life."

There was a new look of appreciation in the eyes of the senior senator. "So, what do you propose?"

"Well, I'll find a way to deal with Bostwick. He'll be too preoccupied with his own skin to follow through on dumping Kapp. That will be the last thing on his mind."

"He's going to squeal like a stuck pig," Stockwell asserted.

"No, he won't. That's too public. He can't handle the embarrassment. He'll work behind me to rally the Trustees' support. That's where you come in, Senator. Don't even acknowledge the issue over Barney Kapp, even if it comes up. Stay above that one. It's me you've got to cover so I can act. You're going to have to find ways to convey to the Trustees that you and your legislative colleagues are four-square in my corner as the Chief Executive of the System. There can't be any doubt in tone or word about your vote of confidence in me. Praise the hell out of them for how well the University System did this year in Carson City. Hell, Senator, this is your wheelhouse. You don't need instruction from the likes of me on how to handle it. The northern Trustees love you. The Las Vegas Trustees don't give a shit about Bostwick. And deep down, they're all afraid to cross you."

The two men sat for a moment, studying each other. Jack looked towards the phone resting on a huge roll-top desk. "May I, Senator?" Stockwell indicated his assent.

"Bonnie." Jack paused, then interrupted. "Don't worry about that right now. Listen, I'm leaving Carson City shortly and want you to get General Counsel to meet me in my office at noon. Don't make it sound like an emergency, just get him there. And clear some time. We may be at this for a while. Also, call your girlfriend over at President Bostwick's office and get him over to my office sometime, anytime, tomorrow. Message is I owe him some face time for that unfinished meeting we cut short last week. Okay? Bye."

They rose, and Stockwell extended his hand. "I'll say one thing, Chancellor. You've got balls. You're not going to be loved much by some folks when this plays out."

"Senator, if I needed affection that badly to do my job I'd keep a puppy in my office. Just make sure I still have a job two weeks from now."

Dan Feldman, placed his half eaten turkey sandwich on his napkin, and looked at Jack with disbelief. "Chancellor, as you know, you have the authority to suspend or terminate a sitting president, but according to the System Code, only for cause. The Trustees can terminate at will upon your recommendation without recourse to cause. Even if you have clear and evidenced cause to act as Chancellor to summarily terminate, a campus president has the right to request a Trustees' review of the action."

"Sure," Jack agreed. "Firing for cause almost always leads to litigation. Up to now we've managed to avoid that."

"Yeah, thanks to you and Duke Butrum. Before you arrived the Trustees would up and terminate a president at will, just because something pissed them off. That was when Padrick O'Banion was Chair about seven or eight years ago before you arrived. He would collect a simple majority and ambush some poor bastard." Feldman emitted a painful sigh. "Big Daddy Paddy. He and his buddies used to show up at meetings half wasted. I was new on the job as General Counsel. God, those were the worst two years of my life. He'd fire the guy, laugh like hell, and hire him back an hour later saying they'd changed their minds. Meanwhile the poor bastard was in the crapper throwing up or on the phone trying to explain to his wife why he'd be home early. The guy is evil."

"So," Jack asked, "what's your take on how Paddy keeps getting re-elected to the Board?"

Feldman thought for a moment. "Well, first, he always runs for the single statewide slot. The rest of the Trustees are regional. So, most of the voters in the state don't really know him personally. You know what they say, distance lends charm. Second, he outspends any opponent five to one."

"Yeah, that amazed me the first time I saw it happen. I know he has money rolling in from a variety of ventures. Does he even have a primary residence? Bonnie sometimes has a hell of a time finding him."

Bonnie finally spoke up. "Well, we know he votes in Clark County, but that doesn't mean he calls Vegas home. He's got three or four places around the State, including Lake Tahoe. I always mail to a P.O. address."

Jack shook his head. "Well, getting back to today's problem. Dan, you say I've got no standing here except for cause?"

Feldman nodded his head in the affirmative. "You had Board support for the other two you got rid of. In fact, I always thought that was the main reason they brought you here. When you cleaned out the System headquarters at the same time, it really took everyone by surprise."

"Those folks needed to go, Danny. You knew it and so did I. Besides, I gave you a heads up that you weren't on the list."

"That may be so but there's a certain chair in your office, Chancellor, that people still avoid sitting in. But I digress. On the matter at hand, as your Counsel I've got to tell you what you already know. No smoking gun, no dismissal."

Bonnie McFall, who hadn't eaten her lunch rose and walked out of the office. Jack assumed she was headed for the ladies' room. He was feeling the urge himself and was about to suggest they take a break, when she burst back into the room and dropped a stack of file folders in front of Feldman. "Here." She stood over them both, hands on her hips.

"What the hell is this?" Feldman asked.

She looked at Jack. "What he's been too busy being Chancellor to look at... until today."

Feldman placed his hand on the stack, continuing to look at Jack, as if for direction.

"It's her Pandora's Box, Dan. If we open it we own it."

Jack gave Bonnie a knowing look. "Why don't the two of you sit here and work a while? I have some things to do. See you in a bit."

Two hours later Jack returned to his office to find it empty. A note was pinned to his chair: "Moved upstairs to my conference room. D.F."

Nodding to the staff as he walked through Feldman's office, Jack reached the conference room, which also served as a legal library, only to find the door locked. He rapped softly on the door. Bonnie's face appeared.

"Oh, he's here." She pulled Jack in quickly, closing the door after him. The long mahogany conference table was covered with scattered files and papers. Most of the chairs had been pulled back against the wall. Half a dozen legal texts and Nevada Codes lay open, bristling with post-it notes and arrow markers. Feldman was scribbling furiously on a yellow legal pad.

"What..?"

"We're not quite ready." He didn't look up. Bonnie was back in front of the computer keyboard, furiously transcribing one after another of the yellow sheets as Feldman tore them away and handed them to her.

"Christ, Danny," Jack said, "why don't you just dictate?"

"He doesn't work that way," Bonnie responded without missing a stroke. Jack recalled that she was Feldman's legal assistant before he stole her away.

"There!" Feldman tore a final sheet away from the pad and placed it in front of Bonnie.

"Somebody fill me in," Jack demanded.

"President Bostwick will meet with you tomorrow at four," Bonnie said without turning away from the keyboard. "He insisted his schedule didn't allow time to come all the way over here, so I said you'd be happy to see him on campus. He sounded very pleased."

"Well, I'm not. Damn it, Bonnie, I distinctly wanted this meeting to go down in my office."

"It doesn't matter where you meet, Chancellor." Feldman smiled up at Jack. "Just remember to bring a jar."

"A jar, what the hell for?"

"To put his balls in when we cut 'em off."

The following day as they drove into the Medical College parking lot, Jack turned to Dan Feldman. "If you don't mind, I'd like to meet alone with the President for a bit. He should know you're sitting right outside, but let me set him up before I bring you in as General Counsel to comment on the legal parameters of the situation. Meanwhile, I'll just take in the chronological abstract of incidents and the letter."

Feldman shrugged. "I'd still strongly advise that I go in with you."

"I understand, Dan. But humor me. I know this guy. I know his type."

Moments later they entered the President's suite. Feldman took a seat while Jack was ushered into Bostwick's office. The room could only be described as baronial in size and furnishing. The walls were covered with an array of recognition placards and framed photos of Bostwick standing next to some grinning dignitary. Jack heard a toilet flush and momentarily Bostwick emerged from his private bathroom pulling on a navy blue blazer.

"Chancellor, how nice of you to come to my humble digs for a change." He motioned for Jack to have a seat opposite his desk, and then eased into his high-backed leather chair. "Can we offer you some coffee or a soda?"

"No, thanks, Hal, I'm fine." Jack noted that Bostwick had shaved off his Van Dyke, but decided not to mention it.

"Okay then." Bostwick opened a folder and peered at the top sheet. "We can pick up right to where we left off last week."

"Before we get to that, Hal, there's something which recently came to my attention that I think we need to discuss." Jack slid a thin manila file folder across the desk. "It's an abstract of alleged incidents involving you and certain female staff. As you can see, they span a number of years and all are logged and dated. The point is, times have changed and in the unlikely event that a formal complaint should arise, General Counsel strongly recommends that it would be prudent for us to be on record as having already engaged in a routine fact finding process." Jack pointed to the unopened folder. "I thought it only fair that you should see what's in there, and we should talk before things get underway."

Bostwick took the folder, opened it, and began to read. His face reddened. "This is preposterous," he exploded, slamming the file on his desk. "How could you even consider..."

"Please, Hal." Jack's voice was calm. "Finish reading it. Then we can talk."

Bostwick's hand was shaking as he turned the last page. The blood had drained from his face. "This is slanderous bullshit, and somebody's head is going to roll, damn it!" He was glaring at Jack.

"That may well be the case, Hal," Jack eyes were fixed on the man, his voice firm. "But before you do anything rash, remember that truth is the classic defense to the charge of libel or slander."

"You can't be telling me that you believe there's a shred of truth to any of this. Why, goddamn it, I'll ..." Bostwick started to rise out of his chair.

"Be careful, Hal." Jack leaned forward raising his hand. "Don't shout and don't threaten anyone. What I believe is that you're the only person in this room who knows the absolute truth. Besides, there's always two sides to every story, right?"

Bostwick sat back, his hands gripping the leather armrests of his chair. "So, Chancellor, where are you in all this?"

"In the middle, Hal, like always, in the middle. I can't permit myself to entertain unfounded assumptions or succumb to my feelings and take sides. That's what's so tough about this damn job. You, on the other hand, have the luxury of a vested constituency. You have your loyal alumni, the faculty, staff, admiring students, community leaders, and, of course, Laura and her family. Hell, you've got the most wonderful woman in the world in your corner. She really respects and admires you, doesn't she?"

Jack gestured again toward the manila folder. "I strongly suggest that you study the contents of that very carefully. Take your time because, as I said, at this point you're the only one who knows what's true and what's not. Christ, Hal, you need to appreciate the position of my office. As I said we're looking at an accumulation of internal reports of accusations and complaints that apparently have been piling up for some time. General Counsel feels strongly that we have an obligation to address this matter. He's right outside. I brought him along in case you have any questions that I can't satisfy."

"No." Bostwick shook his head emphatically. "Right now it's just you and I talking, Jack. I don't want a third party in the room, especially a guy who used to be a state prosecutor."

"I understand, Hal, but he's smart as hell and honest to a fault. We're going to need his counsel to get through this. According to Feldman, if we exercise due diligence by investigating these allegations, however unfounded, then we and the Board of Trustees are on solid ground. Your positive cooperation makes you look good as well. If we choose to continue to look the other way and there's ever a formal complaint filed then everything comes out anyway and, even worse, we'll all be accused of a conspiratorial cover up, especially after today's meeting."

Jack paused to allow Bostwick an opportunity to respond. He waited, but Bostwick sat silent, tapping his finger on the folder. Jack finally leaned forward. "Hal, work with me here." He spoke slowly, deliberately. "For Christ's sake, if you have anything to say to me, now would be the time. Once General Counsel initiates fact finding, you need to realize that it will then be out of our hands. People will be contacted, interviewed, even deposed under oath if necessary. And you know how these things go, Hal. It has to be handled professionally and discreetly. Our offices have to work together, or we'll all end up on Eyewitness News. None of us wants that."

Bostwick folded his arms and leaned back in his chair. "Especially you, right?" He was smiling. "It's true that you have no constituency, Chancellor. The Trustees and the campus presidents do, and we all know that you're hired to keep things safely in the middle, no fuss, no muss." Bostwick paused as if for emphasis. "And I'll bet the ranch that you're going to do just that."

Jack sat for a moment, not believing the arrogance of the man. He rose, walked to the office door, and opened it. "Dan, would you step in please?"

Feldman entered and stood holding his briefcase. Jack extracted an envelope from his inside coat pocket and handed it to him. "Giving you this written directive in the presence of Dr. Bostwick, I believe, constitutes due notification of our intent to immediately initiate fact finding in the matter under discussion. Please leave Dr. Bostwick his copy now, and see to it that the Trustees receive confidential copies by registered mail as soon as possible. Include an explanatory cover note from yourself as General Counsel."

Bostwick sat speechless as the two men departed his office. Jack paused at the door. "Hal, you've been in Nevada long enough to know that you never, ever, bet the ranch against the house."

The following morning Jack was running a bit late. As he stepped out of the shower, he heard the master bedroom phone ringing persistently. Continuing to towel off, he walked to the bedside table and punched the speaker button. "What is it, Bonnie?"

"How did you know it was me?" She sounded a bit edgy.

"Never mind, is Hal Bostwick there already?"

"He was parked in the lot when I got here. I put him in your office with the *Wall Street Journal* and some of last night's coffee. He looks like hell. What do you want me to do until you get here?"

"Nothing. Just tell him that you expect me at any moment. Keep an eye on him. I don't want him near my desk."

"I already took care of that. When will you get here?"

"In a few minutes. And Bonnie, alert General Counsel."

"I already did that. You weren't answering your phone."

"I was in the shower, Bonnie."

"Oh, sorry, sir. Am I being snippy?"

"No more than usual. Listen, I'm half-dressed and on my way. See you in ten minutes. And Bonnie, do you have any of President Bostwick's letterhead stationery?"

"I have it for all the presidents."

"Good."

Ten minutes later, Jack walked past Bonnie and into his office. Hal Bostwick was sitting on the couch. A fresh Danish lay untouched on the coffee table.

"Hal," Jack greeted him. "If I'd known you were coming in ..."

"Never mind that," Bostwick snapped, indicating the open door. "Can we have some privacy?"

"Certainly," Jack closed his office door and walked to the couch, taking a seat across from his obviously agitated visitor. "Are you going to eat that Danish?" He poured a steaming cup of coffee from a carafe and offered to pour a second. Bostwick shook his head.

Taking a bite of the pastry, Jack replaced it on the china plate. He chewed slowly, swallowed, and took a long sip of coffee. "So, Hal, what can I do for you this morning?"

As Chancellor, Jack was obliged to attend and make brief remarks at the graduation ceremonies of each of the System campuses. This spring he took particular pleasure in the proceedings. President Harold J. Bostwick, draped in his elegant academic regalia, presided over and offered his congratulations to the graduates, their families and friends, and announced what the Trustees already knew: that having accomplished the goals he set for himself at the College of Medicine, he would be taking a long deserved sabbatical with his family before accepting a new challenge as CEO of a prominent but yet to be announced medical center. Jack led the platform party in standing applause for the departing president. Later, during the post-graduation reception, he discreetly avoided any discussion of President Bostwick's decision, insisting only that he would be greatly missed.

FOUR

"So, Jack, I'm out of town for a few weeks and you go and fire another president." It was Abe Glassman on the line.

"I didn't fire the guy, Abe. He wanted to leave."

"Yeah, yeah, people fall out of windows, too. Buck Stockwell says you got bullets for balls. He had to really sit on a couple of Trustees. They were pissed as hell, figured you had something to do with it."

"How do you know that old cowboy, Abe?"

"Oh please, Jack, don't insult your elders. Anyway, watch your back. I hope it was worth it."

"It was business, Abe. Besides, everybody knew the guy was an asshole. There, you wanted to hear me say it. I said it."

The old man was laughing now. "Listen, Jack, don't get excited. I didn't call for that. Remember that Russian girl we talked about?"

"Of course."

"Well, I talked with Jake Feingold at the Bar Mitzvah and naturally he didn't know much about the details. His daughter handles that part of the business."

"Was she there?"

41

"Why shouldn't she be? Anyway, we talked to her and it's bad news. They already awarded this year's grants, nearly two million dollars, and there was no Russian girl."

"Shit!"

"Well, I told them the story and she didn't buy it. Gave me a lecture on the integrity of the process. But when she got back to New York, Jake had her check it out and like you suspected, your girl was pulled from the short list. Somebody from the outside was definitely involved. Jake's daughter blew her stack. Some people will get fired, but no matter, the grants are out the door."

"Abe, I'm really grateful that you did what you could. Maybe next year."

"Next year, bullshit. You vouch for this girl, right?"

"Absolutely," Jack asserted, recalling that he was relying almost entirely upon a brief encounter and June Peebles' assessment.

"Okay then. How does Stanford sound? You went there, right?"

"Hell yes. It's a great university, world class. I earned all my degrees there. Best eight years of my life."

"Good, because I already set up the deal. Just listen. First, you impressed Feingold and his daughter with your interest in this thing. They never would have known otherwise. Not to mention I said a few things about you as well. Lisa Feingold did a little due diligence on you herself and is going to invite you to join their academic grants committee, maybe even the board. I don't recall. When she contacts you, say yes and offer to fly to New York to get personally acquainted with the organization and with her. Spend some time and turn on the charm. It couldn't hurt to be nice."

"I'll be nice, for God's sake. But New York, Christ, it's not a good time for me to be out of town right now."

"You work it out, Jack. They've already given out the awards. This arrangement is for Stanford University to get a $300,000 grant with the girl attached to the deal. I don't know how these things work, but Feingold tells me Stanford has been after him for thirty million dollars so getting the girl hooked up should be no problem. When you're back there meeting with Lisa and the Foundation people, you should be in a position to appraise things. That's it."

"Abe, what can I say. It was never my intent to put you to this much trouble. If ever there's anything..."

"Now that you mention it, I could use two courtside seats for next season." The old fox laughed. "Just kidding, Jack, just kidding. Come to the spa and visit for a few days when you get back from New York." He was off the line.

Jack pressed the intercom button on his desk phone and waited. The door to his office opened slowly and Bonnie appeared. "Was that you just now?"

"Yes. Why, what's the problem?"

"It scared the hell out of me. That buzzer hasn't gone off in years."

"Well, I didn't feel like shouting today. I'm a little tired, that's all."

"Now I'm worried. The last man who said that to me dropped dead two hours later."

"Who was that, for God's sake?"

"My second husband."

"Oh, sorry, Bonnie."

"Don't be. He was an ass." She sat down and flipped open her pad. "So, you buzzed."

"Oh, yeah. I'm going to be getting a call from a Lisa Feingold at the Feingold Foundation in Manhattan. Find me, anywhere, anytime."

"She called while you were on the phone with Abe Glassman. Is this about the Russian girl?"

"Yes, but how did you..?"

"Oh, please." She smiled and looked away.

"Of course." Jack sighed. "Then I suppose you even knew..."

"About the lead dancer at the Tropicana, sure. But I knew about Long Island and I figured you deserved a little distraction. She broke your heart, didn't she?"

"Who, the dancer?"

"No, your wife, the violinist."

Jack remained coldly silent for a moment. "Okay, Bonnie, back to business. I need to call Lisa Feingold."

"No you don't. Her administrative assistant and I had a great chat. I cleared your calendar. You're out on tomorrow's early flight through Chicago to La Guardia, business class. They've booked you into the Plaza Hotel. Their offices are within walking distance. And your return ticket is open. It sounds to me like they're anxious to meet with you. Lisa Feingold was pleased at the possibility that the two of you could have dinner at the hotel tomorrow evening."

Jack took it all in, nodding his head as she spoke. "Good job! Now, call back and confirm dinner. Make sure I have June Peebles' phone numbers in New York. Also, see if you can find David Newman's number at Stanford University. There should be a home number on the card as well. Finally, keep the lid on where I am for as long as you can. In fact, why don't you log me on vacation for the rest of the week, since this whole trip is off the books."

As Bonnie left Jack's office, he began rapidly sorting through the papers on his desk. An hour later, he slipped quietly out of the building, pausing only to lean close to Bonnie. "Those two courtside season tickets they sent up to me last week from Vegas... send them to Abe Glassman in a plain brown envelope." He passed and lowered his voice to a whisper. "And for your information, McFall, my heart is not broken.... It's frozen."

Dawn was breaking over the eastern slopes of the Sierras as Jack's plane roared down the runway at McCarran Airport and rotated into a steep climb. Banking to the east, it leveled a bit, and then surged into a steady push to reach cruising altitude. As the desert landscape grew more distant, Jack turned his gaze away from the window and leaned back in his seat. He had just closed the books on a rough and tumble legislative session in Carson City. It had been successful but he'd left a lot of skin on the table politic. And now, he was back on a plane headed east. Exhaustion prevailed. His eyes closed.

As Jack crossed the lobby of the Plaza Hotel, he folded the message he'd been handed by the desk clerk and slipped it into his pocket. Lisa Feingold would meet him at seven-thirty in the bar. He glanced at his watch. Plenty of time for a hot shower and a few phone calls.

"You're in the city! I can't believe this. Ginny was just there today buying flowers." Roy and Virginia Adler were the kind of friends you counted on the fingers of one hand. They lived in Bridgewater, Connecticut, near Danbury where Roy's business was headquartered.

"You've got a nerve, coming back here without calling us first." Ginny was on the other line now. "You rascal, we haven't heard from you in months. How long are you staying? Is someone with you?"

"It was a last minute business trip, guys. Otherwise I would have ..."

"Never mind," she interrupted. "Your timing is great, so you're forgiven. We're having a birthday bash for Roy this Saturday. The big five-o."

"You've gotta come up man." It was Roy again. "I can't do this alone. You know Ginny. It's going to be huge. Besides, everyone will be thrilled to see you again. You'll stay with us, and wait 'til you see the boys. They're young men now. C'mon, Jack, we'll even send a limo. Stay an extra day or two."

"I didn't forget your birthday," Jack lied. "I should get back west, but the hell with it. I'm not going to miss one of Ginny's parties. I should be done here by Friday."

"Great! Wait 'til you see how Ginny redecorated the guest cottage down by the pond. It's rustic eighteenth century, furnishings and all. Except for the plumbing and the kitchen. She kept saying that someday you might spend the winter there, writing the great American novel. It cost me a goddamn fortune."

Jack laughed. "Be careful, I might just take you up on it."

Ginny chimed in. "Still no lady in your life, Jack?"

"Nope." Jack looked at his watch. "Gotta go, guys. Call you tomorrow. And see you Friday evening." They sounded so happy he was there. Jack thought that in a lifetime one was lucky to have even two such friends. But he was running behind and he wanted to be at the hotel lounge bar before Lisa Feingold arrived.

Jack entered the Plaza lounge and stood for a moment surveying the crowded room. It was exactly 7:27 PM.

"Dr. Stark." Jack turned to see an attractive brunette in her early forties approaching him with her hand outstretched. She was wearing a knee length Oscar de la Renta taffeta dress with a short matching jacket and silver open toed pumps. The diamonds on her ears and platinum choker were brilliant but a bit too much for his taste. As he took her hand he could not help notice the Cartier watch on her wrist.

"You must be Lisa Feingold," he said with a smile. "But how did you place me."

"You're the only man in the room wearing cowboy boots, Chancellor."

"Well, I thought a white carnation in my lapel would be a bit too passé."

She laughed and took his arm. "Let's go directly in, shall we? It's a bit noisy in here for civil conversation."

They were seated promptly and as the waiter produced the wine book, Jack motioned toward Lisa Feingold. "The lady may wish to choose."

She smiled in appreciation. "No, please. Choose something from California."

"All right then." Jack looked up at the waiter. "Do you have a Barbera, Charles Krug, '85 or '86? If not, a Mondavi Reserve Zinfandel, same vintage?"

"I'm sure we do, sir." He took the unopened wine book and was gone.

"So, you seem to be aware of my California roots, Ms. Feingold."

"Well, my staff is to blame for that. We haven't filled a seat on our Board for many years, so they were a bit zealous in their research. You have a very interesting background."

"Not the kind you're used to, I'm sure. Any particular event in my checkered past that you might wish me to elaborate on?"

"Well, since you ask, why did you quit high school and join the Marine Corps?"

"Probably for the same reason you left Radcliffe to model in Paris. I was bored."

She laughed and looked away, flushing a bit. "We share another thing in common, as well."

"What's that?"

"We're both divorced."

Jack smiled. "Nothing special about that. What's interesting however is that we haven't remarried."

"Touches, Dr. Stark. They warned me you were fast on your feet."

The wine steward was standing over them holding out a bottle of Mondavi Reserve. "I'm sorry, sir, there was no Charles Krug in the cellar."

"That's perfectly all right. It's all in the same family." Then turning to Lisa Feingold, "I assumed red would be fine, especially after those years in France." He was teasing, and she took it as such, nodding her head and smiling.

They touched glasses in a toast. She rolled the wine in its bowl and took a sip. "Mmm, not bad. You seem to know your wines, Jack."

"Not really. I know this family and their wine. My father was very close to Rosa and her husband in the old days when it was just Charles Krug. Then the two boys grew up, branched off, and the rest is history. The Mondavis won't sell a poor wine. They'll dump it first. I know. I've seen it."

The waiter returned, and they ordered without referring to the menu. She took another sip of wine. "We both seem to know exactly what we like."

"That all depends, Lisa. Are we talking about food or other things? If it's the latter, we'll need another bottle of wine before that conversation unfolds."

Again, she laughed heartily. "We'd better take a rain check on that. You have a nine o'clock appointment tomorrow at the Foundation offices. There are a number of people looking forward to visiting with you... sort of an orientation thing. You and I will get together for lunch at the main offices around one o'clock."

"All right then, how about dessert instead?"

The New York offices of the Feingold Foundation Grants office were not what Jack expected. Their facilities in a converted Brownstone appeared understated for a multibillion dollar operation. The staff was small, friendly, and wasted little time introducing themselves and ushering him through an historical as well as a current briefing of Foundation activities. As noon approached, he was offered a private office and phone. From Nevada, Bonnie assured him that things were unusually quiet there and not to hurry back. He called a delighted Roy Adler at his office in Connecticut and confirmed that he would be rolling up the hill to their home late Friday afternoon. His animated conversation with Roy was interrupted by one of the Foundation staff who informed him that his cab had arrived to transport him to Lisa Feingold's office for luncheon.

As the elevator doors opened on the twenty-fourth floor of the former Union Carbide headquarters building, Jack stepped into what could only be described as mahogany paneled elegance. Antique tables and chairs sat comfortably on plush carpeting. Impressionist paintings adorned the walls. At the far end of the room, large bronze letters set against the wall announced, FEINGOLD FOUNDATION.

A young, primly dressed receptionist smiled and rose to greet him. "You must be Chancellor Stark." Jack nodded. "Please follow me, sir, and we'll go directly to Ms. Feingold's office." They walked past a dozen open door offices until they arrived finally at a suite where Jack was handed over to an older woman wearing a conservative brown suit and low heel tan shoes. "Dr. Stark." She greeted him with a tight smile and escorted him through a pair of oversize double doors into a spacious corner office.

"There you are." Lisa Feingold stepped from behind her desk. This morning she was dressed in an exquisitely tailored blue Armani suit and cobalt blue leather pumps. "Thank you, Elaine."

"No cowboy boots today, I see."

"Sorry, I hope the staff wasn't disappointed." Jack followed her to a table overlooking a panoramic view of the city.

"I gambled that a Cobb salad would please you." She motioned for Jack to sit and then followed suit, crossing her legs.

"You're a mind reader." Jack took note of the fine china, crystal, and Lisa's long legs.

Lisa carefully unfolded a linen napkin. An inch wide art deco sapphire and diamond watch bracelet caught the light. "This is a much better venue. We've a great deal of ground to cover. I assume you abandoned a busy schedule to fly out on such short notice. We appreciate it very much, Jack. As you might guess, this has been a stressful few weeks for us. The Doctoral Studies Grants have an impeccable record. Quite frankly, when Abe Glassman spoke with my father and me in California, I flatly rejected any intimation that outside influence played a hand in this year's awards. The process has such integrity that even the candidates are not aware that they are being considered."

"Abe told me that I'd gotten him in hot water with you. That certainly wasn't my intent. But my sources were very persuasive. The way this girl's name evaporated from the award list at the last moment simply didn't square with the Foundation's reputation. Frankly, Lisa, I was slaying a few dragons of my own at the time, and if I hadn't reached Abe on the first try, the issue probably would have dropped off my radar."

"We're fortunate it didn't. My father adores and trusts Abe Glassman. For that reason alone, I engaged a private agency to do a discrete investigation. In three days we had our answer, and promptly nipped the problem in the bud. It was an unfortunate aberration. I'm satisfied that it won't occur again."

Jack only listened, sipping from his glass and taking an occasional bite of salad. After a moment of silence, he lifted a heavy crystal carafe, and reaching across the corner of the table, filled her glass. "This is marvelous tea." He then refilled his own half empty glass. "It has a touch of peach, if I'm not mistaken."

She lifted the glass to her lips without breaking eye contact. "Yes, it's my personal favorite."

"I'm flattered." Jack carefully set his glass back on the place mat.

"Do they play a great deal of poker in Nevada?" She pushed back her chair a bit and again crossed her legs.

"They play everything," Jack answered. "But slots are the main revenue stream these days. If you're really interested in poker, the best players in the world can be found in southern Indiana, near the Tennessee border."

"My God." She laughed. "How does a University Chancellor come to know such things?"

"Long story."

"Yes, I'll bet it is, Jack, probably only one of many."

She surveyed him for a moment and then reached for a leather case. "Well, we have some things to talk about. Shall we get to it?"

"Please."

"First, one of the members of our board recently submitted his resignation. My father seems to feel that a westerner, like yourself, would bring some balance to our perspective."

"How do you feel about it?" Jack folded his hands and leaned back in his chair awaiting her response.

"I can see his point. We've been characterized, on occasion, as having an east coast bias. It's not the case at all. Besides, we so rarely have a board vacancy. One of my special interests, as you know, has been the annual Doctoral Awards. It's my hope that you would agree to serve on that committee as well. You could chair it by year two, and it would mean a great deal to me and the staff you met this morning."

"That would be my preference, Lisa, if the Foundation sees fit to go through with my appointment. I assume that you would first undertake an exhaustive due diligence process on my background."

"Already done and under review by the appointments committee of the Board as we speak. Your professional background is quite interesting. Your book on the three-year bachelor degree really turned some heads around here."

"Restructuring the Baccalaureate." It's not scheduled for general distribution until next month. How did you manage to get a copy?"

"Your administrative assistant included it along with your other publications and general materials we requested from your office. Didn't she mention it?"

"No, but I've been moving at warp speed these past weeks. Besides, she tends to take such decisions on herself without bothering to consult me. It's one of the things I like best about her."

"Well, we have been moving swiftly here as well. I wouldn't be surprised if, upon your return to Nevada, you find a letter offering you a seat on the Board." Without waiting to gauge Jack's reaction, she pulled another folder from the leather case and passed it across the table.

"Now, one final item, the matter of this young woman, Zoya Chalkin. When you find a moment you can review her file. A case has been made that if her name had remained on the final list, it's possible, even probable, that she would have been one of our recipients."

Jack placed his hand on the folder. "That was my understanding."

"However," Lisa went on, "the grants have been awarded, the Committee has adjourned, and the Doctoral Awards' budget could not accommodate another award, in any event."

Jack weighed in at this point. "Lisa, I believe I have a pretty good grasp of the situation. First and foremost, the integrity of the awards process was compromised through no fault of the Foundation. That, in my opinion, was the primary insult here. I assume from your comments that you have resolved that issue. The fact remains, however, that a totally innocent young woman was deprived of the opportunity of a lifetime. That has to impact your sense of fair play."

"Actually, Abe and my father got sidetracked on that. I think they enjoyed wrestling with the idea and puzzling out some kind of solution. It reminded them of the old days. My feeling at the time was that in a few weeks they would forget the whole thing."

Jack sat quietly. He'd said enough for now.

"Since we can't offer a grant directly to the girl, my father came up with the idea of giving Stanford University an award from the general discretionary funds of the Foundation. The problem would be tying the girl to the grant. My feeling is that Stanford might well reject the offer, and that would be embarrassing to the Foundation."

"Your father can do that?"

"He can do anything he wants up to $100,000 a year."

"That would suffice," Jack said. "Three years times three disbursements, equals one Ph.D. What's the problem?"

"The Foundation shouldn't solicit such a thing, Jack. It could set a bad precedent."

"You need a Shadchen."

"A what?"

"A Shadchen, a matchmaker."

Lisa abandoned her businesslike composure and threw up her hands. "My God, Jack, no wonder Abe Glassman likes you so much. But you can't be serious. We're not casting for 'Fiddler on the Roof' here."

"But Lisa, I'm serious. Put me to work. Let me make a few calls."

"Oh, I don't know, Jack. Poker in southern Indiana is one thing. Stanford University is an altogether different animal."

"Don't be too sure. Besides I'm not proposing to talk to Stanford. I'm going to feel out a few individuals, not the institution. Institutions don't have hearts, people do. If you're worried about it, clear it with your father."

She bristled slightly. "I don't need to clear it with anyone."

"So, it's settled?"

"Let me think about it." She glanced at her watch.

"Time for me to move along." Jack stood and looked out the window. "Is that '666' down there? I love that place."

"It is indeed. They say it hasn't changed in fifty years." She left her chair and was standing next to him. "If you'd like to have dinner there tonight, I'll have Elaine call and make a reservation for you."

"Only if it's for two."

"Oh, I couldn't possibly. Just look at my desk. I'll be here all evening."

Jack shrugged his shoulders. "If I were in Nevada, I'd be saying the same thing. But I'm in Manhattan, thank God. Eight o'clock would be fine, if Elaine can manage it. If you change your mind ..."

She shook her head. "Really, it's out of the question. Sorry to abandon you."

"On the contrary, Lisa," Jack gestured grandly as he departed, "it is I who have failed to liberate you from all this."

Back in his hotel suite, Jack placed a call to David Newman at Stanford University. A melodious voice answered. "Office of the Vice President for Advancement,"

"This is Dr. Jack Stark for Dr. Newman."

"Just a moment please." Jack heard the click of the hold button and settled back on the couch, placing his feet on a coffee table. Dave Newman and he went back to the good years on the Stanford Farm. Each had pulled a tour in the Marine Corps before college. As undergraduates and fraternity brothers, they'd swapped cars and girlfriends like baseball cards and spent endless hours drinking beer and playing shuffle board at Duffy's Pub. They went on to plough through their doctoral studies with the shared conviction that, for the time being, it beat working for a living. Over the decades they'd kept in touch, often expressing incredulity at the other's accomplishments.

"Stark, you worthless bastard!" The voice was Newman's. "Are you still in Nevada?"

"Yes and no, why?"

"I figured you'd be running a fucking casino by now. You're not worth anything to me stuck in that thankless Chancellor's job."

"Well, if you weren't happily married with five beautiful kids, I'd probably be more empathetic. How's my girlfriend?" They had both fallen for the same co-ed while at Stanford and it had nearly ended their friendship. Barbara had brought them together again, threatening a walk out at the wedding if Jack didn't stand up as best man.

"She's great. When are you going to stop sending her valentines, chump?"

Jack laughed. "When it stops pissing you off, that's when. What about the kids? They must be done with college by now, right?"

"All but the baby, Louise. The boys all graduated, but she's got two years to go. God, Jack, you ought to see her. She looks just like her mother, only taller. I swear to God I almost started packing a gun. These guys today, I swear if it hadn't been for the free tuition, we'd have moved to Nova Scotia."

"Just like us, remember Dave?"

"No way. These assholes have no sense of honor. Stanford or not, they've got a long way to go to be like us. We had the Corps, Jack. We raised hell, but there was always the Code. We stepped up to our responsibilities."

"Yeah, I'm with you, but that's ancient history. Listen, Dave, can I talk a little business here?"

"Sure. What's on your mind? You got some Vegas high roller eager to write us a big check?"

"I'm in New York City, Dave. The Feingold Foundation is about to offer me a seat on the Board."

"Holy Mother, Jack. Are you serious? That's huge, man. We'll all be kissing your ass. How...?"

"It'll be announced at their next Board meeting. Meanwhile, keep it in the graveyard, buddy. I'm only telling you this now because I need to ask for your help on something."

"Jack, you're aware that the University's application for a $30,000,000 grant is under consideration by Feingold?"

"That's what I understand and you've got to know right now, Dave, that I've got no juice at all... not yet. I won't even be allowed near something that big right now. I'm going to serve on the Doctoral Grants Committee. Are you familiar with those annual awards?"

"Yeah, but none of the winners are ever placed out here. The word is, there's an east coast bias."

"Well that hasn't changed from what I can tell. None of them will be coming west this year either. But if I go on the Board, next year there'll be a new sheriff in town. As for now, however, I've got a proposition for you. If you're willing to submit a proposal that a student of their choice could matriculate for a Ph.D. with a special spin to it, you'll receive a $100,000 grant for each of the three years involved."

"It sounds too easy, Jack. Are you sure there's nothing in the deal that can come back and bite us on the ass?"

"Word of honor, Dave. It's a slam dunk. The big man himself wants to do this for his own reasons. You know who I'm talking about. And the student will be world class, beyond qualified. Put an international spin to it. That's all I can tell you. Besides, you could do yourself a lot of good personally with the right people. I would see to that."

"I'm thinking here, Jack. If the proposal came from one of the college development offices instead of mine, it would be completely under the radar. None of them share information with each other. Any one of the school or college directors of development would jump at the chance to rack up a $300,000 grant. They all work for me, in a manner of speaking, so I could hand this tip off to someone I trust and want to reward."

"How about the Graduate School of Business?" Jack suggested. Frame it any way you want."

Newman was quiet for a moment. "You implied something international. Can I ask what, specifically?"

"Russian."

"That could work. The Biz school has been on a big Eastern Europe push. I could really do myself some good over there with this."

"So, Dave, can we do it?"

"Send me your ideas for a draft of the proposal and I'll take care of the rest. We'll talk again before it goes out."

"You're sure?"

"Is the Pope Catholic? Hell yes, Jack. Send me an even dozen."

"Sorry, there'll be just the one. And, Dave, I need a really fast delivery on this. We'll turn it around at this end in one day."

"Shit Jack, who do you know, anyway?"

"That's always been the thing, hasn't it buddy. Too bad it took us so damn long to learn it. I'll call you when I'm back in Nevada. Bring Barb to Vegas, complimentary for the whole weekend. We'll do the town. It'll be like old times."

They said their goodbyes, and Jack looked at his watch. Still a couple of hours before dinner. He dialed the direct line to his office. "Hi, Bonnie, it's me."

"And here I thought I was going home early, today." she complained.

"C'mon, this has to go out ASAP. You'll understand as I dictate." In less than an hour she was reading back to him a three page proposal addressed to Jacob Feingold, President and Chair of the Board, Feingold Foundation. Jack was his own worst critic, but even he liked the scope and appeal of the draft. It would do the job.

"Overnight it to Newman, personal and confidential, double envelope. It should be sent from Stanford to Abe Feingold in the same manner. Thanks, Bonnie."

Standing in a hot shower a few moments later, Jack thought briefly about tomorrow's meeting then put it out of his mind and focused on enjoying his solitary dinner at 666.

The following morning he arrived early at the Feingold Foundation headquarters and borrowed an unoccupied office. He had an hour before his scheduled meeting with Lisa and there were always phone calls he needed to make.

"I'm sorry, Dr. Stark," the dispassionate voice on the line responded. "Ms. Peebles is no longer with the Bank."

"Is there a forwarding number where she can be reached?"

"I'm sorry, sir."

Puzzled and a bit surprised, Jack persisted. "Then, connect me to Mr. James Talbot's office, please."

"Mr. Talbot can be reached at our London office next week. Mr. Trimble has assumed his post here. May I connect you?"

"No," Jack answered. "That won't be necessary for the moment... Trimble, you say?"

"Yes sir."

"Thank you very much."

Jack sat for a moment, then snatched up his brief case and began rummaging through the phone cards Bonnie always prepared for him when he went out of town. June Peebles was there, all right, including a home phone number.

"June, it's Jack Stark. I called the Bank. What the hell is going on? Where are you, anyway?"

"On my way to Baltimore, Jack, to interview for a job. There was a hell of a fuss on the top floor about a week or so after we spoke. I don't know any details other than it involved some serious blow back from the Feingold Foundation people. Talbot left the building the same day. A new guy appeared in his office shortly after and handed me my pink slip. Guess I just went out on Talbot's coattails. Collateral damage."

"Christ, I'm sorry to hear that. What about Zoya?"

"I spoke with her on the phone last week. She's all right... graduated MBA with high honors from Columbia. The bank's cutting her loose on June 30, however. Did your office get the stuff I sent?"

"Yes, thank you, June. I haven't had a chance to go through it yet. It's clear that she's not getting one of the Feingold grants. The bus has left on that. I just wanted you to know that I'm not giving up on her. If you talk with her again, please ask her to just sit tight. Did you include her home address and phone number in the packet you sent?"

"It's all in there. And I will call her this evening and relay your message."

"I'd rather you just assure her that there's still hope. Leave me out of it. And June, admonish her to keep all this to herself."

"Have you forgotten, she's Russian?" They both laughed. "I've got to catch a train, Jack. Let's stay in touch."

"Count on it. And June, before you go, did your new boss have a name?"

"How could I forget? Marion Trimble. Why?"

"Just confirming a few things. Good luck in the interview."

The door to the office opened as Jack hung up the phone. Ms. Feingold was ready to see him whenever he was free. He finished jotting a few notes and walked down the hall to her suite.

"How was dinner?" A smiling Lisa Feingold welcomed him into her office. Today she wore a summer weight champagne Chanel suit and as she moved to greet him Jack could not help but notice the perfectly matched 15-inch diamond and gold necklace, watch, and lapel pin.

Christ, Jack thought, this woman must spend my salary on her shoes.

"Dinner was great," he answered. "But you needn't have picked up the tab. That was very nice of you."

"You're our guest, Jack. Whenever you're back here on Foundation business, that's the way it works. Wait until you attend our next annual meeting. It's in the Cayman Islands."

They moved to the window overlooking the city. A small table spread with an assortment of elegant pastries sat waiting. Jack poured himself a cup of coffee and reached for a muffin. "I have not been idle, despite the distractions of this marvelous city."

He offered her a tray, and she shook her head. "What in the world have you been up to, Chancellor?"

"Well, thanks to you, I had some time on my hands last evening and I called a friend in Palo Alto. The Foundation... your father actually, will be receiving an irresistible proposal from Stanford's Graduate School of Business to assist them in securing and supporting an outstanding doctoral candidate for their East European Nations program. Specifically, someone fluent in both Russian and English would best fulfill their needs at this point. The full stipend, including indirect costs, is estimated at $97,500 each year for three years. The School of Business will make an annual request for that amount which will include a full progress report on the overall program as well as the Foundation sponsored candidate."

She stood for a moment without speaking. "You have been busy. When can we expect to receive this request?"

"Next Tuesday... Wednesday at the latest. It will go directly to your father's office and make no reference to your Doctoral Grant Awards program. Someone will have to give your father a heads up on this. I assume that would be you."

"No, I can't have anything to do with this." She was obviously annoyed. "And I must say, Jack, the whole thing has moved much too fast for my taste."

"Lisa, maybe I missed something here. I was under the impression that your father wanted to make things right for Zoya Chalkin. Didn't you tell me that the only impediment to resolving this was that the Foundation could not initiate anything with Stanford University? Well, that's no longer an issue. Everything dovetails together neatly."

"Frankly, Jack, I'd hoped it wouldn't get this far. My father and Abe Glassman are from a different era. Bending the rules doesn't bother them if it gets the job done. They enjoyed doing whatever they did in their day, bless their hearts. But it's a different matter with me. I will have to carry on the work of this Foundation, and its public image is an important part of that stewardship. It was my hope that you, of all people, would appreciate that."

"So," Jack countered, "one of your staff in the Doctoral Grants office sells out to a senior officer of a major investment bank. How does that not put your reputation at risk? How in hell do you square that, Lisa? At least the two old boys are trying to do the right thing, here."

"That person is no longer in the Foundation's employ."

"Right, but there's a new senior account executive at the investment bank in question." Jack handed her a slip of paper. "Do you recognize that name? I noticed it on numerous documents during my orientation with your staff the other morning."

She glanced at the name and looked up at Jack without speaking.

"I can't see how your investigation missed that, Lisa. All one had to do is follow the smell."

She stepped away from her desk, and crossing the office, closed the large double doors. She turned and leaned against them, her gaze fixed on Jack. "So the Indiana poker player has laid his cards on the table."

"Well Lisa, since you brought it up, let's be candid. My resume is good, but we both know that my pedigree would not attract the attention of the third largest charitable foundation in the country. You invited me out here so I would get a good taste of what could be mine, right?"

"Go on, you seem to be dealing the cards, Chancellor."

"Okay, you want there to be no doubt about who' is really running things around here. I figured that out in five minutes. So the guy whose name is on the wall decides to fund a doctoral grant for a deserving kid who got ambushed by two conspiratorial assholes: one, an anti-Semitic banker and the other an over-ambitious member of your own staff. I can't see how your father's righteous act undermines the fact that you make the wheels turn around here?"

Lisa moved away from the double doors and walked past him, pausing by a panoramic window. She gazed out at the city. "Are you finished, Jack?"

"Almost. Just so I understand the game here, if I fold, I get your support for the Board appointment and all the goodies that go with it. It's either one or the other. Am I right about that?"

"As your Nevada friends would say, Jack, it's not personal. It's just business." She turned to face him.

"Dealer's choice, cowboy. For what it's worth, I'd like to see you on the Board.

Jack took in a deep breath and exhaled slowly. "Fuck you, Lisa."

FIVE

Before he checked out of the hotel, Jack put in a call to Abe Glassman and told him the news that Stanford was on board and that Jacob Feingold would have what he needed to act. Abe was pleased and Jack suggested that he call his old friend in New York and tell him to expect the formal request to be hand delivered to him in his office by mid-week.

"I'll call him today." He paused. "This girl, Jack, does she know what you've done for her?"

"I doubt it, and let's leave it that way. It's you who made this happen, Abe. I just ran a few plays. When she gets out west, you should invite her down for a visit. She's a diamond. And you always wanted a granddaughter."

"Maybe so. Why not? You arrange it. Jack, how did the Board thing work out?"

"I'll tell you all about it when I'm in town next week. I could use a day at the spa. How about it?"

"Mazal Tov."

Jack turned the rented Lincoln town car onto the West Side Highway, past LaGuardia Airport, and crossed the Whitestone Bridge north towards Interstate 95. As he drove, the landscape gradually changed to the rolling forested hills of rural New York. He felt himself begin to relax for the first time since left Nevada. He was headed into a land of fond memories and dear friends.

When Jack had arrived in Long Island more than fifteen years earlier to assume the Brockton College presidency, he promptly received an invitation to sit on the board of Adler Enterprises. Eighty-eight year old Samuel Adler, founder of the Long Island based corporation had favored every Brockton president with a similar honor for the past four decades. The aging tyrant's son, Roy, invited Jack to the family retreat in the hills of western Connecticut, and urged him to accept. The two bonded almost immediately and Roy pled the case that he needed an ally. Times were changing, and a small hide-bound contingent of the Board were ignoring reality. As the two young men worked their quiet diplomacy they became fast friends. One week shy of his ninetieth year Sam Adler passed and Roy took the reins of the closely held family business and began building his empire.

After little Gus was born, Joelle quickly returned to the international stage. Jack with his baby boy took every opportunity to retreat to the human warmth and companionship Roy and Ginny offered. To her credit, Ginny never commented on Joelle's sustained absences. While romping with her two boys one afternoon, twelve month old Gus extended his arms and uttered his first word: "Mommy." Ginny gathered him to her bosom and held him close, turning her head to hide her tears. Six years later she would offer a grieving Jack the same comfort.

The Lincoln turned north onto Interstate 84, passed by the city of Danbury and Candlewood Lake to Route 7 before turning on to a narrow country road which wound through the bucolic rolling hills of Bridgewater. He soon spotted the crushed stone driveway leading to the Adler home. It ran for nearly one-half mile, past a huge barn and two large ponds. Moving steadily upward Jack spied the guest cottage beyond a stand of hickory and red oaks. Ginny had faithfully restored the aged eighteenth century farm house while adding every modern convenience. When Roy groused about the expense, Ginny blithely explained that she envisioned gazing down at the distant cottage, smoke rising from its chimney, while Jack spent the winter writing the great American novel.

The main house occupied the crest of a hill carpeted by wild flowers, and looked down on 248 acres of rolling, forested countryside. Roy had built his 13,000-square foot dream home mainly with weathered timbers and siding from seven antique barns dismantled and transported from upstate New York. The sprawling structure combined rustic elegance with a sense of a lived in home. From every vantage point the breathtaking beauty of the Connecticut countryside stretched as far as the eye could see.

The sun was still above the horizon as Jack guided the Lincoln alongside the house. The tires crunched steadily through the wide gravel paddock which led to the far side of the house. Coming to a stop, he noted that the great horseshoe-shaped arbor flanking the pool area was now covered with grape vines. Only four years earlier he had shipped Roy thirty cuttings from California and they had obviously rooted well in the rich Yankee soil. He stepped out of the car and was admiring the scene when he heard footsteps running in his direction. He turned just in time to catch a bear hug which nearly upended him.

"Darling man!" Ginny Adler planted a great kiss on his cheek as they embraced.

"Hey stranger, unhand my lady!" Jack glanced up to see Roy standing on a balcony, brandishing a golf club.

"Don't mind him, he's just jealous." Ginny's arm was still around Jack's neck. She was marching them towards the stairwell leading up to a second story veranda. "Quick. We don't want to miss this sunset."

"Move it, Jack," she admonished, pushing him before her up the stairs. "Roy mixed a batch of Manhattans and refused to take a sip until you arrived. The two men shouted their greetings as they embraced and thumped one another on the back. The three, chatting and laughing, moved to upholstered Adirondack chairs facing west. Roy and Jack set to work on the pitcher of Manhattans while Ginny sipped her usual Pellegrino with lime. As the great golden orb touched the horizon and began its final plunge, they fell silent and clasped hands.

Ginny turned to Jack. "You showed up alone, as usual. Not that we don't love having you all to ourselves."

"I like it this way, just the three of us." Jack extended his empty glass in Roy's direction. "Besides, you know I'm cautious about who I spend time with."

"Oh can it, Jack. Roy told me all about the dancer from Caesars Palace."

Roy shrugged his shoulders as he poured. "Too good a story to keep to myself, Jack. Besides, she would have found out soon enough, and then I'd have caught hell."

"Did you really wear a disguise when you went out with her?" Ginny was not going to be denied any detail.

"No, not really," Jack protested. "It's Nevada, Ginny. And I'm high profile. We dated mostly out of town, San Diego or San Francisco. When we went out in Vegas, I'd pick her up backstage after the last show and the makeup guys would hang a mustache and a few other tricks on me just to confuse the gossip mongers. It was more a game than a gambit."

She rolled her eyes. "And when I think of all the really great women we tried to push your way."

"He wasn't ready for that, Ginny."

"You deserve someone special in your life, Jack"

Ginny was persistent if nothing else. "Don't tell me that with your job and looks, you haven't met plenty of suitable prospects."

"Thanks, and sure, I've met some interesting women."

"So?"

"She's not going to give up, man. Your only hope is to bare your soul." Roy hoisted the pitcher of Manhattans.

The distant hills had turned purple as the light faded. The lamps below blinked on one by one, illuminating the grounds and casting an ambient glow on the porch where they sat. The mood was mellow.

"Okay," Jack moved to the edge of his chair. "You're probably the only two I would trust to understand. To begin, I was born to parents who loved one another unconditionally. I'm sure life placed plenty of challenges in their path., but being just a kid, I simply focused on how they were with each other. Reflecting on it, I can see that they held to a selfless covenant which could only arise out of true love. Every fiber of their being was committed to the wellbeing of the other. You simply can't grow up on a steady diet of that and not have it shape you."

Ginny sighed. "You were a fortunate child, Jack."

"Really? I'm not so sure about that. Just because you two have it together only proves the universal law of random exception. Most folks go to their grave not ever knowing that kind of love."

"Oh Jack, you're being too hard on yourself." She turned to Roy who had carefully avoided joining the discussion. "We know plenty of happily married guys, don't we honey?"

"Well sweetheart, some of them are happy. The rest are philosophers." He chuckled at his own wit and poured another Manhattan.

"Isn't that your fourth, big boy?"

Roy peered at his wristwatch. "In two and one half hours, I'll turn fifty. I do not plan to be conscious to suffer that indignation. Okay?"

"Fine with me. Jack will help me put you to bed. But you'll be hung over big time for the party tomorrow. All our friends are coming."

"They'll understand. But Jack, I want to ask you… what ever happened with that dancer?

"Roy!"

"It's okay, honey, it's a guy thing."

"She married my urologist."

Roy choked on his drink and sat upright. "Can I tell that story tomorrow?"

The following day while Ginny oversaw the grand preparations for the evening's celebration, she suggested that Roy and Jack engage themselves elsewhere. "You're only in the way here. Go have lunch or something."

"So, which one will it be?" Roy had rolled back the doors to a huge car barn where no less than six antique automobiles sat in gleaming splendor.

"You've made some new acquisitions since last I was here." Jack was walking among the vehicles. "This is new, isn't it?"

"Yeah, you're looking at a 1927 Pierce Arrow convertible coupe." Roy was beaming. "I literally stole that beauty last winter. Had to haul it all the way from New Jersey."

"How does it drive?"

"Like a tank. Ginny hates it. She favors that '32 Ford Roadster."

They made a turn around the house, honking the horn and waving before heading the roadster down the hill and away. Within moments they were rolling through the Connecticut countryside with only two missions: to occupy their day and return with a bushel of red apples. The latter chore took them to an orchard near a neighboring town. They pulled to a stop by the roadside stand. As Roy busied himself choosing the fruit that would meet Ginny's sense of color, Jack strolled into the rows of apple trees that stretched away into a distant valley. He could still envision little Gus running among them, his arms outstretched.

Roy's voice brought him back. "Hey Stark, what are you doing way out there? C'mon, we've got to get these back to Ginny before the crowd shows up."

As they jumped into the Ford, Roy thrust a cup of cider into Jack's hand. "Here, just squeezed." They raced through the countryside laughing and shouting over the roar of the engine.

It's a shame," Roy complained, "that you decided to leave all this to go to that god forsaken desert."

SIX

"Did you really tell her to go fuck herself?" Abe Glassman and Jack were sweating it out together in Abe's private sauna at his Las Vegas spa.

Jack gripped his towel and leaned forward to pour a ladle of water on the hot rocks. "Not exactly."

"What did you say, then?"

"I simply said, 'Fuck you, Lisa' and walked out."

"Oh, that's all." They continued staring into the steam rising from the rocks. After a moment they both began to laugh, quietly at first and then uncontrollably.

"Well," the old man coughed and took a breath, "the girl's going to get her scholarship. I had a long talk with Jake."

"That's good news." Jack started to pour more water on the rocks.

"No." Abe put up his hand, and rising to his feet, let his towel drop to the floor. "I've had enough. Let's get a rub down and a shower. Later we can have dinner and you can tell me the whole thing one more time from start to finish."

The waiter at Abe's club opened the bottle of water, filled their glasses, and left. "So, you took a nap like I said?" Abe was looking at Jack.

"Yeah, a whole hour. I feel great."

"Good. You make it a habit, you'll live longer. Look at me." Abe smiled and took a sip of water. "So, Jack, you were surprised when Jake showed up for dinner at 666 that night?"

"Truly, and not much surprises me any more Abe. I was certain his daughter wasn't going to show up. That 'too busy' act didn't fool me. When I asked her if she needed to check the Stanford deal with her father, she really gave it up. The claws came out, and I knew I'd struck a nerve. But, yeah, when I looked up to see Jacob Feingold standing at my table, I was very surprised."

The waiter had returned, and Abe ordered the whitefish for both of them. "So, what did you and Jake talk about?"

"Everything but Foundation business. I stayed away from that. We talked about you and him. He told me some great stories. Christ, I can see why the two of you are so close. You really had some adventures back in the day."

Abe gazed out the window. "It was the times, Jack. What you call adventures were just a couple of guys reacting to the times. We raised the money. We bought the weapons from anyone who would sell, and a nation was born. Did he ask about you at all?"

"About my family, how I grew up. I told some stories about my grandfather, my father and mother… you know, personal stuff, how we got to be what we are." Jack paused and looked up from his meal. "Why are you asking me all this? You already know what went on that evening."

"I like hearing it from your perspective. Jake read the book you wrote. Did he tell you?"

"No. How did he get his hands on that? Lisa sure as hell wouldn't have passed it on to him. Besides, it doesn't matter now anyways."

"Her secretary gave it to him along with all your papers that went to the nominating committee."

"Lisa's private secretary?"

"Jack, she works for Jake. He's the goddamn Chairman of the Board. Everybody works for him."

"That's not the way his daughter sees it."

"Jack, Jack, you're not quite there yet, but you will be. And when you are you will understand. Old players like Jacob and me are generous to a fault. We love to offer our time, our money, even our control over some things. But no one, not even our children, should try to take what we are not yet ready to give up."

"Does he know what I said to Lisa and that I walked out on her Board offer?"

"First, she can't offer what's not hers to give. Second, Jake Feingold is no fool. He knows everything that goes on. She'll run the show someday, but not yet. She's not ready to handle a five billion dollar operation, and he's not ready to give it over. And yes, he's aware of her gambit towards you and of your crude response before you walked out on her. Christ, Jack, you could have simply said, 'No'."

"Yeah, I know, but it just got away from me. And I needed to make my point."

"Well, Jacob is about to make his point, and I'm afraid you're it."

"Should I be worried?"

"That depends on how you look at it. You will be offered the seat on the Board, probably by next week. Jake likes what he saw. But, Jack, you have to handle this situation carefully.

A father is teaching his daughter a lesson. You're that lesson. But she's not going away. He loves her and if you go on the Board, you're going to have to deal with her. You only get one 'fuck you' in this deal. You have to behave if you want to get on with this crowd."

"I understand, but I need to think about it."

Abe carefully separated a bone from the fish on his plate. "Bullshit, you already know."

"The prodigal son returns." Bonnie McFall greeted Jack as he entered the building after a ten-day absence. He paused to place a small gift-wrapped package on her desk, then opened the door to his office.

Bonnie followed him momentarily, clutching the small box. "Wow, Chanel No. 5. Thanks, boss, really."

"I didn't want you to think I'd forgotten you," he said with a smile. "Any mail?"

"Mostly junk." She handed him a half dozen envelopes. "These look sort of important. How was your vacation?"

"Eventful, Bonnie, very eventful. I'll tell you all the dirty details later."

"You better take a look at your calendar." She sat beside him and pointed to some red circled dates. "You're giving the graduation address at Bishop Brunell High School this evening."

"Christ, I completely forgot! I could have given it some thought on the flight back. Damn!"

"I spoke with the Principal's secretary," Bonnie said. "Twenty minutes would be fine with them."

"I'll do ten and they'll like it even better. Oh, and Bonnie, make a note to have me call June Peebles in a week or so."

The rest of the day was busy with phone calls and brief meetings with staff. General Counsel spent an hour going over the final details of Hal Bostwick's resignation. The Trustees were already bickering over which of them would serve on the search committee for Bostwick's successor. Jack dashed off memos to the medical college faculty senate, council of deans, and alumni association, inviting them to elect members from their respective bodies to join with the Trustees in the search process. It was all part of the game. As Chancellor, he knew he would bat last and he had no intention of letting another pompous ass get the job. As an afterthought, he wrote a personal note to the newly elected Med School Student Rep inviting her to join the group. She was smart, feisty, in her fourth and final year, and would add some spice to the tedious search process.

It was still light as he drove into the high school parking lot. The grounds were teeming with graduating seniors in their blue robes, laughing and jousting with one another. It was their night to party. Proud parents were taking photos of their progeny as school staff tried their best to move everyone to their proper place so the ceremonies could begin. Jack walked to the principal's office carrying his academic regalia over one arm. The platform party would robe there before the school band struck the chords that would signal that the ceremony was about to begin. As he entered the office, smiling and nodding hello to teachers and staff, a tap on the shoulder turned him and he grasped the outstretched hand of the Academic Dean of Bishop Brunell High.

"Father Collins, how the heck are you?" The two men were beaming at one another as they shook hands.

"Fine, Dr. Stark, fine. But it's been too long since you visited. You should see the new computer lab. It's an extraordinary facility. And the kids are so into it. Every station is filled every day. They're even coming in on Saturday. We don't know how you managed to find the time or who you spoke to at Apple."

"Father, I simply told your story to the right guy down there, that's all." The "guy" had been a young Steve Jobs.

Jack's thoughts drifted elsewhere as he sat quietly midst the platform party. Little Gus would have been a freshman. The polite rattle of applause as he was introduced brought him back to the moment at hand. He rose, moved to the lectern, and stood for a moment, smiling and nodding to the crowd of jubilant young faces and their families. No one noticed the tears in his eyes.

Hiring a president for a college or university was once a family affair. When Jack first entered the business as a young professor, the Chancellor of a university system simply called around the country and visited with a network of trusted colleagues and came up with a short list of possibilities. He would then talk them over with the Chairman of his Board. Usually, depending on the customs of the state, they might even run it past the Governor. The Board or a committee thereof then gave the Chancellor the green light to secure their choice. It was a time and energy efficient process that satisfied everyone involved. Except for narrowly dedicated institutions, it did not affirmatively solicit women, minorities, or individuals of certain religious persuasions. The fact that the process worked efficiently to procure presidents could not sustain itself against a growing public awareness that at least one half of the nation's potential talent pool was being excluded.

Now, decades later, the process was far more complex and required a substantial budget and time commitment to achieve its goal of equal opportunity. And it usually took at least a full year to bring in a new chief executive. The task of simply composing a politically acceptable search and screening committee exhausted six to eight weeks. All stakeholders within and without the academic community needed to be represented. Moreover, an equal opportunity officer oversaw every step of the process and enforced a strict regime of federal regulations and guidelines. As Chancellor, Jack's first responsibility was to recommend the appointment of an acting president of the Medical College. Nursing the best candidates through the political wrangling of campus vested interests and Board politics was always a challenge. This time he threw them a curve, bypassing all the obvious choices being lobbied for the interim post he selected of the Chair of Primary Care Medicine as his choice for the interim post. Dr. Bryna Nagourney was relatively new to Nevada. She was both a highly regarded physician and a world class scientist. Moreover, she would be the first woman to occupy the post in the history of the state. No one dare publicly criticize her appointment. Moreover it was his private estimate that because she was articulate and popular with colleagues and students alike, she would do well in the job during the interim period and be a top contender for the permanent presidency.

"You crafty son-of-a-bitch." The Chair of the Board of Trustees, Duke Butrum, was cutting into a well done top sirloin. Jack was having his weekly lunch meeting with

Butrum in his baronial office atop the Great Basin Bank and Trust building. "A few of the boys nearly shit their pants when I told them, but the women on the Board were pleased as hell."

"I didn't mean to catch you by surprise, Duke, but she's solid and we're way overdue…"

"Yeah, yeah, I know all about that politically correct bullshit." He carved a slice of steak and speared it with his fork.

Jack broke in. "C'mon Duke, we both know those days are gone. And, frankly, we look like shit to the rest of the country when it comes to women and minorities."

"Hell, Chancellor, I'm fine with it." He carved out another piece of steak. "Besides, setting up the Chair of the Board, to make the announcement of her appointment made me look like a damn hero to the media. Did you read Dolly's editorial in the *Gazette* yesterday? Even the *Las Vegas Sun* had a cartoon of me on a white horse. Hell, I might as well run for Governor."

"Christ Duke, don't even kid about that. You wouldn't really leave me all alone with that bunch."

The big man laughed. "Oh, come on, they like you well enough."

"Oh yeah, 'til they get a wild hair up their ass one day and fire me."

"Not likely, son. Half of them really do like you. The other half are a little scared of you… something about a doomsday file. What the hell is that, anyway?"

Jack avoided the question. "I don't know what they're smoking, Duke, but this Governor thing. You're not serious are you?"

"Maybe. People have been talking to me about it."

"Hell, Duke, with your money, why not just buy yourself a Governor? You don't belong with that crowd."

"Well, I don't know. The state's been pretty good to me. Maybe it's time to give a little back."

Jack took a bite of his club sandwich and chewed slowly. He didn't like what he was hearing. Butrum would have to resign as Chair to run for the office. As Chancellor, he relied on a rock-solid Chair of the Board in order to do his job.

"Six years ago, Duke, I'd only been here a month. And I sat right here and gave it to you straight... what was wrong and what would have to be done. Remember?"

Duke laughed. "I remember you scaring the shit out of me."

"You were scared? Hell, when I accepted this job I understood that the university system needed a tune-up. You told me that up front. But after a couple of months of dumpster diving for jettisoned records and files I realized that I was the CEO of a fucking time bomb. The entire system, top to bottom, was riddled with liability. You remember what I told you when you joshed me about it?"

"Yeah. You said me and some other folks could decide to go to jail if we wanted, but you were going back to New York."

Duke leaned back in his huge leather swivel hair and threw one booted leg on his office table. "It was hard to believe at the time that anyone could learn so much so fast."

"I had help."

"A deep throat?"

"Something like that."

"You never mentioned that."

"I didn't know you, Duke?"

Butrum chuckled. "I always figured some of the board whispered in your ear…"

Jack stood. "That bunch of rabble. Hell no, they were at the core of the problem. Wasn't Paddy Chair before you took over?"

"Right, and he's one evil, twisted son-of-a-bitch. But you know that by now, Chancellor. You've crossed swords with him."

"Sure, but I've had you to back me up. It took some time, but I think he tolerates me now.

"Be careful, Jack. You've been spending more and more tune in Las Vegas the last few years. You know how the northern Nevada trustees feel about the south. Paddy's been scratching their itch about all the attention you've been spending on Clark County."

"Duke, you know I've been brokering a shit-load of corporate interest in relocating operations into Nevada. Hell, Carson City, Elko, Truckee… have all gotten a piece. But the bulk of the interest, especially from California, is focused on Clark County. Things are hot down there, and I promised the Governor…"

"Slow down, Jack." Butrum interrupted. "We all know it's what you do best. That's why the Gov refers to our Chancellor as Nevada's economic ambassador. Christ man, since then you've been living on a fucking airplane."

Butrum stood. Get out of here. Take a vacation, or something."

One week later, Duke Butrum announced his intention to seek the nomination of his party to run for the office of Governor.

SEVEN

Jack was on his final lap at the university track when Bonnie caught his attention by honking the horn on her car. Within thirty minutes he was racing over the Sierras on Highway 80 towards Sacramento General Hospital. Angelique had suffered a massive coronary infarction and was undergoing open heart surgery in a heroic effort to patch the breach between the left and right ventricles.

"We closed it, but there's a leak and we'll need to crack her chest again, or she won't last the night. It's your call, Dr. Stark."

Jack looked at the surgeon. "Technically, why would you want to even try that?"

"It's her tissue. We rarely see an eighty-year-old with such excellent tissue. Otherwise, we'd never consider it. Just look at her skin, even now. There's hardly a wrinkle on her."

"I'm sure she'd be flattered if she could hear us, but I don't want any hopeless surgical heroics here. What are the odds?"

"If we do it now, this afternoon, I give it 50/50 that the patch will hold. I don't want to mislead you. She won't be dancing anymore, but you'll have your mother, reasonably active and well."

Jack didn't hesitate. "What are we waiting for?"

"Just your signature, Dr. Stark."

Jack was dozing in the post-op lounge when he was awakened by the surgeon still in his blue scrubs, his mask dangling from his neck. "She's out of the O.R. Dr. Stark, and it went very well. The patch is holding."

"How long before we're out of danger?" Jack asked.

"The next seventy-two hours are critical. You can see her for a moment, but she's unconscious. I wouldn't expect much for at least a day or two."

The next morning, Jack abandoned his vigil outside the critical care area long enough to buy a razor and a fresh shirt. He returned to find Elizabeth sitting quietly in the waiting room, clutching a small backpack, and staring at the floor. Short cropped hair framed her pretty face and big brown eyes that were puffed from crying. She was wearing faded cargo pants, an oversize grey sweater, and walking sneakers. It had been nearly three years since they had seen one another.

Twenty years ago, the undernourished, ragged three-year-old had been passed to Angelique's loving arms by an itinerant farm worker. He promptly disappeared. Efforts to locate or identify the worker met with no success. One year passed before the Archdioceses foster care office approved Gus and Angelique's petition to adopt the child. She was promptly baptized, Elizabeth Ann.

"Lizzie," Jack spoke softly. She dropped the backpack and threw herself into his arms. He held her for a while, then whispered into her ear. "I missed you, too."

She looked up at him. "Mom… is she going to die?"

"No, honey, it looks like she's going to make it. Right now, she's holding her own. Have you seen her?"

"No, they said that I could go in when you came back."

"Sorry I wasn't here when you arrived," he said, indicating the plastic bag holding the toiletries and shirt. "But I came down with nothing. Just jumped in the car and drove. Bonnie found you and wired the money and tickets?"

"Yeah, thanks. She said you'd meet me here. I love that lady."

They looked in on Angelique who appeared to be sleeping quietly. Elizabeth gave her a gentle kiss on the cheek, and they both stood silent for a few moments.

"Have you eaten?" Jack asked.

"Not since yesterday when I got Bonnie's call. But I'm really not hungry."

"Well neither am I, but we've got to eat. Let's go downstairs to the cafeteria and come back in an hour. They'll be making rounds by then, and we can talk to her surgeon."

The two of them spent the day in the critical care unit sitting with Angelique. Early hat evening they had dinner at a good restaurant and talked about what was going on in their lives. She and Bodie were apparently getting by. He was finding plenty of guide work, and she worked at a roadside gas station and fishing supply store.

"With the money you sent us, we're building a house."

"A house?"

"Well, actually it was an old abandoned cabin. But it's pretty neat now. Bodie winterized it and I did all the decorating and painting."

"Did you buy it?"

"Uh, not exactly. It's behind the store up on a little hill. It belongs to the old guy who owns the gas station and store. He was happy to let us live there and fix it up."

"I'll bet he was." Jack's tone was guarded.

She rolled her eyes. "Oh, Jack, it's not like that up there. People trust one another. He's really a nice old guy. Most of the time he stays with his daughter in Canada. She wants him to sell out and move in permanently so she can look after him."

"Any buyers?"

"Way out there?" No, only a steady stream of hunters and guys who want to fish the rivers."

"Did he ever mention a price?"

"Forty thousand, I think. Yeah, forty thousand dollars. But no one's going to buy it, so Bodie and I aren't worried. Besides, Bodie's a big time guide now, Jack. We can make out, no matter what."

"You two, you're getting along okay?"

"We love each other. Bodie says he can't think of a life without me being there with him."

"So when I call, why won't he say more than three words before handing the phone to you?"

"Because he's afraid of you! Well, not afraid, really. He's not afraid of anything in the woods. More like intimidated, yeah, that's it. He actually thinks you're like some kind of god or something … Stanford Ph.D., university Chancellor, and all that. He knows all about the family and me. We don't get good television reception up there, so we read and talk a lot."

"So, you're happy?"

She cocked her head and just looked at him with her lips scrunched together.

"Okay, Okay, you're happy."

She leaned across the table, pulled him towards her, and kissed him on the cheek. The waiter appeared with their entrees. They ate quietly for a few moments.

"How many acres?" Jack asked.

She looked puzzled for a moment. "I think I heard Bodie say ten or eleven when we were talking about it once. Why?"

"Offer the old guy thirty thousand cash. He'll take it."

She knew her big brother and the tears began to flow. "Oh, I love you for that, Jack, but Bodie won't take a loan from you."

"I don't make loans to family. It's a gift. Tell him he's free to return the check if he can't handle it."

At the hospital, they found Angelique awake for the first time. A few words and kisses were exchanged before she lapsed back into fitful sleep. The intensive care nurse reassured them that all the signs were normal and advised that they get a good night's rest and meet with Angelique's surgeon on rounds early the next morning. Jack took a two bedroom suite at a nearby hotel, so he and Elizabeth could be together. Talking about happier times eased the stress. Soon, exhaustion prevailed, and they both retired for the evening.

"Honey." Jack stood in the open doorway to Elizabeth's bedroom. "It's seven o'clock. I think we better get moving."

It was 8:05 a.m. when they walked into the intensive care ward. Angelique's surgeon was standing by the nurse's station reading charts when he spotted Jack and motioned him over. "I'd like to speak with you alone for a moment."

"Fine." Jack took Elizabeth by the hand and the three moved towards a lighted panel where a number of thoracic x-ray sheets were clipped. "Your mother's heart patch is holding, but another factor has presented itself." He pointed to a frontal shot of the lungs. "See, here at the lower lobes." He was indicating an opaque milky white area. "Fluid. That was taken last night. We noted it, of course, but felt it to be no cause for immediate concern." He moved to an adjacent exposure and pointed with his pen to a much larger patches of white covering the entire lower lobes of the lungs.

"Her lungs are filling with fluid," Jack stated the obvious. "Why, for God's sake?"

"Shock, probably, resulting from the heart attack and the back to back surgeries. Everything went well. She's a strong woman. But I observed this very same phenomenon hundreds of time during the Vietnam War. Young, strong boys with clearly survivable wounds would do well for a few days and then for no apparent reason, their lungs would begin to fill until they went into cardiac arrest. We couldn't save them. It was maddening."

Elizabeth began to cry, and Jack put his arm around her. "What next?"

"That's why I wanted to speak with you now." The physician explained. She's semi-conscious, but in serious discomfort, and soon the pain will become unbearable. You'll need to okay the morphine drip."

Jack sighed and placed his arm about Elizabeth "We should say our goodbyes, then."

The surgeon nodded. "I'm sorry. We had great hopes for her after the last surgery. She came through with such flying colors." Elizabeth had walked away and was sitting in a nearby chair, sobbing.

"Let us visit her a bit, then make her comfortable."

"You have the power of attorney, Dr. Stark."

"Fine. Come on, Elizabeth. Let's go say our goodbyes." Before they went into the curtained intensive care area, Jack took her by the shoulders. "Honey, what you will experience now is part of life. Pay attention. Angelique is not afraid of dying, and your sweet face and words will ease her pain. Tears are fine. They show our love. But smile for her and whisper sweet things to her. She will want to know that we are going to be all right."

A short time later, Jack parted the curtain and confirmed with the attending nurse that the doctor had left the order for a morphine drip to ease Angelique's final agony.

The nurse deftly removed the breathing tube, and checked the morphine drip. Angelique's breathing became painfully labored. She was struggling. The nurse turned to look at Jack. He nodded and leaned close to Elizabeth who was weeping and clutching Angelique's hand.

"It's time now, honey, to let her go. We should say our final goodbyes. Stay close to her. When her breathing stops, keep whispering in her ear. It will be nice for her to leave hearing the sound of your sweet voice."

The morning was crisp and bright as they gathered around the open gravesite next to Gus's resting place. Jack and Elizabeth had taken some time to go shopping and she looked lovely, even in her grief. The faces gathered there were familiar. Jack had grown up among the close-knit ranching families in the valley. Some rose to share a fond recollection of Angelique and Gus. When the time came for Jack to conclude he chose to repeat Samuel Clemens' farewell to his young daughter a hundred years earlier:

Spring raindrops fall gently
On this place.
Bright summer sun shine
Warmly here.
Autumn breezes blow
Softly by this place.
Green grassy sod rest
Lightly here, rest light.
Goodnight dear heart,
Goodnight.

When he kissed Elizabeth goodbye at the airport before driving back to Nevada, he handed her an envelope. "It's a certified draft, enough to buy the entire operation. Make sure you hire a local attorney to validate the title and deed. If you two need anything, call me. Remember, you're a big girl now."

She gave him a crushing hug. He held her close for a brief moment and whispered in her ear. "You lit up her life, sweetheart."

Daylight was fading as Jack began the steady climb up Route 80 through the Sierras and then down to Reno and the empty house he called home. Home is where the heart is, the saying goes. But now, with everyone he loved gone or safely elsewhere, he was gripped by loneliness as never before in his life.

EIGHT

Maxim Ivanovich Popov, was a highly decorated artillery officer of the Great Patriotic War. He earned a chest full of medals for his leadership and courage during the battles of Stalingrad and Leningrad and received official recognition of the government as a Hero of the Soviet Union. He went on to complete his doctoral studies in economics and was quickly marked for high office in the post-war Soviet. While at the university, Maxim met and fell in love with Raisa Mihailovna Azgur. She was a stunning beauty, tall and willowy, with jade green eyes and a laugh that melted men's hearts. During the war, Raisa, at the age of twenty-two, had earned her own credentials as a heroic Soviet woman. She participated in the incredible feat of relocating entire war materials factories to southwestern Siberia, out of reach of the advancing German forces. There, for five long years in unthinkably harsh conditions, she distinguished herself as a brilliant and effective munitions production director.

In the years following the war, Maxim was tapped for increasingly important roles in the USSR's economic development hierarchy. He and Raisa found themselves and their young daughter, Lara, frequently posted to foreign capitals. There, Raisa's brilliance and charm both softened and complemented her husband's formidable demeanor. They were a marvelous pair, she and her handsome diplomat husband. Little Lara was Maxim's diamond, born and nurtured in the bosom of the beloved family of which Raisa was the heart and soul. When Lara reached the age of seventeen and was admitted to the same university attended by her parents, Maxim managed to secure a permanent posting to Leningrad. There, Lara, already a linguist and accomplished pianist, choose to study economics. Four years later on the eve of Lara's graduation from the Academy, Raisa conspired with her daughter to invite a young professor of geology to a large dinner party. Three months later, on the same day that Alexander Chalkin took her hand in marriage, Lara received notice that she had been admitted to the graduate academy to pursue doctoral studies in economics. At the wedding dinner, Maxim's open delight at the news that his daughter would be following in his footsteps served to mute his feelings about sharing her with a son-in-law.

The following summer Zoya Alexandrovna Chalkin was born on July 4, a date held significant only by the fact that it was her birthday. After a brief summer respite, Lara Chalkin vigorously continued her graduate studies. In mid-September her husband Alexander kissed his wife and baby daughter goodbye and set out for the Siberian Steppes to join a routine geologic petroleum exploration. They were last seen flying northwest out of Tomsk on October 3. Neither the plane nor any member of the team was ever seen again. Lara, now engaged in a demanding academic career, and little Zoya moved into Maxim and Raisa's spacious flat. It was common custom in Russia for retired grandparents to play a significant role in child rearing. Maxim and Raisa now had a new diamond to brighten their day.

Zoya's recollections of her childhood abound with memories of affection and security. The USSR may have been viewed as an evil empire by some, but from her perspective, life in Leningrad was good by any standard. As a youth, she rode the electric trolley cars throughout the city in complete safety to her tennis and swimming lessons or on family errands. The quality of her education was exceptional. She was expected to be literate before age seven. For the ten-year period from seven to seventeen, she attended classes six days per week. The class cohort was small and the teachers highly dedicated and respected. No one would ever consider questioning a classroom teacher's authority or standards for performance. Challenging homework was routine and taken seriously as a part of family life. Raisa always had some delicious snack waiting at home after Zoya's day in class. Then it was off to her room to study until dinner. In short, there existed a comprehensive support system for the entire educational process. Students who demonstrated exceptional promise were encouraged to excel. Zoya, for example, opted for English as a foreign language and began her study at age eight. She mastered advanced mathematics long before entering the university's prestigious undergraduate Academy.

When the disintegration of the Soviet Union began, a wrenching decision faced Zoya's family. Maxim and Raisa, now older and in failing health, assessed the coming chaos. Sensing a social and economic disruption of epic proportions, they vowed to get their daughter and Zoya out of the country. Lara refused to leave her ailing parents, but insisted that Zoya immigrate immediately while Maxim's international connections were still viable. In a matter of weeks a weeping, protesting Zoya abandoned her university studies and boarded an Aeroflot flight bound for Oslo and from there to New York City. Initially she lived with friends of her grandparents. Once oriented, however, she moved to a place of her own, worked two jobs, and graduated CCNY with high honors in less than three years. A prominent Manhattan investment banking firm offered her a prized MBA/internship position after a single interview.

Zoya dashed into the foyer of her apartment building just ahead of the full downpour of a sudden summer shower. Opening her mailbox, she stood dripping on the shabby carpet and extracted the contents. Once inside her small apartment, she sorted through the envelopes, carefully setting the bills to one side. There was a letter from her cousin in St. Petersburg. Things were not going well there since the breakup of the Soviet Union. The country she once called home had steadily declined into economic and social chaos. The payroll office at the university academy where her mother, Lara Maximova, now served as Dean of the School of Economics had been closed for months awaiting budget allocations from a broken government.

Still sorting through her mail, Zoya opened an envelope containing a small check and a polite severance letter from the bank. She paused for a moment, sighed, and stared across the room at the summer shower slashing against the window. It would be dark soon. In St. Petersburg it would be light until midnight, then only dim for an hour or two before the dawn returned. She rested her hand on the phone. Her mother would be asleep. Her grandparents had succumbed to their ailments last year, and Lara now lived alone in the flat. The phone rang suddenly, startling her.

"Zoya! It's June Peebles. I've been trying to reach you."

"June! How are you? I received your last letter. Where are you? In Baltimore?"

"I've been here in the city for the past couple of days. When, dear girl, are you going to break down and get an answering machine?"

"I can't afford it. I'm out of a job, remember."

"You mean you haven't received it. You don't know about it yet?"

"About what?"

"Don't you open your mail, Zoya? It must be there by now."

"I just got in and I've been opening bills. What am I looking for?"

"A letter from the Feingold Foundation. It should have reached you by now."

"Wait." Zoya spread the remaining mail on the coffee table. "Here it is."

"Rip it open and read it to me! I'm dying here, Zoya."

Zoya slid her index finger down the envelope flap and extracted the contents. The gold embossed letterhead on elegant sand buff bond read: The Feingold Foundation, 687 Park Avenue, New York, N.Y.

"Dear Ms. Chalkin," Zoya began to read aloud. In a moment they were both screaming on the phone.

"*Bozhe moi*! Oh my God!" Zoya was crying and laughing at the same time. "So much money, June! But Stanford University. I don't know much about ..."

"Call a cab, honey. Meet me at Pardeu's. I'm taking you out tonight and we're going to celebrate. And bring the letter. There's a lot you need to know that's not in it. And don't worry about Stanford. You're over-qualified and totally connected. See you in half an hour!"

"There's really no need to thank me, but I appreciate the call." Jack was speaking with Zoya. Bonnie had pulled him out of an early Monday morning meeting, and he was now standing next to her desk in her outer office. "I only made a few calls. June Peebles really brought your situation to my attention and, with the assistance of a few friends, things seem to have worked out."

Jack glanced at a scribbled note Bonnie had thrust into his hand. "You should plan to stop off in Nevada on your way out. Some people would like to meet you. Have you ever been to the West Coast?" There was a pause. "Ah, well, it's quite civilized. You needn't fear the cowboys and Indians." He laughed and listened a bit before interrupting. "*Izviniti*, (excuse me) Zoya, I need to get back into a meeting. Why don't you speak with Bonnie and the two of you work out something. Okay? You're very welcome. Talk to you soon, and congratulations. Bye." Jack handed the phone back to his assistant and re-entered his office.

"I can see now why you went to bat for her." The meeting now over, Bonnie sat at the conference table next to Jack taking a few notes. "She's remarkable. We talked for more than half an hour. You know she just had a birthday. I sent her a card from you."

Jack gave Bonnie a look. "Well, she's been through a lot for just a kid."

"She's no kid, boss. She certainly sounded like a woman to me on the phone. However I did sense that she's a bit overwhelmed about moving all the way out west. Too bad we can't do something to ease the transition."

"Bonnie, for God's sake don't go all maternal on me." Jack frowned and turned in her direction. "What did you do?"

"Nothing, but like I said, we talked. She's not due in Palo Alto until late September. That's more than two and one-half months from now. She needs to work and earn some money. So I talked with Gloria over in Human Resources. The comptroller is coming up on a big audit. They could use an experienced MBA for a couple of months. Zoya could make some good money and the dorms are empty for the summer, so housing would be no problem."

Jack leaned forward on his elbows and covered his face with his hands. "No, no, no, Bonnie. No way is this office going to solicit this kind of favor from the university. There are some people still raw over my getting rid of Bostwick, and they'd just love a little grist for the gossip mill. Christ, Bonnie! Tell me you haven't talked with anyone yet."

Bonnie raised her right hand. "I haven't. Swear to God."

"Good! Don't."

She nodded her head. "But the way I see it," she persisted, "you got this whole thing rolling. You're too invested in it to just let it drop now. Don't you always lecture me that life is like shooting billiards? Follow-through is everything."

Jack leaned back in his chair and sighed. She was right of course, but since driving up from Angelique's funeral in California last week he really hadn't given a damn about much. It was time to get back on the horse. "Okay, give me a chance to think and let's talk about it tomorrow. Right now, I'm going to the gym."

Early that evening he placed a call to Abe Glassman. The maid answered. "He's dining here at home with Mr. Melcher, Dr. Stark."

"Don't disturb them, Anna," Jack insisted. "It's only a social call. We can talk tomorrow." Jack hung up the phone, walked to the kitchen, and was opening a box of Cornflakes when the wall phone rang.

"What do you mean, only a social call. Messages like that make an old guy like me nervous." Abe Glassman laughed. "Mel says hello. He's right here about to carve up a six pound lobster. Here, I'm going to put you on speaker."

"Hi, Mel. I hear the opening was spectacular. Sorry I couldn't be there to see it. I can't believe you got that place up in only sixteen months."

"Including the knock down," Melcher added. "But don't be silly, Jack. You were where you needed to be. I lost my mother twenty years ago and I still catch myself reaching for the phone to call her. Please, we grieve for your loss."

"That means a lot to me. Thank you both for the wonderful flowers. How could you have known how much she loved pink irises?"

"Never mind. Now, Jack, before our lobster gets cold, what's on your mind?"

"Abe, you remember the Russian girl...?"

"Sure, I was just telling Mel the whole story. Why? I thought that was all settled."

"She needs a job and a place to stay until Stanford in late September."

"And you want it to be down here?"

"Of course," Melcher chimed in. "A kid with class like that. You want her first impression out here to be Reno? She'll run right back to Russia." They all laughed.

"Listen, Jack." Melcher continued. The casino can use all she's got, the MBA, banking experience, and the Russian. Christ, the Russian! Do you have any idea how much traffic we're getting now from that part of the world?"

"God, Mel, I don't know what to say."

"Just get her out here and we'll take care of the rest. Right, Abe?" There was a pause. "He's nodding okay, Jack. His mouth is full of lobster. Stay in touch, and again, regrets on your loss."

Jack put the cereal box back in the pantry and instead opened a bottle of zinfandel. The label showed a pastel of hillside vineyards with a river winding far below. It read 'Famiglia Stark Reserve, 1983'. He noted that there was only half a case left. Two glasses into the bottle, the phone rang again. He was tempted not to answer.

"Jack." Abe was obviously on the speaker. "Mel and I have been talking." It was also obvious that they had been downing a few martinis as well.

"Hello again to you both." Jack raised his glass.

"Listen, Jack. Like I said, Mel and I have been talking and we feel like having a little fun with this. You know, give the girl the red carpet treatment."

"Why the hell not, I say." Mel broke into the conversation. "She's had it tough, worked her ass off all of her short life. Why shouldn't two old farts have some fun?"

"What are you guys up to?"

"Jack, you just get her ready to travel by next Friday. Mel's coming up to New York from Miami in the Lear and he'll fly her out to Vegas. I may even join him, so you better warn her. Everything is arranged. She's going to work in the accounting department and live at the new hotel. Then it's off to Stanford and back on the job during vacations if she wants. Let me know. Mazal Tov."

ROBERT M. BERSI

The next morning, Bonnie was surprised to see Jack's car already in the still empty parking lot when she arrived early for work. His door was closed when she walked into the outer suite, and she noted that one of the phone buttons was lit. She brewed some coffee, pulled two huge bran muffins from her bag, all the while keeping an eye on the phone. As soon as the light went off, she knocked once and walked in. "Breakfast," she announced, placing the tray on Jack's desk, and sitting across from him. "Dig in, they're still warm."

"Thanks." Jack took a cautious sip of the hot coffee and proceeded to break off pieces of his muffin with a plastic fork. He sat quietly eating and sipping for a few moments.

Bonnie held her peace as long as she could. "So, who was that so early on the phone? Had to be East Coast, right?"

"It was June Peebles in Baltimore. I called to congratulate her on her new job."

"You already wrote her a note day before yesterday."

"Well, I wanted to call her."

Bonnie just sat, looking at him. Staff was beginning to trickle into the building now. Jack could see the cars pulling into the parking lot below. He leaned back in his chair and smiled at his assistant. He'd tortured her enough for one morning. "Okay, shut my door and I'll fill you in."

Bonnie listened without comment as Jack went over the last evening's events. When he finished, he waited for her reaction. "What's wrong? I thought you'd be all smiles."

"Las Vegas?"

"Yeah, I know, Bonnie. You wanted her up here so you could play mother hen. But that's not going to happen. This is the arrangement, and I was lucky that Abe and Mel were in their cups and feeling frisky."

"That's what I'm worried about."

"Give it a rest, will you, Bonnie. The girl's been living in Manhattan on her own for five years. She can take care of herself just fine. Besides, I've pushed this thing far enough. She has a hell of a deal now, and I'm done with it."

Bonnie could see that Jack was annoyed. He still hadn't recovered from the emotional stress of the past few weeks and he appeared physically exhausted. He needed a break from solving other people's problems. Pushing his chair back, he stood, turned away from her, and gazed out the window. "Listen, I'm going to take a few days to settle my mother's estate and tie up some loose ends down there. Then I'm going to disappear for a week or so. We're into the summer break now so that shouldn't be a problem, and if it is, I don't give a damn. Okay?"

Bonnie nodded.

"Also I want you to personally handle the logistics of getting Zoya up to Westchester Airport to hook up with Melcher's Lear jet next week. June Peebles is probably talking with her now, but you call and make damn sure everything gets done right and on schedule. If you need money to bridge some gaps, use your personal credit card. I'll cover your costs. Once she's in Las Vegas she'll be just fine. But you make it clear to her that if she has any problems or questions at any time to call you. Give her your home number. I don't want her calling here. You know all the players, Bonnie, and they know you, so there should be no problem handling this. Any questions, ask them now, because I'm leaving this morning."

She finished jotting notes and looked up. "Where will you be?"

"Connecticut."

NINE

"You look terrific!" Bonnie was obviously delighted to see Jack. He did look fit and rested. He was tan, wearing a new Brooks Brothers suit, and not carrying his briefcase. Nearly three weeks had elapsed since he walked out of the office that morning.

"Sorry I never called. Everything alright here?" Jack paced about his office as if he were seeing it for the first time. He dropped onto the corner couch and put his feet up on the coffee table. "All this is new."

"You just forgot. We ordered it months ago." Bonnie was looking hard at him. Something was different.

"Thanks for not bugging me. How did you manage?"

Bonnie sat down on the couch. "Well, for the first week I just bluffed. No one really pushed to see you. Then I sent out the memo that General Counsel was in charge for a week, and by the third week people were starting to gossip."

"That must have been hard on you. I'm sorry, but you never called."

"I tried Connecticut, but they said you'd gone fishing."

"They lied."

"I thought so, but it made a good story, so I just told people you were on a boat in Nova Scotia and couldn't be reached."

"Good for you. Let's use that again sometime."

"The Presidential Search Committee met without you. I took notes. They elected a chair, bickered over procedure for an hour or so… then scheduled another meeting."

Jack was leaning back, hands locked behind his head, staring up at the ceiling. He dropped forward and surveyed the stack of mail on his desk. "Anything in there you haven't already taken care of?"

She scooped the pile of mail from the desk and handed him a couple of pieces. "Just these, read the handwritten one first. She has beautiful script."

Bonnie rose to leave his office. "Thanks for the promotion. You didn't have to do that. The raise would have been enough."

"Pissed some people off, did it?"

"Oh, yeah." She moved towards the door, leaving him to his reading.

"Good," he said with a smile. "And Bonnie, about Connecticut…"

"That's okay, boss, just give me a heads up if you decide to take the job." She was gone.

One glance at the impeccable Cyrillic script disclosed its author. On a single page of plain bond, Zoya not only expressed her gratitude, but by writing him in Russian, revealed her insight into the true role he had played and that her sentiments and expressions were personal and for his eyes only. Jack read the note again, then carefully folded it and slipped it into his coat pocket. He glanced through the other correspondence and was about to buzz Bonnie, when she opened the door and stepped into his office.

"The Chair of the Presidential Search Committee is on the line. She's insisting on speaking with you. I've been putting her off for weeks, so you really should talk to her."

Jack nodded, sighed, and picked up the phone. He was back.

"Dr. Conseline, should I offer my congratulations or condolences?" Dr. Debra Conseline, Professor of General Surgery and Chair of the College of Medicine Women's Coalition, had not been a particular fan of former president Bostwick.

"I'm happy to accept both, Chancellor. You've been a hard man to reach. We missed you at the first search committee meeting."

"Oh, I doubt that. The group seems to have done well enough without me, and after this past year I sorely needed some out of touch time in the boondocks."

"How was the fishing in Nova Scotia?"

"Very therapeutic."

"Before we get down to business, Dr. Stark, I want to express my approval of your choice of Bryna Nagourney as acting president. You surprised some people with that choice."

"Favorably, I hope. Anyway, it sent the right message. *The Chronicle of Higher Education* gave the appointment unusually good coverage, so I think you can expect a good pool of candidates. And Debra, we're obviously going to be working together closely on this, so I'd be more comfortable if we were on a first name basis."

"Okay, so let's begin by talking about the search budget, Jack." Her tone was definitely less formal now.

"Good point, and only one of many issues we should discuss before the committee convenes again. We need to get started before my calendar gets clogged. Are you free for lunch today?"

"I guess that would be all right." Her voice gave away her sense of surprise.

"How about the River Club at noon?"

"One o'clock would work better for me, Dr. Sta... I mean, Jack."

"Perfect. See you there. And thanks for calling, Debra."

As soon as they hung up, Jack told Bonnie to reschedule his lunch with General Counsel and push back his afternoon appointments. He was about to make a new and politically valuable best friend.

When Dr. Debra Conseline was shown to their table Jack was already seated. He was gazing out the window at the Truckee River as it rushed through downtown Reno. Out of the corner of his eye, he spotted his guest being shown to the table and he rose to greet her. A tall, imposing woman in her mid-fifties, she was dressed in a Native American woven shift, belted at the waist with a silver link chain. Jack noted that she was wearing boots, even though it was mid-summer.

She extended her hand. "I'm a bit late."

"Not at all." Jack resisted the impulse to pull out her chair. He shook hands and waited for her to sit. "I've been lounging here day-dreaming about how many wedding rings have been tossed off that bridge into the river."

"I don't think they do that very much anymore." She nodded to the waiter who had arrived at the table carrying a glistening pitcher of iced water.

"You're probably right. It always seemed a bit environmentally repugnant to me anyways, polluting the river with shattered dreams."

She laughed. The ice was broken. "That was quite a surprise to the faculty when president Bostwick announced his resignation at commencement. I thought the Trustees liked him."

"Oh, I think they did."

"Why the abrupt departure, then?"

Jack, aware he was being pumped, just shrugged his shoulders. "Who knows, he might have been considering it for some time. My grandfather used to say that when good things happen we should simply accept them and move on. Let's talk about your budget."

"My budget?"

"Well, getting right to the point, I already authorized a substantial budget for the search and screening process." Jack passed a sheet of paper to her. "The funds will be in a designated account in the controller's office. He'll need an authorized signature for all expenditures. That should be the search committee chair, not me. I and one or two Trustees serve on the committee in an ex-officio, non-voting capacity. We'll participate in the process and discussions, but your committee will present your choices to me for recommendation to the Board."

"How many finalists are usually put forward?"

"Oh, over the years, here and elsewhere, I've seen as many as five or as few as one."

"That seems a bit extreme."

"It is. In one case it appears as if the committee hasn't done its job, and in the latter it appears to the Board that they are getting someone shoved down their throat. Two or three strong, acceptable candidates is a good number in my opinion."

"Rumor is that when you received your appointment as president in Connecticut the faculty committee told the Board that they wouldn't serve under anyone else. Is that true?"

"Well, they sent up two candidates, but yes, I learned afterwards that something like that occurred. Actually, it could have cost me the job. I don't recommend it. There are other, better ways, for the College of Medicine faculty to get the person they want."

"Do you think the Trustees will approve our top choice?"

"Probably, yes."

"How can you be so sure?"

"Well, the committee chair and the Chancellor are sitting here having lunch today. That's a good start."

"You know, Jack, I get the gut feeling you've done this before." She was smiling.

"Always trust your feelings, Debra."

Paddy O'Banion insisted that his first meeting as interim Chair of the Board of Trustees be scheduled in Las Vegas in August. When the northern Trustees called to complain that, for obvious reasons, the summer meeting was never held in southern Nevada, Jack politely reminded them that they elected Paddy to fill in as their Chair, not him. The agenda was light, and he reassured them that it probably would only be a one day session. Paddy's perverse ego, however, trumped any such hopes. He had grand plans for his debut as Chair. There would be a Wednesday evening outdoor poolside reception at his club. The entire day on Thursday would be devoted to public committee meetings. The Board would convene its regular session on Friday with full attendance by the media. They would adjourn at approximately 3:00 p.m. to an open bar reception for the press and general public. When Jack relayed the objections of the northern Trustees to such a lengthy stay in the heat of August for only a six-item agenda Paddy's comment was, "Fuck 'em." He would hold the Chair for sixteen more months until the next scheduled election.

Jack arrived in town a day early, booked into his usual low profile off-strip hotel/casino. He met Paddy there to go through the agenda as he had always done with Duke Butrum. Paddy seemed more interested in the hotel than the agenda. "Why don't you stay on the strip, Chancellor, like everyone else?"

"Oh, this place is quiet… not too pricey. It has everything I need and it's actually only a block from the strip, for that matter."

"Smart politics, huh?"

"Yeah, that too."

Paddy leaned in closer. "I got a meeting with somebody later today. This would be just right, you know."

Jack beckoned the waiter. "I'll get you a suite, Paddy. You're Chair of the Board now. You're entitled."

"No, don't bother. I only need it for a few hours. You've got a room. I can use that." Paddy's hand was extended, palm up.

"It's only a standard room, Paddy. Not even a decent table to sit around. Besides, my stuff is all over the place. Get a nice suite." Jack removed an envelope from his briefcase and placed it in Paddy's outstretched hand. "Here, I brought your new university credit card. You're the Chair of the Board now. You'll need it."

Paddy opened the envelope and looked at the card. "Huh, my name and everything. Not bad." He slipped the card into his shirt pocket. "But I don't want to blow it on a suite when I only need it for an hour or so. Your room will do."

Jack sat for a moment. When he spoke his tone was level, without emotion. "Listen, Paddy, you're the new Chair of the Board and I'm the Chancellor, right?"

"So?"

"So, we should be clear about the relationship… you know, get a good start. As I see it, my job includes making your job easier as Chair of the Board. It doesn't include personal concierge services."

A slow smile spread over Paddy's face. "Don't you like being Chancellor?"

"It's a tough job. Some days are better than others."

"Yeah, I can see that. Maybe I should just fire you and start fresh."

"We both know it's not that easy, Paddy."

Paddy's smile slowly faded. "I don't quite know how to read you yet, Stark. Just be careful."

"Always." They parted without shaking hands.

Jack made a few phone calls from the lobby. Despite the heat, he decided to walk the six blocks to Melvin Melcher's new palace on the strip. He hadn't seen it yet and was unprepared for the extravagant opulence of the place. Amazing what one could do these days with a billion dollars.

One of Melcher's security lieutenants recognized him. "Chancellor Stark, welcome."

"Hi, Tony." Jack smiled and extended his hand. "I thought we agreed to drop the Chancellor bullshit years ago."

Tony Mundo had been with Melcher since the beginning. His short, powerful build belied his age and, of course, there were stories. Jack liked and respected the graying little man.

"Are you staying with us this trip?"

"Just admiring the place, Tony. I had to miss the opening. Wow, this is something, even for Vegas."

"Mr. Melcher isn't around right now. Is there anything I can do for you? Have you had lunch?"

"Yeah. Listen, Tony, do you happen to know a Zoya Chalkin? She's a young..."

"The Russian girl, sure. She's here for the summer. Mr. Melcher told me to keep a special eye on her. Easy to do, too. She's a doll, and a nice kid."

"Where is she working?"

"Well, she was helping to look after a bunch of Russian guests a while ago. But she works most of the time in the cash control center. Why, do you know her?"

"We've met. She's going to Stanford this fall. Thought I'd drop by and see how she's doing, that's all. It's no big deal. I can catch her some other time."

"Well, at least let me give you a quick tour of the place. If I don't, when Mel hears you were here, he'll be pissed at me."

Jack laughed. "Hell, Tony, he'd be pissed at both of us. Let's go."

Even for Jack, it was an incredible experience. The hotel and casino amenities were beyond belief. They had just finished viewing one of the six thousand square foot suites reserved for special guests, when Tony's beeper went off. "Got an issue in the back. Tag along and I'll give you a glimpse of what's behind all the scenery."

As they were walking through the maze of offices and control centers that monitored the functions of the massive operation, Tony pointed a stubby finger. "Hey, there she is." A young woman dressed in tailored black slacks and a white, long sleeve blouse had just stepped into the hall and was walking away from them.

"Zoya!" The girl turned and recognizing Tony, stopped and waited.

"Zoya Alexandrovna." Jack extended his hand. *"Ochen rad vas vidit. Kak dela?"* (So happy to see you. How are you doing?)

She had obviously not placed Jack until he spoke. Quickly regaining her composure, she grasped his hand and beamed a smile of recognition. *"Harasho,* Chancellor Stark, *ochen harasho. Spaciba.* (Good, very good, thank you.)

Tony kept walking. "Zoya, why don't you show Dr. Stark where you work? I'll only be a minute."

She nodded and led Jack through a double door and into a vast carpeted area clustered with computerized work stations. "This is part of our financial controls system," Zoya dutifully explained as she entered a small side office. "I'm in here."

Jack took a chair near a bank of three wide-screen monitors spread over a table. Zoya sat next to him. "Sorry about the disorder, but we never get visitors in here, so I sort of spread out when I'm working on a project."

"Like what?" Jack asked, waving his hand at the crowded desk. "What's this all about?"

"Oh, I came up with an idea for cross-auditing cash flow. Mr. Melcher had me set up in here so I could work on it in my spare time. He's been very good to me. I can't thank you enough."

"Your letter said it all, Zoya. I was quite moved." Jack noticed a large calendar on the wall with September 17 circled in red. He pointed. *"Krasnyi den, da?"* (Red-letter day, yes?)

She beamed. "Oh, yes!" My first day at Stanford University! I'm excited and anxious, all at the same time. You know, I've never been to California. I intended to read up on the history of the state and Stanford, but I've been so involved here with my job and I really want to finish this cash flow model before I leave."

"Well, Zoya, I'm a native Californian with all three degrees from Stanford."

"Yes, I know."

Jack reached up and with his pen and drew a line under the week prior to September 17. "I'm in Silicon Valley only a few miles from Palo Alto for this entire week. If you can arrange to arrive a day or so early, there are some people you should meet."

She looked somewhat conflicted. "That would be wonderful, but I feel so obligated here."

"Don't worry about it. If what I hear about you is true, you'll manage. I hope Mr. Melcher appreciates such loyalty."

"Excuse me." A young man was standing at the open door. "Dr. Stark, Mr. Mundo will be tied up for some time. He asked that I finish the tour."

Jack stood. "Thanks, I've seen enough for one day. If you would guide me out to the lobby." He turned to Zoya. "Good luck with the project. I imagine advising you not to work too hard would be a waste of breath." He smiled, turned, and was gone before she could respond. She stood in the doorway and followed him with her eyes until he was out of sight.

TEN

September arrived with the northern Trustees still exorcised over the August meeting in Las Vegas. Paddy O'Banion rejected Jack's counsel and insisted on being the sole architect of his debut as Chair. The result was a media disaster. None of the hastily scheduled Thursday committee meetings had published agendas, placing them at risk of violating Nevada 'sunshine' laws. Being political animals, most of the Trustees stayed home. On Friday a few of them pulled a 'sick out'. Las Vegas Trustee Judi Chang had a flight delay out of Chicago, and Paddy's general meeting of the Board of Trustees was without a quorum and could not convene to conduct business. Paddy forced everyone to hang around for hours waiting for Chang to show. Finally the ice sculpture melted, the food table was picked clean, and the press drifted away to write their scathing reviews. Most had a field day ridiculing the Board of Trustees and their new leader with editorials and cartoons. Some called for an investigation into how much of the taxpayer's money had been wasted on transporting, feeding, and housing scores of staff from the nine campuses for three days. Even Jack, as

Chancellor, drew a few random barbs, but it was worth it to teach Paddy a lesson.

The evenings were really not chilly enough in Reno yet to justify a fire, but the house seemed cold and empty, and Jack indulged himself with a cheery blaze and a snifter of brandy. He had just touched a match to the tinder when the phone rang.

"Boss, sorry to intrude on your inner sanctum, but I just finished speaking with Zoya, and I think you need to give her a call."

"Bonnie, we talked about this, remember. Can't you handle it?"

"Not this. Melcher just made her a near six-figure offer to stay on, and the girl's head is spinning."

"Well, I'm really not too surprised, to tell you the truth. She's got the background and the brains to be worth plenty to them down there. Did she ask to get in touch with me?"

"Not in so many words, but she needs your counsel. I can hear it in her voice. Christ, boss, she's got no one at all to talk to. I never had a good feeling about this Vegas thing. Here, write down her number in case you decide to call. By the way, it was her birthday last week."

Jack sat slouched back on the couch, staring into the flames. He swirled his second brandy, downed it with one gulp, and reached for the phone.

"Zoya, it's Dr. Stark."

There was a moment of silence. Then a quiet, tenuous response. "Yes. Of course I recognize your voice, Chancellor.

"Bonnie called me with the good news. Do you want to talk about it?"

"Very much. A day ago I was preparing for my move to Stanford and now..." She stopped.

"I know. You're caught in the middle of two very exciting prospects. And to complicate things, you're conflicted about disappointing any number of people, including me, right?"

"Yes, I think so."

"Zoya, *slushai!* (Listen!) *Ya hachu pravdu, panimaesh* (I want the truth, do you understand?)"

"*Da, ya panimau.* (Yes, I understand.)"

"You're facing a life-defining decision. It's not your first and it certainly won't be your last. Believe me, I've been there myself. Tell me, how do you feel right now?"

"How do you say, like the deer in the lights?"

Jack smiled. "Like a deer in the headlights," he corrected.

"Yes, that's it, and I am so confused that I can't think clearly. This is not like me. I'm ashamed to admit it, but I feel frozen."

"Then you need to talk with someone you trust. What about your mother?"

"I can't burden her with this. I know her. If I share these feelings, she will abandon everything to be beside me. It would take weeks to get a visa, and even then, what does she know of such things American?"

"So, who then? June Peebles?"

Jack thought he heard her say something, but he wasn't certain. Her voice was so subdued. "Say again, please, Zoya. I couldn't hear."

She was barely audible, but he heard, "You."

"Me? Zoya, this decision could set your course for life. Why me?"

117

"Do you still have my letter?"

"Yes."

"That is why."

"Because of what you said in your letter?"

"No, because you kept it."

Jack sat in silence for a moment, thinking. "Okay, you're facing a tough decision… alone. I can relate to that. Can you get away for a couple of days?"

"I've never asked. But, yes, I guess I could."

"Good. Throw a few things in a bag: a skirt, a few tops, whatever. Wear jeans tomorrow and tell your supervisor you need to take some time off. Something's come up and you'll be back, say, Wednesday night. Don't ask him. Tell him on your way out the door. Then take the 9:20 United shuttle to San Francisco Airport. There's always plenty of empty seats. I'll meet you on the curb outside arrival/baggage. Look for a silver BMW coupe. We'll talk more then. You need some perspective, so we're going to be busy for a couple of days. Okay?"

"Yes. Thank you. I feel better already."

"Good. See you tomorrow morning."

Jack looked at his watch. It was still not too late to phone Dave Newman and ask him to set up a few things. It would be a good chance to gauge how high they'd jump for an alumnus who happened to be on the Feingold Foundation Board. Later, as he packed and prepared for an early start the next morning, he was unaware that he was humming to himself for the first time in months.

Three hours after departing Reno, Jack turned into the SFO arrival underpass and maneuvered into the passenger pick-up lane. He was scanning the crowd of arriving passengers, when a rap on his windshield startled him. He lowered the passenger window and Zoya, her long auburn hair pulled back into a pony tail, leaned in and smiled. "I saw you coming up the ramp, but you drove right past me."

She was wearing navy blue culottes, flats, and a white pullover top. In her right hand she carried a small Prada bag. Jack stretched across and pushed open the passenger door. "I was looking for a girl in jeans."

She slid into the car. "Sorry, I left in such a rush, they're still wet."

As she closed the door and snapped into her seat belt, Jack took her bag and carefully placed it on the rear seat.

She managed a slightly guilty look. "It's a knock-off."

"Well, it's a good one." Jack glanced at her and smiled as he pulled the BMW into traffic. Thirty minutes later they entered the Stanford campus and drove down the mile long palm-studded avenue which led toward the main campus. Zoya craned her head in all directions, admiring the rose gardens, flower beds, and clusters of blooming shrubs and trees which punctuated the vast expanse of manicured lawns.

"It's beautiful," she kept repeating, "so beautiful."

"You're seeing only a fraction of the campus. The buildings up ahead are the central quadrangle. We'll be walking through them on our way to your first meeting with David Newman. He's an old friend and anxious to meet you."

Jack parked in a restricted zone close in the quad, and placed his card under the windshield wiper. Zoya, meanwhile, had unzipped her bag and extracted a pair of Kenneth Cole clogs, a small makeup case, and a hair brush. She touched up her lipstick, slipped into the high heel clogs, and stepped out of the car. Jack stood watching with fascination. She reached back and released the clasp holding her hair and with one shake of her head the flowing mane fell about her shoulders and down her back. A few strokes of the brush completed the transformation from cute graduate student to stunning young woman. She looked up and smiled. "I'm ready."

Jack glanced at his watch. "We're a bit early for lunch, so let's use the time for a short tour and history lesson."

They strolled past statuary, through arched walkways, and paused by a fountain. Jack kept up a running narrative about his alma mater. Now one hundred years old, Stanford was built to memorialize Jane and Governor Stanford's only child, Leland Jr., who, before his sixteenth birthday, succumbed to an infection during a visit to Florence, Italy. The bereaved parents finally settled upon the idea of building a distinguished university where promising young men of California could attend tuition-free. After a number of challenges, on April 6, 1892, the "Leland Stanford Jr. University," reported it the *New York Times*, "…opened its empty halls to the empty minds of the far west." Jane Stanford, now widowed, became its first and only trustee. As the decades passed there was enormous growth and change. Inevitably, tuition became a necessary reality. Women were finally admitted after World War I and for decades restricted in number to what was jokingly called "the frozen 500". After World War II, such practices evaporated, and Stanford moved rapidly to secure a position of world prominence. Still affectionately referred to as "the farm", the 8,000-acre campus sits on the original Stanford horse ranch.

Zoya had been listening intently to Jack's narrative. "You love this place, don't you?"

"Oh yeah," Jack answered, rising to his feet, "every blade of grass, every moment of time. There's something about it that never leaves you."

They walked a bit further. "Here we are." Jack opened a heavy brass handled door, and Zoya preceded him into a marble foyer. A modest polished metal sign read, "University Advancement, Office of the Vice President." The receptionist looked up and smiled as Dave Newman burst out of his office. "I saw you from my window."

"How are you, David?" Jack grasped his friend's outstretched hand.

"This, of course, must be Ms. Zoya Chalkin." Newman smiled. "*Dobro pazhalovat!* (Welcome.)

"Yes, Dr. Newman. *Ochen priyatno* (It's my pleasure)."

Newman motioned towards the hallway. "Come, come. We have a lot of catching up to do, and I'm so looking forward to getting to know you, Zoya. We've plenty of time for lunch. Your appointment with Dean Chukmajian isn't until three."

As they walked, Jack joked, "What's with the Russian, Newman?"

"That's the only word I know. In fact I can say it in six languages... comes in handy in this job. Here we are." Newman led them through a tiled patio into a beautifully appointed, carpeted dining room ringed with arched windows opened wide to the surrounding gardens. A slight breeze moved through the room fluttering the white tablecloths. "Let's sit here, where we have a good view of the Chapel. Zoya, you must have Jack take you inside before you leave. You would appreciate the art. There are even a number of authentic icons. Thousands of Stanford grads have been married there. Beth and I were." He looked at Jack. "I venture that's probably the only time you ever set foot in the place during your eight years here."

"Oh, I dropped in from time to time. Good place to study."

"Study? He never studied, Zoya. He was a fraternity rat and an accomplished dilettante, always running in those hills, playing golf free on the university course, or hanging out in the city. I never saw you crack a book, old buddy. Remember how we would crash all the campus receptions for the free food and booze?" He turned to Zoya again, who by this time was not sure whether to be amused or embarrassed. "That's why Beth married me. It was obvious that Jack had no future."

Jack jutted his chin. "You left out Phi Beta Kappa, Magna Cum Laude, and, oh yes, that Hoover fellowship."

"You just knew the right people. Anyhow, we can haggle over old times later. We're embarrassing Zoya when we should be going over her schedule."

"Agreed. Let's stop showing off in front of the young lady, David. Go ahead."

"Well, Zoya, you meet first with the Dean of the School of Business and a few key faculty who are very impressed with your resume. The dean's bio is in this folder. Just relax and enjoy yourself. The faculty want you in the program and that's all that matters. After your visit you'll be delivered back to my office where a grants coordinator from the controller's office will take you through the financials. Then you are on your own until tomorrow. I'll meet you for breakfast at 8:30. Jack knows where. Oh, and I've set you both up in suites at University House. Sorry to abandon you but, unfortunately, I'm tied up tonight."

Zoya took the folder and glanced inside. "I can't thank you enough, Dr. Newman. You've gone to so much trouble."

"Don't mention it. Besides," he added while looking at Jack, "I want this guy indebted to me for reasons of my own."

They had a leisurely lunch during which Jack remained mostly silent while David and Zoya conversed. At the Dean's office there were introductions and an exchange of pleasantries with a couple of department chairs before Jack and David departed for the Advancement Office.

"Christ, Jack, I was prepared to be impressed, but she is really a piece of work. And she appears to be as brilliant as she is beautiful." He was laughing as they walked. "I thought for a moment, there, that the Dean was going to wet himself."

"I tell you, Dave, I've come to respect that, with Zoya, you have to look past those big green eyes. A thousand years of mother Russia lays buried in her soul. There's a chord of aristocracy about her that belies her Soviet background. It's elusive at this point, my friend, but I'll wager she's more of an imperialist capitalist than either of us."

"Maybe so, but meanwhile she's eye candy with brains. You can't deny that. Now, let's talk about you and Feingold. You're really in?"

"Oh yeah, it's official, even been appointed to the steering committee. Seems they want a fresh perspective at the annual meeting next month."

"Where's it being held this year?"

"Somewhere in the Cayman Islands."

"Christ, give me a break! Is the Stanford proposal on the agenda?"

Jack smiled broadly. "You know I can't tell you that."

"You just did. Thanks."

As the two men entered Newman's office they found a young woman from the university controller's office waiting. She rose to meet them. "Dr. Newman, I'm a bit early, but there's a small problem I thought we should discuss before we meet with Miss Chalkin."

"Fine, Rachel. First let me introduce Chancellor Jack Stark. Dr. Stark is a member of the Feingold Foundation Board. He can sit in with us on this."

As they sat down, Newman waved away his assistant's offer of coffee. "What's the problem, Rachel?"

The young woman spread some financial forms on the table in front of Newman. "Well, Dr. Newman, as you know the university charges an overhead cost for every grant received."

Newman nodded his head. "Sure, all universities do. That's how they cover costs of administering the grant."

"Well, sir, as you can see here," she pointed with her pen to a line on one of the forms. "The School of Business is planning to charge a 49% indirect cost per annum."

"What!" Jack's exclamation startled the girl.

Newman was scanning the sheet. "There must be some mistake. Scholarship grants are always limited to eight percent."

"The School of Business sees this as a grant to its Eastern European Studies Program, rather than a scholarship grant directly to the student. They could call it either way, but technically they're correct." The young woman was avoiding looking at Jack, who had now stood and was pacing about the room.

"Goddamn it, David. Their skimming nearly $152,000 off the grant. Jake Feingold will be furious. After tuition and fees, it leaves her with almost nothing to live on. I thought everyone understood the spirit of this grant?"

"So did I, Jack. I walked this through every step. This shouldn't have happened. Rachel, leave these papers with me and I'll get back to the Controller on this." She nodded and scurried out, closing the door behind her without bidding farewell to an obviously furious Jack Stark.

"What the fuck is going on, David?"

"It's Chuk, that asshole."

"Chuk?"

"The Dean, Gary Chukmajian, the greedy son-of-a-bitch. He was all smiles when I told him of the grant to his precious program. Moreover, he understands the University's position with the Feingold Foundation. But he just couldn't resist reaching for the money. It goes right into his discretionary account. The worst thing about it is that he's within his rights. Technically, it's a grant to the School and not to the student. But he understood the deal. The arrogant little bastard double crossed me."

"So, make him change his mind."

"I can't, Jack. It's an academic issue. You of all people know how that works."

"So, who around here can?"

Newman thought for a moment. "Probably the Provost. All the academic deans report to him. He'd have the most leverage, but I can't approach him with this."

"Does he know I'm on campus?"

"Oh hell yes. Getting a visit from a Feingold Foundation Board member who is an alum is a feather in my cap. You can bet I let him know that I got you here."

"I'd like to meet him."

"That's great. But I don't like the tone in your voice, Jack."

"Relax. I won't compromise you. But Christ, Dave, we're running out of time here."

Newman's assistant informed him that Zoya was outside, having just returned from her meeting at the School of

Business. "Have her wait for a moment, Claire, and see if you can arrange a meeting for Dr. Stark with the Provost. You know what to say."

Zoya was ushered into Newman's office and proceeded to tell them of her meeting. Apparently she had spent most of her time there with the Chair of the Finance Department and the Chair of the Information Systems Department. Both had apparently vied for her interest in their respective Ph.D. programs. The three way exchange had been substantive and they were so impressed with her that they suggested a combined program with concentrations in both areas. Jack nodded and smiled at her excitement about their competitive interest in her.

"What about the Dean?" he asked.

"Oh, he didn't stay on after you and Dr. Newman left."

Newman's assistant interrupted. "Dr. Newman, the Provost is free and would very much like to meet with Chancellor Stark."

"Now?"

"Yes, sir, if that's possible."

Jack was on his feet. "Zoya, you'll have to occupy yourself for an hour. I need to see this fellow."

"Oh, we'll take care of her," David offered.

Zoya shook her head. "No, please. Just give me a map and let me explore the campus by myself."

Jack shrugged his shoulders. "Okay then. I'll meet you by the Chapel in one hour. Have fun."

Jack never had occasion to be around the University Provost's office during his eight years as a student on campus. As he was shown in, he was surprised at the modest simplicity of the spacious suite. This is an unpretentious fellow, he thought. He was immediately greeted by a short, somewhat portly man, dressed in a rumpled blue blazer, grey pants, and scruffy penny loafers. Ted Benedetto extended both hands in welcome. "Dr. Stark, what a pleasant surprise."

"It's my pleasure, sir, being back on this campus."

"So let's walk while we talk." Benedetto led the way out a sliding glass door and onto a pathway which wandered through a eucalyptus grove. They exchanged stories of one another's adventures in academe. Benedetto was intrigued with Jack's tales of Nevada. Inevitably the topic of Jack's appointment to the Feingold Foundation Board arose.

"It's uncharacteristic for a westerner to be invited," Benedetto commented.

Jack finally saw his opening. "Well, circumstances arose which enabled me to be of some service to Mr. Feingold. We became well acquainted and learned that we shared some highly regarded mutual friends. The rest was, well, Ted, you know how it goes ..."

"I assume David Newman has discussed the University's current proposal before Feingold?"

"It wasn't necessary. I had already read it the last time I was in New York. Thirty million, as I recall. He did ask if it was on the agenda for the annual meeting next month. Of course, I couldn't discuss that, but the agenda is still a work in progress, as far as I know."

"Of course, we understand."

"I need you to be assured of one thing, however," Jack went on. "I truly love this university. Students can accumulate a treasure here that will sustain them for a lifetime. It's a pity that Zoya Chalkin won't have that opportunity."

The University Provost stopped in his tracks. "I don't understand. Newman informed me that she's here for a few days meeting people in preparation for..."

"Yes, but unfortunately we encountered an unacceptable impediment to those plans. We'll be leaving tonight." Jack looked at his watch. "In fact, she's meeting me in front the Chapel in five minutes." Jack extended his hand to the dumfounded Benedetto. "You've been very gracious. I've enjoyed our talk."

"Please." Benedetto clung to Jack's hand. "What happened? Is there anything I can do?"

"Well," Jack turned back towards the Provost's office. "Let's talk about it as we walk."

When Jack finally arrived at the University Chapel, Zoya was nowhere to be seen. He pushed through the heavy baroque doors and stepped inside.

Late afternoon sunlight was filtering through the stained glass windows. Soon he spotted her sitting alone midway down the middle aisle.

"Beautiful, isn't it?" The sound of his voice startled her.

"Oh, yes," she whispered.

"Sorry I was so late."

"Oh, don't be. I've been sitting here thinking of home."

They sat silently for a moment. Finally she turned to him. "Is everything all right?"

"Yes," he answered softly. "Everything is just fine."

As they exited the Chapel, Jack turned to Zoya. "We still have plenty of time before sunset. I'd really like to visit an old haunt, for sentimental reasons. It's a bit of a drive, but you might enjoy it. I can drop you off at the guest house. You can you jump into something more casual and be ready to go in, say, an hour?"

"Of course, easily."

Jack laughed and shook his head.

"What's so amusing?" she asked.

"Oh, nothing. I was just chiding the gods that you weren't here when I was a student." Before she could respond, Jack stopped walking. "Here we are. I'll be back in..."

"One hour," Zoya completed his sentence and disappeared into the foyer of the building.

She was standing by the steps wearing jeans and a red t-shirt as Jack pulled up in the BMW. A white tennis sweater was draped over her shoulders. "You're late," she joked, dropping into the seat of the BMW. She noticed that the moon roof was open.

"Don't worry, I'll make up the time. Buckle up." The car surged forward, tossing gravel, as Jack turned sharply onto a narrow road that curved away toward a distant ridge of forested mountains. Within moments they were out of sight of the campus and beginning to climb into the trees.

"We're going to a dinner lodge atop the far ridge. There's a lot of history there for me." They were climbing sharply now through a deep redwood forest. Jack deftly guided the car around scores of hairpin turns, accelerating out of each before shifting down for the next.

"We're in the La Honda redwoods now," Jack closed the moon roof without taking his eyes off the narrow road. The great trees thrust upwards into a wet mist, and Zoya began to feel as if she were being transported to a different world and time. They suddenly broke onto the crest of the mountain. Jack slowed, peering quickly in both directions, and turned sharply right. "Below us, miles to our left, is the Pacific Ocean and behind you, to the right, is civilization." He had turned on the headlights and was cruising slowly through the mist searching for familiar landmarks.

"Ah, there it is." He eased the BMW off the road, coming to a stop next to a slightly tilted neon sign. The neon letters

"BELLA VISTA" cast their glow upon a half dozen cars parked randomly outside the entrance. Jack set the brake and stepped from the car. "C'mon, kiddo, let's see if time has forgotten this place."

They walked briskly through the chilly mist, and Jack pushed a heavy oak door open and followed Zoya inside. Pausing for a moment they surveyed the huge wood paneled room. To the far right a fire blazed in a fieldstone fireplace that covered half the wall. A crescent of rough cut reclining chairs, some with faded pillows, sat on a great rag carpet near the hearth. A young couple shared a battered Adirondack love seat, sipping beers and staring silently into the flames. A polished wooden bar with a bass rail and stools stretched down the left wall and dog legged right in the direction of the fireplace. Every manner of western memorabilia festooned the walls on all sides.

"Oh, thank God," Jack exclaimed under his breath. Taking Zoya by the arm he moved further into the room. As they reached the bar Jack boosted Zoya up on one of the tall stools. She caught her breath at the scene which stretched before her. Beyond the bar a cozy windowed dining room jutted out from the mountain revealing an endless chain of lights blinking like stars in the far distance below them.

A grizzled old bartender slowly approached. "Two Manhattans on the rocks," Jack said quickly. Then turning to Zoya, "Indulge me, please?" She nodded and smiled. Their hurried departure and whirlwind drive up the mountain had distracted her until now. Standing next to her with his foot on the rail was a totally different man. No longer shrouded in a Brooks Brother's suit and academic credentials, she could appraise him from a totally different perspective. He was tall, athletically built, and surprisingly handsome in his boot cut jeans and Pendleton shirt. She sat studying his profile, for the first time noticing the cleft in his chin. The strong, rugged hands gripping the bar hinted of tales not yet told.

"Here you are, folks." The bartender put down their drinks. "If you're planning to have dinner, I should let the kitchen know. It's been sort of a light evening."

"Do you still serve that sixteen-ounce rib eye?" Jack asked.

"Couldn't stay open without it." The bartender looked at Jack. "I feel I should know you, fella, but ..."

"It was a long time ago." Jack pointed past the window in the direction of the Stanford campus.

"Oh, hell yeah, you're one of the old gang. These college boys today don't make it up here like they used to. They're not much for raising hell like your bunch. Anyways, welcome back!"

He turned to Zoya. "Young lady, I should have asked for your I.D. before serving that drink." Zoya, smiled, opened her purse, and produced a couple of cards.

The old man held them up to the light and studied them for a moment. "Damn, I never would've guessed it." Handing them back to Zoya, he smiled at Jack. "She don't talk much, does she?"

"Well, that's my fault. You haven't been properly introduced." Jack gave the bartender a questioning look and waited.

"Virgil."

Jack nodded. "Thanks for reminding me. Virgil, I'm Jack. Allow me to present Zoya Alexandrovna Chalkin. She's from St. Petersburg, Russia." Zoya gave Jack a feigned look of disapproval.

The old man stiffened in surprise, stepped back, and began to walk away. "Hell, I've got to tell cook. You two find a table over by the corner window. Pick out a bottle of red and two glasses. We'll be right out with your salad." He disappeared into the back talking to himself. "All the way from Russia. Christ almighty."

Three hours, two steaks, and two bottles of wine later, they waved goodbye and set off down the mountain towards Stanford. Less than an hour later they pulled up to the campus guest house.

Before getting out of the car, Zoya turned to Jack. "Thanks for letting me drive. I loved it."

"Well, you earned it, speaking Russian to old Virgil and his wife. Sorry if I embarrassed you." Jack stepped out of the car. "Keep the keys. I need a good walk across campus. Say, we meet right here tomorrow at eight?"

"All right, if that's what you'd like."

"I'd like." He began walking away. "I really had fun tonight, Zoya. You're a terrific girl."

She stood by the car watching him until he was out of sight. "I'm not a girl, Jack."

Newman was already seated and sipping coffee when Jack and Zoya walked into the Waffle House on University Avenue in downtown Palo Alto. He looked up and waved them over. "I thought you'd forgotten me."

"Sorry, man." Jack let Zoya slide into the booth opposite David, then sat beside her. Zoya and Newman were already engaged in morning greetings as the waitress dropped two menus in front of them and poured coffee without asking.

"Have you ordered?" Jack asked without opening the menu.

"No, been waiting for you two."

Jack looked up at the waitress. "Belgium Waffles, fresh strawberries over, and two scrambled eggs on the side.

"All around?" The waitress asked.

Jack handed back the menus. "And the lady would prefer hot tea, not coffee."

"Same old Jack," David nodded his assent then looked at Zoya who smiled and shrugged her shoulders.

"What's on the agenda today?" Jack asked.

"Well it's changed a bit." David gave Jack a look. "What in the hell happened over at the Provost's office yesterday afternoon?"

"Nothing much," Jack said innocently. "We walked and talked for an hour. Nice guy, Benedetto."

"Well somebody sure as hell lit a fire. The Controller's office called and said the indirect cost percentage has been waived completely. So, Zoya, it appears that the entire $292,500 grant inures to your doctoral study activities. The Business School Dean's secretary has scheduled you to meet with the two department chairs again. Seems they have something exciting to propose, and it has to be today. Have you decided on an area of concentration yet?"

Zoya looked up from the huge waffle the waitress had placed in front of her. "Well, I'm torn between Banking and Finance or Information Systems. Frankly, the two fields are so interdependent, I'd like to do both."

"I think that will be up to you. You're scheduled for two hours with them from ten to twelve, so it appears they're anxious to do some serious planning. Hell, I don't know. These are world class guys, with international reputations, so you should enjoy yourself. The three of us can meet in my office at noon for a sandwich and hash out what you've learned."

"What was the grant amount, again, Dr. Newman?"

"Two hundred ninety-two thousand, five hundred."

Zoya pushed her waffle away. "Wow. So much money."

"Don't worry," David chided with a smile. "This is Stanford. You'll need it all."

An hour later, as they exited the restaurant, Newman turned to Jack. "What in the hell did you do, Stark?"

Just before twelve noon, Newman's secretary stepped into his office and announced that Zoya would be lunching at the faculty dining room and wouldn't be returning until one-thirty or two.

David gave Jack a knowing look. "Oh, money is honey, my little sonny." They both laughed and opened their box lunches.

Jack was on the phone when Zoya finally returned to David's office. He waved her in, and she sat for a few moments while he finished what appeared to be a heated conversation. She tried not to listen, but couldn't help noticing the tone of command in his voice as he concluded the call.

"Sorry," he said, spinning the chair in her direction. "Still have a University of my own to run."

"Not a serious problem, I hope?" She set her thin leather case on the coffee table.

"Yes actually, but it'll work out."

Newman walked in. "Zoya. How did your meeting go? We thought they were never going to bring you back."

"I'm so sorry, but Dr. Brukner and Dr. Koachin wanted me to meet some of their colleagues. They said they called your office."

"Not to worry." David looked at Jack and dropped into a nearby couch. "We both enjoyed our sandwiches and wondered what mischief they were up to. You didn't sign anything, did you?"

Zoya looked confused. "Uh, no. We just talked and talked. It was all quite exciting."

"Relax, I was just kidding. Tell us all about it. Jack's been on the phone the whole time, and I had some business of my own to tend to. Did you get something accomplished?"

"Oh my, yes! I had no idea how extensive the Eastern European Program is. We talked about a hybrid doctoral concentration in both international banking and finance conjoined with information technology. Both of them agreed that it should be no problem and that, indeed, I would be ideal for that format. They wanted to know all about my Academy studies in Russia as well as my MBA/internship with the bank in New York. At lunch a Russian speaking member of the faculty joined us along with some others from Prague and Minsk."

Jack raised his hand slightly. "What firm commitments, if any, did they make?"

Zoya opened her case, extracted a pad, flipped a few pages, and began reading. "First, the hybrid Ph.D. is a go, no problem. Everyone thought that it made sense. Second, because I have the MBA from Columbia University, they offered to let me test into much of the first year curriculum. We could use the time saved for faculty-directed projects here and abroad. Third, for obvious reasons, my foreign language requirement will be considered met. And finally, both department chairs offered to serve jointly on my dissertation committee. Everyone had interesting suggestions for research projects we could do together." She looked up waiting for their reaction.

Jack looked across the room at David who had been jotting notes. "So, what do you think, Dave? Sounds to me like they're going to 'fast track' her."

"Pretty damn good. The terms need to be set forth in the Doctoral Study Contract with the departments involved and the School of Business, but it doesn't sound like that's going to be a problem."

"So it seems," Jack added. "It's obvious that they want to piggy-back on some of that grant money, but that's all right if it serves Zoya's priorities as well. My only concern is who will have the signature authority over expenditures of her account."

Newman had been studying a memorandum just given to him by one of his staff. "Make a couple of copies of this, Myra, will you?"

A moment later, Jack and Zoya were reading a staff directive from the Controller's office that Dr. David Newman, Vice President for University Advancement, was to have sole expenditure authority over the Feingold Foundation doctoral studies grant for Zoya Chalkin.

"Shit!" Newman waved the memo at Jack. "This is going to really piss off the Dean. I've already got enough problems with that asshole! Pardon me, Zoya."

"Relax." Jack folded the memo. "You and Provost Benedetto are going to enjoy your upcoming visit to the Big Apple for a friendly tour of the Feingold Foundation offices. On your way back you can stop off in Vegas and we can have dinner and take in a show. In fact, why don't you invite the wives to meet you in Vegas and make a weekend of it as my guest?"

"Your guest?"

"Well, Caesar's Palace's guest, actually."

Newman threw up his arms and stood. "I'm late for a meeting. Zoya, *ochen priyatno* (it's been a pleasure). When you get settled here, Beth wants to have you over for dinner. She's dying to meet you. Meanwhile, look out for this guy. You see now how he operates."

"It is very Russian actually." Zoya smiled and reached for Newman's hand. "*Bolshoe spasibo* (many thanks), Dr. Newman. You have been so helpful."

"Hey, Newman, did you get that thing I asked for?"

"It's right outside. Bye."

Resting against the curb, facing outward was a shiny new golf cart, Stanford colors and all, with the key dangling from the dash. "That's my boy! Come on, Zoya. You're going to see plenty in the next couple of hours... from horse stables to concert halls. I'll narrate. You ask questions. Meanwhile, have a Coke." The cart lurched forward and they were off.

Later that evening, Jack stood beside her as passengers boarded the United flight to Las Vegas. He again apologized for cutting the trip short. "That damn phone call."

"Please, Jack. It was a grand experience. I know everything I need to know now. I am no longer helpless in the headlights." She was smiling up at him, her green eyes glistening with unshed tears.

"Zoya, if you need..."

She put her finger to his lips, kissed him quickly on the cheek, and disappeared into the passageway.

Jack stood watching until the aircraft pushed away and taxied onto the tarmac. "Steady, boy." He turned abruptly and strode onto the moving walkway, quickening his pace as he raced away from what once might have been and toward the relentless responsibilities which were his life. Hours later as he raced over the crest of the Sierras towards Reno his hand touched his cheek and fell away.

ELEVEN

The annual meeting of the national Association of Governing Boards convened in Washington, D.C. in late September. The northern Trustees always attended, and this year Judi Chang from Las Vegas would join them for the first time. Judi Lee Chang's family had been in southern Nevada since before air conditioning. A widow in her mid-forties with two children, she directed much of her time and family wealth to local humanitarian causes. The delay of her Chicago flight a month earlier had spared her from Paddy O'Banion's board meeting debacle. Nevertheless, she had been tarred with the same scathing statewide media criticism as her colleagues, and Paddy had made it no secret that he blamed her for his failure to produce a quorum. Jack had stopped off in Detroit to meet with officers of Burrows Corporation and planned to join the Trustees at the conference where he was scheduled to speak. His lead article on corporate/college cooperation in a recent *AGB Journal* had sparked a great deal of interest. He professed an aggressive, highly personal and entrepreneurial approach in dealing with private corporations. The shortest distance between two points, he maintained, was a straight line. Chief executives, he maintained, talk to chief executives and direct CEO to CEO contact should command a University President's agenda. It saved a great deal of time and energy and accelerated the decision-making process. Moreover, a hand held out palm up is not nearly as well received as a handshake. He advised university leaders to think partnership.

While in D.C., Jack planned to have a few side meetings to discreetly explore an exit strategy from Nevada. Duke Butrum, though no longer a Trustee, had given Jack a head's-up that Paddy O'Banion was working hard to gather the votes to "can your ass". Jack made a mental note to use the conference to gain some ground with Trustees who understood and supported his university advancement strategies. His forty-minute presentation was extremely well received and concluded with a powerful message: when a major corporation gains confidence in a university CEO and the Board, it invests not only its money, but its reputation and organizational zeal in support of the mission of that university. Those colleges and universities determined to hold their place at the cutting edge of American higher education should master the art of recruiting to their cause the wealth, reputation, and influence of powerful private sector organizations.

As usual, however, most of his Trustees were occupied with their own agendas, and except for the day he spoke, Jack made himself unavailable, preferring to enjoy a short holiday from their care and feeding. Instead, he took a shuttle to New York and dropped in briefly on the Feingold Foundation, being careful to avoid crossing paths with Lisa. Dinner that evening was spent at 666 with an old friend and University of Connecticut Board Chair, Larry Blyn.

"Have you given any thought to my proposition?" Blyn persisted. "You like the northeast and it likes you."

Jack sighed. "That's the trouble, Larry. I've been living among barbarians for too long. I've developed a pretty edgy style."

"Bullshit. You're packing a heavy resume now, pal." He went on, "You could be CEO of the entire Connecticut University System. I'd like nothing better than to have a reason to get rid of the empty suit we have now. Or, in six months, the Commissioner of Higher Education is going to retire. I swear, that's yours for the asking. The folks in Hartford would love you. Just think of the fun you could have with the boys at O'Mally's Bar. They damn near run the whole State from there."

"Larry, you're just the tonic I needed. How's Adrianna, by the way?"

"Gaining weight."

"How's business?"

"Like always, a pain in the ass. Lots of problems with the new stores. And people, they don't know how to work anymore."

"So, things are fine and you're making money. Good! What about the trotters? Still winning blue ribbons?"

Blyn's face lit up. "God, Jack, they're gorgeous. One of the mares just dropped twin fillies. Such angels! The trainer says in two years we're going to sweep the board with them."

"I miss watching them run. Maybe I can come back for part of the season. Send me a schedule, will you?"

"I'll send you more than that. Just give me the word when you're ready." They touched brandy glasses and relaxed into the rest of the evening.

On the flight home, Jack made some notes on the discussions he'd had with various people during the conference. Larry Blyn had been such a mensch for pressing him to move to Connecticut. Hawaii, North Carolina, and Tennessee were also probing for new system executives, but he found it difficult to picture himself in the same old job at a different venue. Anyone who walked a day in his shoes would understand.

The seat belt sign flashed on, and he stored his papers in preparation for arrival at McCarran International. As he viewed the familiar landscape from his window seat, he reached into his shirt pocket and extracted a folded piece of hotel stationery that had been given to him during check-out. It was from a veteran Chronicle of Higher Education reporter who covered the national scene. Both men had been kid Marines and over the years they'd become good friends. They had somehow missed each other this trip.

"Jack," the note read. "Watch your six. L/C."

"Well," Bonnie handed him the opened envelope. "It's postmarked Palo Alto and addressed to you, but the rest is in Russian."

Jack was amused by her exasperation. "When did it arrive?"

"The day you left for Washington."

"You poor thing." Jack unfolded the handwritten note. "You must be dying of curiosity."

He began reading aloud in Russian and Bonnie gave him a look that would kill.

"Oh, I'm sorry." He began again, in English. "Everything here is even more wonderful than expected. I am feasting with scholars at a banquet of knowledge and excellence. When you can, come see for yourself. Bring butter and toast. Zoya."

"That's it?"

"Yep."

"Butter and toast... What's that, code for something?"

"It's harmless, Bonnie. Relax. She's safely on her way to a new life now."

"Well, at least she made the right decision."

"We did well, Bonnie. Thank you for putting your heart into this."

"You're welcome, boss." She placed a huge folder on his desk. "The agenda for the October Trustee's meeting in Elko, next month."

"Thanks a lot." Jack slapped his hand on the four inch binder. "Shall we go through it after lunch?"

"Okay by me." She paused as if deciding whether or not to continue.

"What?" Jack said. "Spit it out."

"Well," she went on, "it's the media. Public Affairs says we've been getting three times as many calls as we usually do for schedules, location, and copies of the agenda. I can't figure it out."

Jack opened the binder. "After Paddy's last meeting in Vegas, you can't blame them. What else could it be?"

"Yeah, you're probably right." Bonnie turned to leave. "Back at one o'clock?"

Jack nodded his head and kept scanning through the agenda items. When he heard the door close he reached for

Zoya's note and read it once more before slipping it into his shirt pocket.

"*Darago*i Jack (Dear Jack)," it began.

It was nearly five before he and Bonnie completed going over the agenda book. She had pages of notes.

"Why don't you do those tomorrow?" Jack rose and stretched.

"I'd better do them now," she answered, while walking towards her office. "Half the stuff is in my head, and I'll forget it by then."

"Okay, that's why you get the big bucks, I guess."

She gave him a dirty look and closed the door. Jack reached for the phone and dialed Duke Butrum's direct line at the bank.

"Yeah!" Butrum's cowboy drawl was unmistakable.

"It's Jack Stark, Duke. You sound busy or pissed. Is this a bad time?"

"No, hell no. You back in town?"

"Yesterday. Got something I want to show you."

"C'mon over. You know the back way up."

Twenty minutes later Butrum was peering at the hotel note. "Who the hell is L/C?"

"A stringer for the Associated Press and the Chronicle. He has friends in Vegas. We were both in the Corps at different times. L/C stands for Lance Corporal. Seems he's picked up the same scuttlebutt you have. I can't call him though. This is all I get, but he's good for it."

"Didn't know you were a jar-head, Stark."

"Don't let the degrees and the fancy robes fool you, Duke. Who else would be gung-ho enough to do this fucking job?"

Butrum snorted. "Well, looks like Paddy's up to his old tricks. He probably thinks he's corralled enough votes to give you problems. How long has it been now, five years?"

"Seven, next spring."

"Do you give a shit anymore? I'll bet there are people looking at you from other places."

"A few, but what really bugs me right now is the prospect of losing a fight to a goon like Paddy. You know what I'm talking about, Duke. There's a big difference between walking away with pride and getting run out of town."

"Let me get this straight. It's really not about the job. It's about turning the tables on Paddy? Damn Jack, now you've got my interest. Like what?"

"Like getting him voted out as Chair and getting someone decent in there to fill out your term. Let's call it doing a service for the people of Nevada. You're stepping away from the leadership of the Board of Trustees to run for Governor. Do you have any idea what a public joke this character is making of the Board you chaired for so many years? Nevada has always had an image challenge. The rest of the country is eager to believe the worst about us. I guarantee you that within the month we'll make the *Los Angeles Times* and not long after that we'll be national… *Chronicle of Higher Education*, the wire services. It'll be a goddamn media feeding frenzy and the only one enjoying the whole show will be Paddy. You know him. Tell me I'm wrong, here."

"You're telling me I have more to lose than you do in this."

"Hell, Duke, win or lose, I'm out of here. It's only a matter of time. But you, this is your home, man. Your years as Chair of the Board are your legacy of public service that you plan to point to with pride when you run for Governor.

145

But this asshole is about to shit in your hat. I guarantee you that everything you've accomplished will be yesterday's news. Your opponent in the race will be pointing his finger at you, not Paddy. You'll be the one answering questions in front of TV cameras."

Butrum's face was glum. "Christ, Stark, when you get going you really strip the hide off a guy."

"Sorry, Duke, but it's nothing compared to what the Nevada media will do to you. You're a candidate now and when you kick off your campaign, it'll be open season. You can't blame them. It's their job. Not to mention that your opposition will miss no chance to take every shot they can. I don't want to be around when they claim you abandoned your educational leadership responsibilities for political ambition."

"Shit, Jack, it sounds like you could write the fucking speech for him."

"Not me, Duke. You've got my vote already. No, somebody a lot better at it than me will swing that hatchet."

Butrum threw up his hands. "Hell, I just bought $500,000 of TV time." He hauled his big frame up from his office chair. "Okay, you made your point. Give me time to think here." He walked slowly across the room to a huge picture window that looked out to the distant Sierra peaks covered with an early dusting of snow.

After a few moments, Jack walked over and stood next to Butrum. "I'm sorry, Duke. Maybe I said too much. You know how much I appreciate…"

The big man draped his arm around Jack's shoulders. "You can't leave, Jack," he declared. "Not 'til I'm Governor."

"What? I don't follow."

"I brought you here to Nevada. You told me what had to be done and what you needed and I backed you up. You brought in corporate interests and the outside dollars. How much by now, fifty, sixty million?"

"Closer to a hundred, if you're counting."

"Okay, so we did some good things for the state, and I cut the ribbons and made the announcements. But if I'm Governor, goddamn it, I intend to really ramp up on economic diversification and development. And that's not just campaign rhetoric."

"Good for you, Duke, but win or lose, I'll be packing my bags. It's just a matter of time. That's how it works in my business."

The big cowboy grasped Jack by his shoulders. "Not an option, Chancellor! Hell, even the women like me now because of that gal you had me appoint acting president. No, you can't leave just yet. That dog won't hunt. Paddy needs his wings clipped. I'll take care of that. I may not be the Chair of the Trustees anymore, but I am going to be the next Governor, goddamn it, and they know it."

"But how..."

"Hell, Jack, the guys on the Board owe me big time, and the four ladies have all been insulted by Paddy at one time or another. You let me handle that part of it. Now, tell me, do you have anything big you can bring in before the next Board meeting?"

Jack thought for a moment. "Well, I've got some deals in the pipeline. If I spend all my time shuttling between Silicon Valley and Nevada, I'm sure I could bring in something big and sexy like a few corporate relocation announcements. I'll be away a lot, on the road 24/7 for weeks. I would need a codicil to my contract spelling it all this out: duties, responsibilities, expenses, and so forth. Also, I'll need to borrow one of your pilots and the small plane now and again."

"Done. But not the Lear. I need that for my own stuff and to get one-on-one face time with certain people." Butrum was scribbling something on a scrap of paper. "Here, look at this. If it's okay, then shake my hand and go close some deals."

Jack read the text carefully. When he reached the bottom line he raised his eyebrows. "That's not necessary, Duke."

"Hell yes, it is. The new Mercedes sport sedan... it's a fucking ride, man."

The Board of Trustees bi-monthly meetings had always been news. Nevada newspapers and television stations gave the two-day events blanket coverage. They jammed the media booths and cluttered the arena floor with cables, power lines and cameramen to catch every gaffe and heated exchange or insult. Trustee bashing had been a blood sport for years. Their public grandstanding and disagreements had provided endless fodder for editorial page cartoons and media lampoons. During recent years, however, a tough Duke Butrum supported a new Chancellor who brought about a semblance of civility and business-like conduct to University System governance. In time, a skeptical media relented and began offering up grudging praise. Paddy O'Banion's debacle at the August Board meeting in Las Vegas changed all that. The circus was back in town. Everyone wanted a seat to the next show. Adding fuel to the fire, O'Banion had ordered the meeting venue changed from Elko to Reno, where he could count on much broader media coverage.

Jack, true to plan, had been working around the clock to bring a number of deals to closure. With only two days left before the Board meeting, a weary Chancellor assured Butrum that he'd signed three solid agreements with more in the pipeline.

"Bring 'em home, Jack!" Butrum had shouted into the phone from his Lear jet. "The game is on back here. Pour on the juice. We need to look good, buddy!" He was laughing heartily as he rang off.

The Reno meeting opened to a packed house. The level of media interest and public attendance was so high that the floor of the university basketball arena was pressed into service to accommodate the crowd. Chair of the Board, Paddy O'Banion, pounded the gavel for a moment, then leaned into the microphone and shouted for the meeting to come to order. His voice echoed through the vast space of the basketball arena and slowly the din of voices and clatter subsided. A few Trustees still visiting in the crowd scurried to their places.

The Board members occupied a long semi-circular table so that they might easily address one another while at the same time being visible to the gallery and media cameras. The Chair presided from a center location with the Chancellor seated to the immediate right. Board members spoke into foam capped microphones which sat directly in front of them. Thick Board agenda binders lay open and note pads and papers were already scattered about. The campus presidents sat at a table immediately to the right of the Board.

"This meeting of the Board of Trustees of the University Nevada System is hereby called to order," O'Banion began.

"The Secretary will please read the minutes of the last meeting."

"Um, there are no minutes, Mr. Chairman," the obviously embarrassed secretary announced. "Absent a quorum, the Board was unable to convene." A wave of laughter went through the crowded arena. O'Banion scowled and rapped his gavel for order.

"Mr. Chairman." Judi Chang had her hand held high and was leaning forward so she could be clearly seen. O'Banion acknowledged her quickly, as if he'd been expecting the interruption.

"Mr. Chairman," Chang repeated, "I move that a procedural exception allowed under the bylaws be made so that an unscheduled item may be placed on the agenda at this time."

"Second the motion." Leo Paladanos did not wait for the Chair's recognition of Judi Chang's motion. Paladanos was a Las Vegas businessman with a three hundred pound frame and a reputation for good nature and an even better appetite.

"The motion has been made and seconded," O'Banion spoke quickly. "Is there any discussion? Being none, the vote is called by a show of hands. Those in favor?" Hands rose in agreement. Carson City Trustee Tuck Doty, nursing a hangover, had left the table to pour himself a cup of coffee and waved his arm in assent. Paddy smiled and banged down the gavel. "The motion is carried." His head swiveled about as if looking for another motion.

Judi Chang spoke again. "I move that the Board retire briefly from its general session and reconvene in executive session."

The press table erupted in a flurry of whispered exchanges. The presidents shifted uncomfortably in their seats. A few cast their eyes briefly in Jack's direction.

"Second the motion." Tuck Doty had returned with his coffee and muffin.

Paddy quickly accepted Doty's second. "Discussion? Being none, the vote is called by a show of hands." O'Banion banged down the gavel. "The vote being unanimous, we are now adjourned for executive session. The Board will move to the adjacent conference room." He was now shouting over the crowd. "If everyone will be patient, we will reconvene the general session very shortly. Please partake of the refreshment table in the meantime." He turned to Jack with a smile. "That goes for you too, Chancellor. You won't be joining us this time."

Jack picked up his briefcase and walked toward the nearest exit. It would be crisp and sunny outside and the October air would help clear his head for what was to come. "Hey, Chancellor!" He turned to see Duke Butrum headed his way. "Let's sit down over there." Butrum motioned to an empty bench away from the main walkway. "What's going on inside?"

"Well, everyone is confused as hell. The media smells blood though. Some of them picked up on my not going in with the Trustees to the executive session. I didn't see you."

"Oh, hell no. I just drove in and sent a couple of my guys to look for you. I knew Paddy would shut you out of the executive session. He expects to walk out in a few minutes with your head on a platter."

"Really."

"You don't want to be in there anyways. It's not going to be a pretty sight." Butrum reached over and patted Jack's briefcase. "You got it all in there?"

"Yep." Jack opened the case and extracted three folders. "Your script is clipped to the outside of each folder. Abstracts of the agreements are inside for you to hand to the Trustees. I have the originals. Also, there's a dozen press releases covering each deal in case you need them. There are some great quotes from the corporate CEOs about you. I know, because I wrote them myself. Now, where's my new contract?"

Butrum was scanning the brief sheets intently. "Jesus, Jack, you've got the touch. Can I really stand up there and say all this?"

"Absolutely! All the ground work was initiated while you were Chair of the Board. The dates will check out. I simply closed quickly on what was in the pipeline. Hell, Duke, how many miles did I log over the past month? How many times did we conference call CEOs from your office? They reacted to the picture of a Chancellor of the University System and the former Chair of the Board, soon to be Governor, working together as a team. They bought in. No other university brought that warranty to the table. Hell, if it had been football, we'd both be wearing Super Bowl rings."

"Goddamn it, Stark, you got to write some speeches for me."

"Duke, the codicil to my contract?"

Butrum reached into his jacket pocket, pulled out an envelope and laid it on the bench. Jack read through the document carefully. It was all there: expanded duties and responsibilities, augmented expense account, even the new BMW. It was signed, Judi L. Chang, Chair of the Board and bore today's date. An unsigned acceptance statement awaited Jack's signature at the bottom of the second page.

Jack pointed to Chang's signature and the date. "What...?"

At that moment, a roar came from the basketball arena. One of Duke's men stepped out of the side entrance and waved in their direction. "We better get in there." Butrum stood and propelled Jack along by the elbow. "It's show time."

Entering by the side entrance they witnessed a scene that Jack will not soon forget. The crowd was on its feet applauding. Judi Chang was seated, smiling and nodding, as she banged the gavel for order. Flanking her, a number of Board members were also standing while looking in her direction and applauding. Paddy O'Banion was nowhere in sight. Butrum took a seat nearby, and Jack walked to his regular seat next to the Chair. Judi Chang looked over at him and smiled. She leaned into the microphone and called for order. "Before we open our published agenda, the Chair would like to recognize the long serving former Chair of the Board of Trustees, Mr. Duke Butrum." The crowd again broke into applause. A shrill whistle or two punctuated the acclaim.

Butrum stood and moved to the podium facing the Board. "Thank you, Madam Chair. As you and the members of the Board know, I am here today as an emissary of this body to present a number of outcomes from years of hard work supported by the Board of Trustees and intended to benefit the University of Nevada system as well as the State of Nevada. With the Board's indulgence I will briefly review three separate agreements recently finalized with national corporations which are expected to add thousands of jobs into Nevada's economy and millions of dollars in grants and contracts to our university system."

As Butrum spoke, Jack quietly re-read his new contract, signed it, and slipped the folded document into his coat pocket. Giving it a gentle pat, he leaned back and made plans to reinvent his life.

TWELVE

"The Carnelian Room, at the very top of the Bank of America building in San Francisco. You can see both the Bay Bridge and the Golden Gate at the same time. It's a spectacular view in the evening, and the food is five-star." Jack was in Sunnyvale, California, tying up some loose ends after last week's Board meeting in Reno. Dave Newman's secretary had located Zoya for him, and she was now on the phone in Newman's empty office.

"You're celebrating something, then?"

"Oh yes, and I don't want to do it alone. You must join me for dinner. Besides, we haven't talked for more than a month. I want to hear everything about what's going on at Stanford."

"I'd like to, really. But I don't have a car yet and it's getting late in the day to catch the train. Tomorrow would be so much easier."

"I'll be on a plane to New York tomorrow. The Feingold Foundation Board is having their annual meeting in the Caymans Friday, and I'm spending a day with my Connecticut friends first."

"That sounds nice. You're very close to them, aren't you?"

"Very, very close and a special part of my life. You must meet them. They're rare people, the kind you should have as friends."

"Someday, perhaps."

"Now, Zoyechka, no more excuses about this evening. *Lavi moment*! (Seize the moment). I'll pick you up at six in front of the School of Business. Will you be there?"

"Of course. But I have to find something to wear."

"I'm sure you'll manage. Just look for a black limo."

"That's her," Jack announced. The limo slowed to a stop. Zoya was standing alone, bathed in the soft light of the wrought iron and glass carriage lamps which illuminated the broad granite steps. She was wearing a simple black boat-neck dress and black lizard pumps. A short double strand of pearls embraced her long graceful neck. A snow white pashmina wrap covered her back and draped over her arms. A cloud of long auburn hair cascaded about her shoulders. The limo driver looked back at Jack through the rear view mirror.

"If you're wondering if she's my daughter, you're fired," Jack said with a smile. The driver stepped out immediately and opened the door for Zoya.

She peered in, accepted Jack's outstretched hand and settled into the seat. "*Spaciba, Jack. Dobruy vecher. Kak dela?* (Thank you, Jack. Good evening. How are you?)"

"*Ochen harasho, Zoyechka.*" (Great) There was something different about her, something subtle and indefinable. "You look different, Zoya."

"Really?" She smiled back at him and looked around the interior of the limo. "This is lovely, Jack. Where's the BMW?"

"Ah," he said, handing her a glass of champagne. "They bought me a new Mercedes."

"I liked the BMW." Her voice was wistful.

"I know you did." He touched the brim of his champagne flute to hers. *"Per questa notte e due cari amici.* (To this night and two dear friends.)"

"Italian," she exclaimed, sipping from her glass. "It's so romantic. Say more. Make another toast!"

Jack lifted his glass again to her. *"Per la vostra bella occhi verdi, Princepessa Zoya.* (To your beautiful green eyes, Princess Zoya.)"

She blushed and turned away. "You haven't told me what we are celebrating."

"Your good beginning at Stanford. Don't look surprised, I have my sources. And last, but not least, my emancipation."

She was both pleased and puzzled at his ebullient demeanor. "I've never seen you so happy and carefree. What has happened?"

"Carefree, indeed. Such a good choice of words, Zoya." He pointed out the limo window. "There, look, we're approaching the city. Have you taken the time yet to see San Francisco? Knowing you, Zoya Alexandrovna, it has been all work and no play."

"I've wanted to, Jack, but there's been so much to do since I arrived."

"Panimau, ya tozhe (I understand, the same with me). But tonight let's put all that aside and enjoy one another's company and good fortune."

As the elevator rocketed towards the fifty-second floor, Zoya caught her breath and clung to Jack's arm. "I never got used to this, even in New York," she explained. They slowed to a sudden stop and the doors parted to reveal an elegant foyer. Jack guided them towards the sound of voices and music. The receptionist desk was unoccupied, and Zoya stayed close by his side as he walked directly into the cocktail lounge, past a few crowded tables and stopped in front of a huge panoramic window. Far below, the lights of the city stretched for miles in all directions.

"Oh, Jack," she gasped. "What an introduction to San Francisco!"

"Dr. Stark." A cultured, indulgent voice broke in. They turned to see the smiling face of the maître d' wearing an impeccable tuxedo and white carnation.

"Jean Luc, my old friend." They clasped hands, and Jack turned to Zoya. "Allow me to introduce Zoya Alexandrovna Chalkin. Originally from St. Petersburg, Russia, via New York, and this is her first visit to San Francisco."

Jean Luc beamed at Zoya. "How lovely to meet you. Welcome to the Carnelian." He motioned to a young man who presented Zoya with a single red rose. "You must excuse my obvious delight at meeting you, Miss Chalkin," Jean Luc said as he led them through the dining area. "This one," indicating Jack, "has never appeared here for other than business." He wagged his finger at Jack. "Finally we have you as it should be, with a beautiful companion. Ah, here we are." Two waiters pulled back their chairs, and they were seated at a table which seemed suspended over the scene below. Zoya could see lights glittering on the suspension cables of the distant Golden Gate Bridge and to the far right tiny headlight beams streamed in both directions across the Bay Bridge between San Francisco and Oakland.

Jack was pleased at her obvious fascination with their venue. "Thank you, Jean Luc. This is perfect."

"But, of course." A champagne cork popped, and Jean Luc carefully filled their crystal flutes. "Now, Miss Zoya, if you do not object there will be no menus. You are both in my care this evening. We do not plan to release you for hours."

Zoya appeared fascinated with the scene below her, and Jack took the opportunity for a long appraising look at the stunning young woman sitting across from him. "You're pleased you decided to come, then?"

Zoya lifted her gaze in his direction. Her eyes sparkled as she smiled and nodded. "Oh, yes. Thank you for being so insistent. Everything is so different than our last outing. You are a man of surprising contrasts, Jack Stark."

"And you, Zoya Chalkin, "are a beautiful enigma."

"How so?"

"Your pearls, for example. Did you notice how Jean Luc looked at them when we met? They are royal, and at least a century old."

"They belonged to my great grandmother. My mother gave them to me when I left St. Petersburg. They are my only treasure."

The waiter arrived with a small crystal bowl of black caviar, sweet butter, and thin triangles of toast on a gold rimmed china plate. Zoya buttered and spread a thin layer of caviar on two pieces of toast. "Do you remember?"

"How could I forget?" Jack took the delicacy from her outstretched hand. "The Russian way. That seems like a long time ago, doesn't it?"

"Mm," she responded enjoying her caviar and nodding. "Only because so much has happened since we met. I do wonder sometimes about where you came from, Jack, and how it is that you are always alone."

"Well, Zoya, I have my thoughts about you as well. After all, you're young and beautiful. I suspect that men must be swarming around you. But then I console myself that you are also intelligent, well educated, and possess an almost regal demeanor. You'd be surprised how guys are intimidated by the latter."

She laughed and raised her hands as if to ward off his compliments. "Yes, yes, I know. My mother worries about my future prospects over here. Americans, she warns, prefer silly girls who are blondes, and you are neither. Poor mama."

"It's an unfortunate stereotype," Jack admitted. "But not entirely inaccurate."

"When I was fifteen, in St. Petersburg, boys began showing up and my grandmother took me aside and explained the difference between boys and men. She advised caution and patience. My grandfather used to terrify them. He was such a formidable man." Her expression softened with nostalgia for a brief instant. She wagged an index finger in Jack's direction. "You haven't addressed my question."

"Your question?"

"Yes. You know so much more about me. I want to hear stories about you, the boy and the man. Start at the beginning, please. It will help me to understand."

Jack leaned back in his chair and looked at her for a long moment, as if deciding. Then, he began, slowly at first, about Gus and Angelique and life on the ranch. She seemed fascinated, hanging on every word, so he talked on about quitting high school to join the Marine Corps at seventeen, the years in the jungle, finding himself at Stanford, the casual Ph.D. years, the unplanned year in mountains of northern Mexico, and finally, his two decade journey as professor, young university president, the loss of his son and failed marriage, and now, as Chancellor in Nevada. In the telling, it became clear to Zoya that this man respected much, feared little, and possessed a capacity for honor and commitment which, until now, she had only encountered in the classics.

"So, there you are," Jack concluded. "It's only the shorthand version, but I think that's more than enough for one evening.

"Did mademoiselle enjoy the duck?" Jean Luc stood looking down at Zoya.

"It was exquisite," she lied, unable to recall a single bite.

"Now, you must indulge me, please, Mademoiselle Zoya." Jean Luc extended his hand. "The dessert chef has been preparing something special, but refuses to allow it to be served without your personal approval." Jean Luc leaned closer and whispered, "I think he is smitten. Please, he has just arrived from Europe."

Zoya gave her hand to Jean Luc, rose, and cast a helpless look at Jack, who shrugged as if unwilling to interfere. She was led away to the kitchen, and Jack thought he heard the faint clapping of hands. Moments later, Zoya and Jean Luc emerged followed by two waiters bearing a huge baked Alaska crowned with twin flaming Russian Onion spires.

A beaming Jean Luc seated a slightly stunned Zoya and nodded to the two waiters to begin serving. "It was but a ruse," he explained to Jack. "The kitchen has been buzzing about the Russian beauty, a true reincarnation of the Princess Anastasia. What could I do?"

After the entourage departed, leaving them with their flaming desserts, Jack raised his glass to Zoya. "Well, *daragoi tovarish* (dear comrade). If your classmates back in mother Russia could only see you now."

It was after midnight when the limo stopped in front of Zoya's apartment on campus. The driver got out to have a cigarette and walk a bit. Jack and Zoya sat close together all the way back, chatting and laughing. Zoya had finally fallen asleep, her head resting against Jack's shoulder, his arm about her as he gazed thoughtfully out the window. The champagne, the fume blanc, and the port may have helped evaporate their inhibitions. But the magic carpet of that evening had been woven with subliminal strands of admiration and affection. The way Zoya clung to Jack's arm as they bid farewell to Jean Luc and her kitchen admirers evidenced the transformation.

Jack gently brushed away a strand of hair from her forehead. "*Zoyechka. Tu doma* (you're home)."

She stirred slightly, opened her eyes and looked up at him. "Oh, Jack. I was dreaming." She did not move. Instead she raised her hand to his shoulder and drew him down to her. "Jack," she whispered.

Her skin was warm, soft as satin, and the scent of her hair, overpowering. He kissed her gently on the cheek.

She moved slightly so their eyes could meet. "*Mne kazhetsa chto ya ...* (I feel that we...)"

"*Ya tozhe, sladenkaya Zoya. Ya tozhe* (So do I, sweet Zoya, so do I)." Their lips came together in one long, tender kiss so sublime in the moment that it defied description. They talked for a while, before parting, making plans for staying in touch, and how and when they might be together again.

Early the next morning as his plane departed for New York, Jack wrote to Zoya, reflecting on the evening. It was not so much a love letter as an expression of his feelings. She was unique and precious, as bright and fragile as spring flowers on a lakeshore. He vowed to himself that, regardless of his own feelings, he would bear the burden of responsibility for her best interests. Once convinced that she was safely secure in what she wanted, only then would he open a floodgate of love and devotion that most women only dream about.

"My God, I've never seen him like this." Ginny Adler was sitting with Roy in the den enjoying the fire and a hot toddy. "He's been on the phone for nearly an hour. Who is that woman he's talking to?"

"What makes you think it's a woman?"

"The tone of his voice or whatever. I can just tell, that's all."

Roy groaned. "There, he's off now. For Christ's sake, don't cross-examine him. You know Jack. He'll tell us when he's ready."

"So, come sit." Ginny shouted up the stairs. "I want to hear all the mischief you've been up to since you were here last summer."

Jack slumped onto the couch across from them. "Sorry, guys. I walk in, drop my bags, and disappear." He accepted the mug Roy handed him and took a sip, breathing in the brandy vapor. "Wow, this is what I need." He stared at the fire. "So, you two look great. How are the boys?"

"Jack."

"What?"

"She's going to explode if you don't tell her what that was all about."

Ginny gave Roy a scathing look, then turned to Jack, shrugged and raised her eyebrows slightly.

"So, I met someone. You said it would happen, didn't you?"

"Someone?"

"Yes, a young woman in California."

"How young?"

"Ginny! For God's sake, what did I just tell you?"

Jack raised both hands slightly. "It's okay, I'll get around to that, but first you should let me tell you more about her."

"Oh Christ, she's really young." Ginny was on the edge of her seat.

The fire was burning low by the time Jack finished bringing them up to date. Roy just sat there, listening, but Ginny interrupted repeatedly with questions of one kind or another.

"Let the man tell his story, Ginny."

"That's okay," Jack gestured. "She's just worried that I might get disappointed."

"After everything he's told me," Ginny barked at Roy, "I'm more worried about the girl. You say she's Russian?"

"Yes, but she's an American citizen."

"Jewish, you said?"

"Correct."

"Good. So, when do we get to meet her?"

"I don't know, Gin. There's a host of geography and schedules to reconcile before..."

"You'll come for the holidays. She'll love it, with the snow and the sleigh rides. I'll redecorate the guest house. Her favorite color must be red. You can stay here at the main house, unless, of course..."

"Wow, Ginny, it sounds wonderful, but that's only a couple of months away." Jack turned to Roy who was obviously enjoying the whole exchange. "Aren't you going to help me out here?"

"You're having the romance of a lifetime with a drop dead gorgeous young woman half your age, and you're asking me for help? Go to hell!"

"So, you'll work it out, Jack. Talk to her and then call me with the dates. Just be sure to travel a few days before the twenty-fifth."

Jack threw up his hands and fell back on the couch. "Okay, I promise."

"Good." Ginny stepped around the coffee table and gave him a big hug and a kiss on the cheek. "You can't fool me, Jack. You're really smitten. And if everything you say is real, well, this is it, big boy, and you can't blame us for wanting to be part of it."

Roy stood up and stretched. "It's late. C'mon Gin, you've tortured Jack enough for one night. Let's get some sleep." He walked toward the staircase. "Jack, you know where your rooms are. See you at breakfast. I'm making waffles."

It was late the following evening when Jack checked into his hotel near the Feingold offices. Before unpacking, he was on the phone with Bonnie going over business.

"I've got a stack of clippings here about the Reno meeting of the Board. Do you want me to read them to you or just give you a summary?"

"The latter, please, Bonnie."

"Well, it seems everyone likes what happened, especially the corporate deals and Judi Chang as the new Chair. The media ate it up. Butrum is quoted everywhere and yesterday the *Gazette Journal* endorsed him for Governor."

"Anything about me?" Jack's career-long code of conduct held that any damn fool could get into the papers, but it took real skill to stay out.

"Only a mention or two, just the way you like it. The *Las Vegas Sun* did named you at the close of a long editorial praising the Trustees and Butrum. Quote: 'Always, standing in the wings, out of the spotlight, is Chancellor Jack Stark. As we celebrate, we must not fail to acknowledge his quiet genius.' Not bad, huh?"

"Yeah, I'll take 'genius', anytime. Thanks, Bonnie. Anything else that merits my attention?"

"Yeah, you forgot to memo who is officer of the deck while you're away. Doyle Hennigan has been bugging me about it. You know, boss, he's an overly ambitious weasel. It's no secret to anyone that he's after your job. And after all you went through to promote him to Vice Chancellor for Academic Affairs. He's constantly kissing up to the Trustees."

"Don't worry about him, Bonnie. He does run a big operation, but everybody, including the Trustees, see him for what he is. He's no threat. And I don't want to shake things up right now. I'll nominate him to a couple of presidencies elsewhere, and he'll be gone by next summer. Just hold your nose and play along. Whenever I'm away for more than a few days, just memo the office that General Counsel is in charge. That'll send the right message to all parties."

"Okay, boss. Everything else will keep until you get back. Oh, I almost forgot. The new Mercedes arrived yesterday. You can pick it up at the dealership when you get home."

Jack unpacked and ordered a club sandwich from room service. It would be nearly six in California.

"Zoya. *Hi bebchik. Kak dela?* (Hi, gorgeous. How are you?).

"Jack! I was just thinking about you. Are you still in Connecticut?"

"Last night. I'm in Manhattan now. It's so beautiful back here in the fall."

"Oh, I know. Did you have a good visit with your friends?"

"Actually, now they're your friends as well. We spent the entire evening talking about you."

"*Bozhe moi* (My God), what did you tell them?"

"I didn't have to tell them anything. Ginny took one look at me and knew. After that she pulled it out of me. You have to remember, Zoya, these are my closest friends. We've known one another nearly twenty years. They can read me like a book."

"They must be close. You're not an easy book to open, Jack."

"Neither are you, *moya malenkaya Ruskaya* (my little Russian)."

"I got your letter this afternoon. It was beautiful. Do your really feel that way about us?"

"Absolutely, that and more. It's okay to be in love, Zoya, and to spend time together."

"I know, Jack, but not in Palo Alto or Nevada. It's too risky."

"Zoya. *Tot kto ne riskuet, tot ne pjet champanskovo* (If you don't take risks, you will never drink champagne)." Jack could hear her laughing as she tried to protest.

"Don't worry, I was only kidding. We'll be very, very discreet. I'll phone you tomorrow, same time?"

"A little earlier would be better. I don't want to miss your call."

THIRTEEN

"It's a category four hurricane headed directly for the Caymans." Jack was sitting in Jacob Feingold's office as the old man chaired a conference call with the Executive Committee of the Board. Another voice on the speaker spoke up. "I'm not flying anywhere near that thing, no matter what my pilot thinks."

A woman's voice chimed in. "Even if it misses the island, the place will be a mess."

"Yeah, Jake," a male voice agreed. "We went through a near miss in Boca once, remember? It's no party, with all the crap blowing around and the power outages."

Feingold finally spoke. "Okay, so before we start getting members dropping out, let's agree on a new venue and notify everyone within the hour. We'll begin a day late to allow people a little extra time. Shall we just do it here in the city?"

There was a lot of grumbling on the line. "The annual meeting is supposed to be a retreat from the city, somewhere different and quiet."

"I hear you," Jake said. "Let's take a few minutes to think about this, and we'll hook up again and decide. Any objections?" The voices were quiet. "Okay, thirty minutes then."

Jake Feingold looked up at Jack. "You see, it's not easy to give money away."

"I can see that. Listen, Mr. Feingold, wasn't Nat Ancell on your Board at one time?

"No, that was Bonds for Israel. The greatest salesman I ever knew. He founded the Ethan Allen Corporation in 1934 and he's still going strong. Why?"

"Well, I've got connections at the University in Danbury, Connecticut. Nat is the primary donor of the most spectacular School of Business you've ever seen. It's a stone's throw from his corporate headquarters and the Ethan Allen Inn. Fairfield County corporations like Union Carbide and Perkin Elmer use the facilities there for major meetings all the time. It's only a one-hour drive from La Guardia or Kennedy and only thirty minutes from Westchester Airport. The meeting rooms are beautifully appointed as only Nat would have it. There are six conference rooms and a large interior amphitheater with a glass roof. It's rural, forested, with walking trails, and the leaves are turning now. There's even an outdoor concert venue by the lake. Hell, Nat owns the Inn and the Business School bears his name. What do you think?"

Jake sat quietly for a moment. "Do you know the university president up there?"

"I do. He recruited the first Dean of the Ancell School from the university I headed in Long Island. If Nat likes the idea we'll get concierge treatment for our board meeting."

Jake gazed out the window, obviously visualizing Jack's unorthodox suggestion. He punched the intercom. "Dorothy, see if you can get me Nat Ancell up in Connecticut." He turned to Jack. "He'll be there. He won't let go until they carry him out."

The intercom buzzed. "Nat, you old futz. How much was that wager we made on who would retire first?" There was a pause. "Well, double it! We have a little problem here. Maybe you can help."

Forty minutes later the Executive Committee of the Feingold Board approved the plan, and Jake gave the order to immediately contact every member with the details. After the speaker was off, he turned to Jack. "Great idea. I think they'll like it. By the way, Abe Glassman called and gave me an earful about your recent board meeting. He's impressed with the way you handled the play."

"It's no big deal, Mr. Feingold. Just business."

"Of course, Jack. I understand. If you don't mind my asking, how long do you plan to stay with it out there?"

"Well, the job they brought me in to do is more than done. But my handshake with the former chair is to stay on until he becomes Governor next January."

"Handshakes are sacred."

"Yes they are, sir."

"Well, we should talk about it sometime." Feingold stood and extended his hand to Jack. "Welcome aboard and please, it's Jake, when we're not with strangers."

Jack spent the rest of the morning on the phone. Afterwards he walked over to 666, where he was scheduled to meet Lisa Feingold for lunch. He hadn't seen or spoken with her since their unpleasant parting months earlier.

He arrived to find her already seated, sipping on a martini. She was dressed in a tailored asphalt suit and wearing a ruby studded platinum bracelet and matching broach. "Jack." She smiled and extended her hand. "It's good to see you." She leaned a bit to one side and peered down.

"No boots, Lisa. They belong in Nevada along with the cowboy." He took her hand. "You're stunning as usual. I like the pin."

"A birthday gift from my father. Also, a belated thank you for the flowers! You surprised me."

"It was my way of apologizing for my language."

"Oh, dear," she mocked him. "And all this time I thought your comment was an interrogatory. You do have a way of making a lasting impression, Jack Stark."

The waiter appeared, and Jack pointed to Lisa's martini. "Bring me a double." He smiled at Lisa. "It appears I've been checkmated."

"Don't be silly. I was a total bitch that day and I don't blame you for walking out."

"You're being too gracious." Jack leaned forward as if to extend his hand across the table. "Friends?"

"Colleagues," she corrected, crossing her arms and smiling. "Father told me about the new venue for the Board meeting. Jack Stark to the rescue, what?"

"Well," Jack responded, "it's a bit more rustic than the Caymans. And I admit to being a bit disappointed. I've never been to the islands. But you can't argue with a category four or five hurricane. I've had that experience."

"Really, where?"

"Luzon, the Philippines, a long time ago. It was a typhoon actually, but just as deadly."

"That's right, you were a boy soldier over there."

"U.S. Marine. How in the world did you know about that?"

"Oh, Jack, the background check, remember. Our people are very thorough when it comes to new members of the Board. You're interesting reading. They did encounter a couple of blank spots, however."

"Really?"

"Yes, after you graduated Stanford there's an entire year that's been blocked."

"That's odd. I was doing some post-grad work."

Lisa shook her head. "Not a matter of record… anywhere. May I ask in what and where?"

"Deep immersion Russian language program somewhere in Virginia. Didn't hear or speak a word of English for a year."

"Virginia, how interesting. Then you show up at Stanford again. Earned a Ph.D. in economics."

"I did that, yes."

"You were on a full grant fellowship, Jack. Very impressive."

"Jack smiled. "Yeah, I really enjoyed those years."

"Then you disappear again for a year, Jack. All we could find was that you left for Mexico."

"I did. Grabbed that sheepskin and ran."

Lisa leaned forward. "Now I'm really curious. Why Mexico?"

"Why not? Maybe I wasn't ready to get serious about life yet."

"You speak Spanish. We know that."

"Since I was a kid, working on my dad's ranch. We all did."

"Well, we couldn't ascertain what you did in Mexico."

Jack shrugged. "Just a last adventure before settling down. Some evening after a few of these," indicating his martini, "I'll tell you all about it."

"Oh, I'm sure you've had plenty of adventures. That's why my father and Abe Glassman like you so much."

"I'm pleased to hear that, Lisa, but I can't hold a candle to those two. They lived and played the game through heroic times."

"Sounds like you envy them."

"I do."

"Men." She looked away. "Here's our lunch. Since you appear unwilling to share much more, let's talk about me. What do you already know?"

"Well," Jack began cautiously, "only that you're a native New Yorker; left Radcliffe to model in Paris; quit abruptly when you were hot to return to Harvard; finished your BA/MA in art history and served on the faculty of two colleges. Married and divorced. And for the past decade, you've been your father's right hand at the Foundation, evolving to the point of functioning as its chief operating officer. If I might echo your own words, you've covered a lot of ground for such a young woman."

Jack paused without looking up from his plate. "Other than that, I'll leave it to you to fill in the blanks."

Lisa cocked her head to one side and smiled at him. "I'll give you this, Jack, you're straightforward."

She glanced at her watch. "Listen, I hate to cut this short when it's getting interesting, but I'm due back at the office. This annual meeting relocation is driving us all crazy."

"Need any help?"

"No, we're good, but thanks. If you're free this evening, my father is having a few friends over for dinner. Why don't you join us?" Eight o'clock... east coast casual." She scribbled an address on a cocktail napkin and dashed off.

Jack finished his drink and paid the check. East coast casual, he thought. What the hell is that? He was pleased that he hadn't bothered to pack his tuxedo.

The evening at Jake Feingold's Central Park West residence turned out to be a pleasant surprise. The dinner guests were few, and clearly made up of close friends. Jake seemed pleased to see Jack and did not spare the kudos during his introductions.

"Jake," Jack remarked privately, "Lisa invited me to drop by, and as gracious as you've been, I feel as if I'm intruding on your hospitality."

Jake put his hand on Jack's forearm. "Jack, if that were the case, you wouldn't be here. How was your lunch today?"

"Truth be told, Jake, I don't think your daughter likes me very much."

"Jack, you're tough, smart, and she can't intimidate you." The old man laughed. "How could she possibly like you?"

"Well, I'll try to be more accommodating."

"No, don't do that!" Jake gripped Jack by the forearm tightly. "The Board lets her walk all over them. I need you to take a leadership role. Challenge her at every meeting. Push back just enough to make her work for it. Promise me you'll do this?"

"Sure, Jake, I get it. A kite rises against the wind, right?" Jack looked long and hard at the old man. "You're a good father. You want her ready when the time comes."

"All fathers want that." He shrugged his shoulders. "We can only try and hope. Now, go spend time with my guests. You're a man with a lot to offer and you should know such people."

It was midnight by the time Jack returned to his hotel and placed a call to Zoya. After a dozen rings he hung up and headed for the shower. He stood under the needles of hot water, turning slowly and replaying the names and faces of the people he'd met that evening. It had been a small gathering, but he knew that he'd been in the presence of great wealth and power. Lisa Feingold sat next to him during dinner but paid little attention to him. Lester and Lorraine DeWalt, both founding members of the Feingold Board, occupied most of his time. By evening's end, they were insisting that he join them at their lodge in Vermont this winter and spend weekends with them in the Hamptons next summer. It was only later that he learned that they had an unmarried daughter in her mid-forties.

Back on the Stanford campus, Zoya could lay claim that same day to concluding a full week of grueling exams. To the utter amazement of her two departmental advisors, she had successfully challenged most of her first year doctoral course work. The consequence would be a significant acceleration in her progress toward the Ph.D. The foreign language requirement would be waived due the fact that she was already academically and commercially literate in Russian.

Before finally retiring, Jack tried ringing her again. He was about to hang up when she answered.

"Zoya! I was about to give up on you."

"Oh, Jack!" She sounded breathless. "I was at the door when I heard the phone. I'm so glad I caught you in time. Isn't it late back there?"

"It's been a long day, but I want to hear about you. What's going on?"

Zoya told him the news about her fast-track week. "I didn't want to burden you with it before. Apparently, it's somewhat unorthodox."

"Well, to the extent that they've let you run with it, I would agree. But the program, after all, is unique and privately funded, so your two Department Chair advisors can afford you a lot of flexibility. Knowing you, I'll bet you're looking to burn your way through in record time. Just make sure you have them sign off on every move. Anyhow, congratulations."

"*Spaciba* (thank you) Jack. I want you to be proud of me."

"*Kaneshno, moya krasivaya, umninkaya devachka* (Of course, my beautiful, brilliant girl). I just want there to be something left of you when I get back to California next week. Have you even eaten tonight?"

"Sandy and Roman took me to dinner."

"Who?"

"My department chairs. They wanted to talk about an idea they have for next summer."

"Oh, yeah. What kind of an idea?"

"A joint venture with Moscow University and some emerging Russian banking entities."

"What's in it for you?"

"Advanced research for my doctoral dissertation."

"My God, Zoya, you just got there and these guys are already talking about your dissertation. Did they mention a topic?"

"In general terms, something to do with Eastern Bloc investment banking and designing support technology and financial control systems that would accommodate multinational activity."

"They want a piece of your grant, Zoya."

"*Ya znau* (I know) Jack. And I want their Ph.D. It's a game."

Jack laughed. "I forgot for a moment *tu Ruskaya* (you're Russian)." They clearly missed one another and continued the conversation for another thirty minutes.

"What if I fly straight to San Francisco this Sunday? I'll have my new car delivered to me at the airport, pick you up in Palo Alto, and we can spend a day or two. Let's drive up to the ranch. I haven't visited in months and want to show it to you. I've some decisions to make and it would help to have you there. How about it? Will it work around your schedule?"

"I'll make it work!" She was genuinely excited. "I'll be home studying Sunday afternoon. Just call when you land and I'll be ready. I have to be back by Tuesday night, though. Wednesdays are booked back to back."

"Fantastic. All you'll need is some jeans, a few tops, and a jacket. It can be chilly up there sometimes."

"I'll be ready. *Spakoinoi nochi, moi geroi.*" *(Good night, my hero.)*

FOURTEEN

The Feingold Foundation Board of Directors met quarterly in New York City. The annual meeting, however, was traditionally more focused on recreation than business. The members were used to retreating to a remote, placid environment where they met briefly each morning and spent the rest of the day and evening indulging themselves in more pleasant activities. The three-day gathering offered them every opportunity to interact socially and generally enjoy a good time together. The Westside Campus of the university offered 290 acres of woods filled with walking trails and fitness runs as well as a beautiful terraced lakeside amphitheater. The two existing buildings at the time were the College of Business and an enormous indoor/outdoor sports complex.

Nineteen of the twenty-four member Foundation Board confirmed that they would arrive on Thursday in time for the opening luncheon meeting. The Inn would accommodate them in luxury suites. The university was ready as well. Every coach, trainer, and physical therapist on campus had been diverted to its bucolic Westside Campus. Along with bountiful, healthy cuisine, each member of the board was assigned a personal trainer for the entire stay. Walking, jogging, indoor aqua sports, fitness instruction, and even a brisk round of golf at the local country club filled their daylight calendars. Every evening they were treated to a concert or theater performance. By the time they departed, they were praising Jake Feingold for his efforts, claiming they never felt better in years.

Early Sunday morning as Jake's limo dropped Jack off at JFK Airport, the old man shook Jack's hand. "It was a hit. And you, you mensch," he said shaking his finger. "You always escape taking credit."

"It's one of my few talents, Jake. Mazal Tov."

Moments later as Jack checked in for the flight home, he was informed that he'd been upgraded to First Class.

"Where are you?"

"At the airport. Are you ready to go?"

"I will be by the time you get here. I can't wait to see the new car and hear about the meeting."

After swinging by the Stanford campus to pick up Zoya, Jack sped southwest on the Bayshore Freeway towards Gilroy and the Pacheco Pass. The pass roadway would wind its way for 35 miles through the coastal hills before dumping them back on the freeway east to Highway 12 and the ranch. Jack was eager to see how the big Mercedes would handle on the snakelike curves. Zoya was snuggled deep in the lush black leather passenger seat, eyes glued to the road, and emitting small sounds of delight every time Jack accelerated around a curve.

"It smells so new." She caught her breath as Jack stopped suddenly on a wide spot in the road. They were poised at the crest of the hills and far below them stretched the north central San Joaquin Valley.

Jack set the brake, opened the door, and stepped out. "C'mon, scoot over the console and get behind the wheel."

"You mean it?"

"What am I standing out here in the road for? Of course I mean it, unless you don't want to try this beast."

She had already scrambled into the driver's seat and checking out the controls by the time Jack opened the passenger door and took his seat. "Adjust your seat. Controls are on the lower left. That's it. Now set your rear view and let's go."

She eased the big black machine back on the road and after a few cautious moments was cruising through the curves.

"It's true then," Jack exclaimed. "Russians love German cars."

"Only BMW and Mercedes. Besides, we conquered them, remember?"

"Oh, I thought the Americans had something to do with that."

She made a face without taking her eyes off the twisting road. "The Red Army broke the back of the Wehrmacht long before you guys came along. You can claim Japan, Jack, but you must tip your hat to mother Russia for the other."

"Are you sure about claiming to be American?"

"Absolutely! *Ya Amerikanka*! Are you sure about your history? Just do the math on the body count and talk to me then." She flashed him a knowing smile.

Jack shook his head and looked out the window. "Okay, remind me not to take you to any American Legion conventions."

"Huh?"

"Nothing, just talking to myself. Drive." They were coming out of the hills into low rolling countryside covered with vineyards and walnut groves. Jack put his hand on her arm. "Slow down and take the next exit. That's Highway 12 east. We're only about thirty minutes from the ranch."

As they drove, Jack regaled Zoya about the history of the area and how everything had changed so dramatically since his childhood. With the worldwide recognition of California wines, Napa and Sonoma became famous for their vintages, drawing international acclaim and tourism. The less glamorous vineyards of the San Joaquin Valley were, in fact, the belly of the beast and the true production centers. Without their limitless acreage and vast harvest capacity, the industry could never have met the explosive appetite of recent decades.

He touched her arm. "Soon you need to turn left onto Plumtree Road. Slow down now, we're coming up on it. Here! Now follow it for about a mile towards the river. There, you can see the trees in the distance. Go slowly, now, slowly."

A weathered metal sign hanging from a six foot high T-post came into view. In faded letters it announced 'Stark'.

"Here," Jack said, and Zoya wheeled the Mercedes onto a long gravel driveway flanked by rows of tall Eucalyptus trees.

"We are there?" she asked.

"This is it," Jack answered. "We used to grow the best damn zinfandel in the county. I've only found time to visit once since mom died." He was craning his head in all directions. "It doesn't look like a thing has changed. See, there's the cottage and beyond it the sheds and barn. The main house is out of sight behind those eucalyptus trees. Christ. It's like we've gone back in time."

Zoya slowed and came to a stop in front of the cottage. A dog ran towards them barking. "Be careful," she warned as Jack opened the door and stepped out of the car.

"Don't worry. He's wagging his tail." One of the shed doors slid open and a grey-haired old man wearing a tattered straw hat and faded blue denim bib overhauls stepped into view. He walked slowly toward the car, and as he drew near, he paused for an instant and broke into a shuffling run.

"Jack? *No creo que si* (I can't believe it's so)." Zoya watched from the car as the two men fell into each other's arms and embraced. "Marta," the old man shouted, still clinging to Jack. "Marta, *venga, venga horita. Mira quien esta aqui!* (Come, come quickly. Look who's here.)"

The screen door of the house opened. A small woman wearing an ankle-length cotton dress with her long grey hair wrapped into a bun atop her head stepped out. She pulled a pair of eyeglasses from her apron pocket, slipped them on, and clung to the wooden banister with one hand as she walked down the steps. "*Que pasa, viejo? Quien es el?*" (What's going on old man? Who is it?)

"Jack, Marta. *Juanito, Mira!*" (Little John, look!)

"*Hijo mio* (My boy)!" The woman was on Jack now, arms about his waist, pressing her face to his chest. He lifted her off the ground and kissed her on both cheeks. The three of them proceeded to have an animated exchange in Spanish. Jack was waving one arm in the direction of Nevada. He finally noticed their eyes darting to the Mercedes.

"Ah, *perdonami* (pardon me). Marta, Felipe," He helped Zoya out of the car. "*Mi novia, senorita Zoya Chalkin.*" He put his arms around Marta and Felipe. "Zoya, this is Marta and Felipe Martinez. Their son, Hiro and I grew up together as brothers. They are my family now that everyone is gone." Zoya exchanged kisses on the cheek with Marta.

Felipe grasped her hand. *"Ay, que bonita! Jack, tiene una novia, finalmente."*

Jack looked at Marta, then at Zoya. *"Felipe, mi amigo, la verdad es yo tengo dos novias."* Marta burst into laughter and the old man shook his fist at Jack.

Zoya cocked her head and gave Jack an inquiring look.

"He said that you were beautiful and asked me to please tell him truthfully that I finally had a sweetheart. They worry about me. What can I say?"

"And?"

"I admitted that I now have two sweethearts, you and Marta."

Zoya quickly stepped next to Felipe and kissed him on the cheek. "Now, I have two as well." The four burst into laughter.

Marta put her arm around Zoya's waist and began walking toward the cottage. "Come," she said in perfect English. "While the men walk around, we will have some tea and talk."

They dined that evening in Marta's tidy kitchen. Zoya was regaled with stories of the two boys growing up together on the ranch, and the happy times before anyone had money and life was uncomplicated. Marta and Felipe had lived in the cottage for as long as Jack could remember. The story was that they had arrived with the Braceros one year when Jack was still a small baby and stayed on. They worked the land alongside Gus and Angelique. After Jack's father died, they were a great comfort to Angelique. Now they were waiting for Jack to decide what to do with what was left of the ranch. As evening approached, Jack's plans to stay at the Inn were summarily dismissed. Marta, without commenting, led Zoya to a tiny bedroom in the cottage. Jack and Felipe were banished to the main house. As they parted Zoya gave Jack a kiss on the cheek and an amused smile.

The next morning after a breakfast of huevos rancheros, Jack set out with Zoya on a tour of the property. Marta had insisted that she wear a huge straw hat to protect her fair skin from the sun. Jack wore jeans and an old denim shirt and work boots that he'd found in his dad's closet. Only forty acres remained of the original property. The plot of land was shaped like a wedge of pie. The point consisted of about three acres of high ground. The cottage, sheds, and barn occupied half of it. The other half sat high above the rest and through the eucalyptus grove one could see the great house perched on a steep slope. It had been unoccupied since Angelique's death, the furniture stored or covered. The living areas, kitchen, and dining room occupied the lower levels. The beamed living room was dominated by a great stone fireplace and a sweeping view of the vineyards. Below, a huge basement, wine cellar, and personal family winery had been carved deep into the hillside. Standing on the long, banister porch outside the living room, Zoya could see the entire panorama. Beyond a small orchard of fruit trees, the vines stretched in neat rows all the way to the distant river, which flowed in a lazy curve along the entire breadth of the lower property. Far to the left she spied what appeared to be a large pond encircled with a single row of eucalyptus saplings. A half sunken row boat lay tied to a wooden wharf.

Zoya squeezed Jack's hand. "I can almost see you here as a boy. It's so special, Jack. I understand now. The only thing

I really miss about Russia is our family dacha... so many wonderful memories of summers in the country with my family."

"You haven't seen the best part yet." They descended the outside stairwell from the porch and walked through the vineyard towards the river. When they approached the wide belt of California oaks which flanked the river, Jack helped Zoya climb a steep earthen levy. Reaching the crest, she caught her breath at the scene below. A thousand feet of sandy beach stretched along the river which flowed past them until it disappeared behind the band of oaks. Two giant poplar trees shaded a pair of picnic tables flanking a stone-lined fire pit.

Jack led Zoya down the slope and across the beach to the edge of the water. "See how the river curves here in a long semi-circle. As it slows to make the turn it drops sand and over the years this beach was formed. This was Hiro's and my special place." Jack fell silent.

"I was going to ask you, where is Hiro? No one mentioned him yesterday."

"He's gone, drowned by this river during the hundred year flood... the summer we turned seventeen."

Zoya rested her head on Jack's shoulder and squeezed his hand tightly.

"The day after the funeral, I quit high school and joined the Marine Corps. Damn selfish of me, leaving the four of them here with no one. But my father understood. It helped me get past it. I spent nearly three years fighting in places that denied our existence and for people who resented our presence. When I came home I was twenty. I couldn't or wouldn't live on the ranch and somehow found my way into

Stanford. I returned here often, but never stayed. And yet I love it so."

For moment, Zoya's gaze followed the steady flow of the river. "At our Dacha during summer I would fall asleep each evening to the sound of the breezes drifting through the birch and apple trees outside my bedroom window. I loved the deep tone of my grandfather's voice and my babula's arms about me. But that's all gone, Jack, for both of us. When I graduated from the Academy, my mother and grandmother explained to me that their world was passing and that now I must build a new life in a new place." She smiled up at him through her tears. "Oh Jack, standing here together finally makes sense of it all." He cupped her face in his hands and kissing away her tears, lifted her into his arms.

"Zoyechka, This can be your dacha now... our refuge." He lowered her to the sand and knelt beside her. "Together, we can make it so. We can swim and garden in summer and in the winter lounge in front of a roaring fireplace. No one will ever find us."

Zoya was quiet.

"What?" Jack asked.

"Marta," Zoya answered. "I should sit first and have a proper talk with Marta." She looked up at Jack and smiled reassuringly. "After that we can make our plans."

That evening they had dinner next to the fire pit in the red brick patio of the main house. Marta had brought all the cooked dishes from the cottage and they sat beneath the vine covered arbor that Gus had built fifty years earlier for his beloved Angelique. Indian summer had brought color to the elm trees which Felipe and Gus had planted when Jack was still a small boy. Two glasses of sangria soon brought the conversation around to the ranch.

"Jack," Felipe spoke haltingly. "You are an important man, now, with many burdens. You must do what is best for ..."

Jack raised his hand slightly, interrupting the old man. He opened a pouch which lay on a nearby chair and extracted what appeared to be a legal document. He handed it to Felipe and Marta. "To begin, I could never bring myself to sell this land, so banish that from your minds. This document gives you a life estate in this property."

Felipe looked at Marta and then at Jack. He was obviously puzzled.

Jack pushed the folded document across the table. "You now own what you always had with Gus and Angelique... the right to live on this land for the rest of your lives." He reached out and tapped the paper. "Now, no one can force you to leave what has been our family home since Hiro and I were babies. *Comprende?*"

Felipe nodded his head slowly. Tears were beginning to form.

"*Ahora!*" Jack raised his glass. "*Sallud, a los dos hombles superior, Gustavo y Felipoe, y tambien Angelique y Marta, a los dos ninos, Hiro y Jack. Y finalmente, con su permiso, a la Corazon de mi vida, Zoya!*" (And finally, with your consent, to the heart of my life, Zoya.) Everyone lifted their glass and drank.

"What did you say?" Zoya asked softly.

"Maybe Marta will tell you later."

What Jack did not mention was the pension that was included in the papers he gave Felipe and Marta. As Angelique's successor trustee, he had provided for his family.

The following morning Jack insisted that they leave early. He had business in town, and Zoya needed to be back to the university campus by the late afternoon or early evening.

They bid their farewells with kisses and hugs all around and promises that they would soon return.

"How was your talk with Marta?" Jack headed the Mercedes toward town.

Zoya smiled. "We spoke about what you said last night." She paused. "And other things."

"Like what?"

Zoya sighed. "The house will be ready for us in two weeks."

"That old matchmaker! She has plans for us."

Zoya laughed. "Of course. They love you."

As they entered the outskirts of town, Jack pulled into the parking lot of a large auto repair and detail shop.

"Hey, Stark," someone shouted as he exited the Mercedes. "That Nevada gig must be working out damn well. I like your new wheels. Big son-of-a-bitch, though, isn't it?"

"Hi, Rolly." Jack thrust out his hand to the three hundred pound mechanic. "I see you haven't been missing any meals." They both laughed, and Jack motioned for Zoya to join them.

"Is it ready?"

"Like a gem," the big man answered. "It's over here." They walked to the rear of the garage, and Rolly stripped the tarp away from a silver BMW coupe. The car glittered from every inch of chrome to its shiny black leather interior.

"You want to sell it? I've already had a couple of offers. It's a beauty."

"Isn't that your car?" Zoya asked.

"Nope." Jack took the keys from Rolly and dropped them into her hand. "It's yours."

"*Bozhe moi* (my God), Jack. No. I can't."

"Okay, I just thought it would make it easier for you to get to and from the ranch. If you have a problem with owning it, I could just loan it to you." He reached for the keys.

Zoya turned away quickly and smiled back at him. "Let me think about it."

"You do that, on the drive back to Stanford. Now let's have lunch."

Before leaving town Jack stopped off at the Farmers and Merchants Bank and checked the account from which Felipe would draw for the maintenance and improvements on the ranch. He toured Zoya through the small rural community where he'd spent his boyhood: St. Teresa's Elementary School where the nuns had struggled to educate a bunch of wild country boys full or mischief, the high school where he'd boxed and played football until Hiro's death. Nothing much had changed. They talked and laughed as he told of a young boy's misadventures. Neither wanted their time together to end. Finally they returned to the garage.

"Well, I guess this is it for now. Do you have the map I sketched for you?"

She nodded, gave him a quick hug and a kiss, and stepped into the silver coupe.

"Enjoy the ride," he called after her. "We'll talk tonight."

FIFTEEN

"You picked a good time to get away." Bonnie was responding to Jack's phone call that he would be back in the office the next morning.

"Why, have things been quiet?"

"Dead. No one is pissing and moaning about anything. The Trustees haven't called once. The press has forgotten us."

"What's your take on it?"

"Well, boss, I think that Board meeting when Judi Chang took over the chair from O'Banion really stunned everyone. Too bad you left so quickly. People were looking to pat you on the back."

"You know I avoid that crap. They're the same ones who'll put a blade in you a week later. Speaking of that, what's the news on Paddy, anyway?"

"He dropped out of sight. Gossip is that he's talking about resigning from the Board."

"Bullshit. He's just off licking his wounds, that's all. Sorry to call so late. See you in the morning. Oh, and if General Counsel is in, I'd like to have a talk with him."

"Sure, I'll give him a heads up, and speaking of lawyers, Ted Bitner called and wants to get some time with you this week."

Theodore 'Bit' Bitner headed one of the state's leading law firms and was considered to be among the top trial attorneys in the country. It was to his firm that the newly-appointed Chancellor turned when he swept his headquarters clean during his first months in office. That ordeal had evoked great mutual respect and welded them as trusted friends. Jack became close to the family, even personally campaigning Bit's son Greg into Stanford two years later.

"Set that up please, Bonnie, ASAP. Look forward to seeing you bright and early tomorrow."

"Greg's graduating from Stanford next May, can you believe it?" Ted Bitner and Jack were munching on club sandwiches in the law firm's oak paneled library.

"You must be proud of him. That place is no cake walk these days."

"Oh, I am, Jack, proud as hell. He's got great prospects."

"Then why the long face?"

"Well, it's Carrie, Jack. I've never seen her so unhappy. I'm actually afraid she might be thinking of leaving me."

Jack sat in stunned silence, preferring to stare at the leather bound volumes in the stacks across from them. Finally his eyes focused on Bitner. "Leaving you?"

"You heard me."

"But you're up for the Democratic congressional seat next election. For Christ's sake, Ted, what got into her? Please don't tell me that you..."

"I did nothing, not a goddamn thing. And that congressional bid... Truth be told, I haven't made up my mind. The folks here at the firm are panicked about it."

"I don't get it. If you didn't screw up, what's the problem?"

"From what I can gather, the issue is that she's 'done nothing' but service the family for twenty-five years. Now, she's turning fifty and she wants to express herself. You know the drill. The kids are raised, and she wants to make her own mark in the world before it's too late. I see her point. I'm just afraid she's about to declare that she can never do it living in my shadow."

"As I recall, you two met in law school, right?"

"Fell in love, got pregnant, got married, graduated, lived happily ever after."

"Did she finish her law degree?"

"Oh, yeah," Bit laughed for the first time. "Top of her class and editor of the *Law Review*. She marched across that platform, grabbed her Juris Doctorate, and her water broke an hour later. That was Christina. She's married and living in Chicago now."

"Then David and Greg?"

"Yep, eighteen months apart."

"But Bit, in the years I've been here I've seen her all over the state, highly involved in one thing after another. Last year, didn't she chair the Governor's Commission on Human Rights? And I recall something about the Democratic Central Committee and the statewide women's caucus."

"Yeah, that last one lost me a few clients, but what the hell."

"So, Bit, why am I here other than to lend a sympathetic ear?"

"She always liked you, Jack. I thought you might be willing to have a chat with her. If anyone can talk her down, it's you."

"You know I'd do anything for you, Ted, but..." The look of despair on Bitner's face overcame Jack's better judgment.

"All right, I'll take a run at it. But she's going to have her guard up. Just listening and hand holding is not going to cut it. I'm going to have to come in heavy. Are you okay with that?"

"Sure, Jack, whatever. Listen, you've got a free hand to speak for me... anything. But please don't waste any time. I'm dying here."

Jack nodded, stood, and the two men walked into the hall. "You know, don't you Bit, that my degrees are all in economics. I don't know crap about relationship counseling."

Bitner responded with a wry smile. "That's what I'm counting on. Try and get to it right away, Jack. I'll do anything to keep from losing that lady. I love her, you know."

"Yeah, I know."

"That was one hell of long lunch." Bonnie jumped up from her desk. "I had to push back your two o'clock with 'you know who' and she's pissed as a stepped-on rattlesnake."

"You call her and reschedule, but not today. I've got something more important to straighten out." Jack walked into his office, slammed the door, and reached for the phone.

Luncheon the following day at the Smith Valley Spa provided the perfect venue. Jack and Carrie Bitner had known each other since his first month in Nevada. Carrie was an attractive woman with a steel trap mind and the wit to go with it. She'd been a tremendous asset to Bit's career. The Bitners were the couple to admire in northern Nevada. When the conversation got down to the issue at hand, Jack didn't mince words. He was dead serious and made it clear

that he understood her position completely and that he bore
an offer which not only validated Bit's love for her, but met
her own needs as well. He didn't bother to mention that he'd
been sleepless until three A.M. until the obvious solution
came to him. He began to speak, slowly at first. When he'd
finished, he sat silent.

"He actually would do that?" Carrie Bitner's blue eyes
were boring into Jack.

"It's his idea, Carrie, and it's not just a gesture. Think
about it for a moment. It would knock people on their ear
and most importantly, with a little push from the right places
it would work. I love it, myself!"

She sat for a time sipping her drink. "You know I care
for him, Jack."

"I know, Carrie. And he loves you. This isn't just a mink
coat or a new Mercedes convertible. Ted's not the kind of
man who would disrespect you that way. It's a gesture of love
and sacrifice. Hear me, darlin'. The man gets it."

She nodded her head slowly.

"Carrie, do it. Do it for Bit and the kids. Do it for yourself.
For Christ's sake, do it for me!"

"He really does get it doesn't he, Jack? That means more
to me than anything. Tell him it's a deal."

"Tell him yourself, tonight."

Jack walked into Bitner's office less than an hour later. "Is
he in?" he asked Bitner's secretary without breaking stride.

"Yes, Chancellor, but he's on a conference call with..."
Jack had already entered the private office and closed the
door behind him.

Bitner looked up startled, and quickly punched a button
which knocked him off the speaker phone discussion. He
reached for the intercom. "Charlotte, get to the group

somehow, and explain to them we're having technical difficulty."

He started to get out of his chair, but Jack motioned him back. "You'll need to be sitting down for this, Ted, and tell your secretary that if Carrie calls, put her right through. I'm not here; get it?" Bitner sat back, a look of bewilderment on his face.

"Relax," Jack began. "I'll make this fast. First, I just spent three hours with your wife and delivered an offer of proof of your understanding and love. I've got to hand it to you, Bit, not many men would make such a sacrifice."

"What the hell are you talking about, Jack?"

"I'm talking about your joint announcement with Carrie that you have stepped aside. I'm sure you can come up with a credible reason. And that Carrie Bitner has thrown her hat in the ring for the upcoming congressional race. Moreover, you, as her campaign chair, are calling on the State Democratic Central Committee to endorse this highly qualified individual as the first woman to be elected to congress from the State of Nevada."

Bitner regained his composure. "What about..."

"Bit, she loves the hell out of you. And every woman in this damn state is going to love you by tomorrow evening. Now get home to Carrie and go to work. You and your staff are going to be pulling an all-nighter on this."

Jack held out his hand to his friend. "She's not in your shadow any longer, pal. But she's in your life forever." Jack opened the office door and was gone.

The Chancellor's office was deserted by the time he returned. Only Bonnie sat doggedly at her desk.

"How'd you know I'd be back today?" Jack asked his loyal assistant.

"I had a hunch. Besides, the paperwork is piling up, and I would have called you tonight at home anyways."

"Well, I appreciate it, Bonnie. Seems like the last two days have been sort of a blur. Do you feel like plowing through some of that stuff?"

She sat down across from him and placed a pile of correspondence and file folders on his desk. "Sure, but not before you tell me what the hell is going on."

Jack quickly briefed her. "Things were moving too fast for me to put you in the picture like I usually do. Sorry."

"That's okay, I covered for you." She leaned back in her chair and gazed at him for a moment. "You look really drained, boss, but what you did for those two, well, only you..." She picked up the papers from his desk and stood hefting them in her arms. "I can tell that you're really getting stretched. Just promise me you'll warn me before you walk out of here for good."

He nodded his head and smiled up at her. "You'll be the first to know, my dear."

"Oh, before you shut down for the day, Duke Butrum called. Wants to talk today, if possible."

"I'll call him now." Jack heaved a huge sigh. "You go home. These talks can go on for hours." Jack reached for his private line.

"Duke, sorry it took me so long to get back to you."

"What the hell have you been up to, Jack? You're never in the goddamn office when I call."

"Only good things, Duke, I assure you, only good things. And hanging around this fucking office is not how they get done. What's on your mind? We haven't really talked since the Trustees' meeting."

"Thought I'd give you a heads up. Anyone telling you that Paddy O'Banion is resigning from the Board of Trustees is blowing smoke up your ass."

"Why? What's he up to now?"

"You. That's what he's up to. He's got a year left on the Board before he has to run again and he's sworn to have your head as a campaign trophy. This is no bullshit. The guy is capable of anything, and you need to watch your back. I wish I could give you more to go on but I'm up to my ass in my own shit right now. I barely have time to wind my watch and take a piss these days."

"You'll be Governor of Nevada by next January, Duke. Everybody knows that."

"Yeah, everybody but me."

"I understand, and thanks. I can take care of myself. You just take care of those voters. You've done enough for me."

"Okay, but keep your eyes peeled, Jack. I won't be talking with you 'til after the election, probably."

"Go get 'em, Duke! And thanks again."

Jack leaned back in his chair and sighed. He truly was tired of this pathological comedy. He'd talk with Zoya tonight when he got home. That would be good therapy. Opening his desk calendar he drew a line across next Friday. He'd be on his way early to the ranch to see what Felipe and Marta had accomplished before Zoya arrived later that day. Meanwhile, he resolved to roll up his sleeves and spend some serious time with the Medical College presidential search committee. This weekend he'd fly to Vegas to pay his respects to some good friends and show up at the football game on Saturday and slap some backs.

Bit and Carrie Bitner's press conference caught the state's most savvy political observers by surprise. Even the Las

Vegas media headlined the story. As he watched the two of them smiling and waving on every television news broadcast, Jack chuckled to himself. It was a perfect gambit. Bit was a seasoned politician with plenty of juice in the district. Besides, there wasn't time to build up another viable candidate. There would be a Bitner on the ticket, all right. It just wouldn't be Ted.

The drive over the Sierras from Reno to the Stark Ranch took about two hours, depending on weather conditions. When Jack's dad was dying and later when Angelique was alone, he made the trip weekly. At that time his mother was coping with the abyss of widowhood, and he recalled the day they were having lunch after a visit to the cemetery. He was struck with the realization that the person sitting across from him was not simply his mom. Suddenly he saw the young college flapper with her spit curls, flawless complexion, and big brown eyes; the girl who had warded off countless suitors to adventure west with Gus; who had birthed a son and struggled alongside her husband to build a new life far from family and friends. That Sunday morning he suddenly saw that talented, courageous young girl, stealing time from endless chores to spend hours teaching her three year old son to read. She had always been 'mom' to him, and now she was gone. On that memorable day, however, he saw and heard the whole woman. It taught him a lesson he would not soon forget.

Nobody was in sight as Jack drove slowly down the long tree-lined driveway. The cottage, outbuildings, and barn appeared unchanged. He parked near the eucalyptus grove and walked through the trees in the direction of the main house. It felt good being back in jeans and boots with the early November sun warming his back. He could hear Marta's voice calling out to Felipe. What a scene. The entire exterior of the great house had been washed and the window sashes repainted a gleaming white. He could see that the porch had been stained and the old reclining chairs and swing sofa sat facing the vineyard as they always had when he was a boy. Stepping into the house he encountered a vision from the past. The wide planked hardwood floors gleamed. Huge rag carpets lay centered in each room. Furniture and family antiques not seen for years had been carefully placed. The long dining table and twelve oak spoke back chairs with needlepoint seats dominated the area along with a massive china cabinet adorned with hand carved grape clusters. Two matched mahogany side boards completed the room. A six foot tall black and nickel potbelly stove sat in one corner of the expansive country kitchen. Nearby, stood a small round oak table with carved eagle claw feet and four matching chairs with woven wicker seats. His mother's copper bottomed cookware hung suspended and gleaming from iron hooks. The open cabinets displayed stacks of old mixed family china and glassware.

Stepping into the beamed ceiling living room, he noted Felipe struggling to position a leather sofa near the fireplace. Jack startled him by coming from behind and grasping one end.

"*Hola, Jack. Bienvenido!*" Felipe looked around. "*Donde esta la senorita Zoya?*"

"She won't be here for hours," Jack responded.

"*Bueno,*" the old man puffed and waved his arm about the room and towards the stairwell. "There is still work to do.

Marta wishes everything to be *perfecto*. She is so happy that you will be coming each week *con su Zoya*."

Marta appeared at the top of the stairwell and motioned Jack to come up. *"Mira,"* she walked him to the master bedroom and stood with her hands upon her hips.

"It's wonderful," Jack exclaimed. "You know, Marta, I never slept in that great bed with the pillars."

"But remember, Jack, you were born in it." She grasped his arm and led him back down the hallway to another smaller room. "This was yours. You used to climb out the window and slide down the roof at night and go hunting with Hiro."

"You knew?"

"Hijo, Felipe used to follow until you were both back home safely."

The room was simple with a single brass bed, chair, and round-top trunk where he'd stored his comic books and other boyhood treasures. A gun rack with a .22-caliber rifle and a double barrel twelve-gauge shotgun hung next to a small closet. Jack hoisted the shotgun, opening the breach and peering down the barrel. It had been cleaned and oiled. The walnut stock felt familiar in his hands and the memories came tumbling back. No one hunted then for sport. You brought back game for the table. He could still see his dad standing and placing four cartridges in his small hand. "That should do it," he'd say. "There's just the family tonight."

The other bedrooms were untouched, the furniture covered in old sheets and dust blankets. Jack gave Marta a big kiss on the cheek. *"Muchisimas gracias*. Zoya will love it all." She gave him a hug and a smile, and removing her apron, disappeared down the stairs and headed for the cottage.

Felipe moved to the lower slope and opened the great oak doors to the basement wine cellar. Jack had forgotten how cool the temperature stayed there: 56 degrees, year round. Nothing had been touched since his father's illness and death. The French oak barrels lay on their mounts. The crusher, redwood vats, and bottling station stood waiting for the master's hand. The deep graveled floor crunched under Jack's boots as he walked about touching and caressing the rows and rows of dusty bottles.

"Felipe," he spoke softly, "is it holding up, aging well?"

The old man shrugged. "*Creo que si* (I believe so). We have not opened any of these since your father..." He broke off and fell silent.

"Well, amigo, let's see for ourselves." Jack grasped a single bottle, wiped the dust away carefully and set it gently on a small table just outside the open doors. "Hand me a corkscrew and two glasses."

The two men sat exchanging looks of approval with each tip of the bottle. "All we need now, Felipe, is some hard cheese and peppers."

Felipe nodded. "And your father."

They were sitting silently staring at the empty bottle when Marta's voice called from above. "*Donde estas* (Where are you)?"

"*Aqui, mamacita,*" Felipe shouted up to her as Jack grabbed the bottle and glasses.

"She has brought the food for your weekend," he told a surprised Jack as they closed the cellar doors quickly and scrambled up the side stairs to the kitchen door. There was Marta, carefully storing everything in the old refrigerator. The air was rich with the aroma of freshly baked bread loaves.

"Marta, you are an angel." Jack threw his arms around her.

"Enough for two days, Jack." She gave her husband a look. "Since you are here to watch things, Felipe and I are going to visit my sister in Fresno. *Esta Bien?*"

"Of course, Marta. And *mil gracias* to both of you for what you've done for us. You know how much I love you."

"*Te amo, tambien*, (I love you too). But you have been alone long enough. This young woman *es preciosa* (precious), and I see how she looks at you and I hear her voice when she speaks of you to me. *Oiga me, hijo mia* (Hear me, my son), treat her gently, with love and devotion, and she will light up your life."

"I know, Marta, and I promise. Just be sure to tell sweet lies about me when the two of you go for your walks."

Marta gave him a slap and a kiss. "Felipe," she announced, "*Vamanos*. My sister will be waiting." Jack walked them back to the cottage and waved goodbye as they drove away in Felipe's pickup truck. He walked about for a while, surveying the entrance to the property and the cottage and outbuildings. Things appeared a bit shabby, but Felipe had insisted that whatever could be viewed from the main road should remain unchanged for now. The sound of tires on the gravel driveway caught his attention as the silver BMW appeared with Zoya at the wheel. He stood leaning on a shovel as she drove alongside.

"Ma'am," he drawled, "that's a pretty fancy automobile you're driving out here in the dirt."

"Well," Zoya responded with a big smile, "I was looking for a guy in a blue suit, but you'll do." She hopped out of the car and gave him a big hug and a quick kiss. "I've missed you."

Jack, his arms about her waist, lifted her off the ground and swung her in a half circle. "That makes two of us, kid.

Let's go back and close the gate before we park your car in the barn."

"I noticed it when I drove in. It wasn't here two weeks ago."

"Felipe dragged it out of the barn and hung it. We've been trying to get him to do it for years. Something must have gotten into him." Jack laughed, and pointed toward the gaping barn. "Later we'll park the car right in there and we'll cover it. Did you bring the cowl?"

"In the trunk. I leave it covered on campus." Jack followed her as she bounced along the path toward the main house. She was wearing jeans, Nikes, and a short sleeve sweater, with a small backpack slung over one shoulder. He smiled at having to remind himself that this gamine was indeed a twenty-six-year-old young woman. She stopped abruptly as they exited the grove of trees and stared at the house.

"Oh, Jack."

"Da, Zoya, our dacha."

She slipped off the backpack, dropping it to the grass, and ran to the porch. Running her hand along the varnished banister rail, she touched every piece of furniture, finally arriving at the swing couch where she sat and looking up a Jack, patted the space next to her. She hadn't said a word, but placed her arm through his and gently began to rock back and forth. The creaking of the chain and springs was the only sound to be heard as they looked out over the vineyard to the distant river.

"This is where your mother and father stood when you were little?"

"Over there." He pointed. "Against the rail."

"Oh," she sighed, and rested her head on his shoulder.

"Are you hungry?" He whispered into her ear.

"Yes!" She popped upright.

Marta had prepared tostadas for them. They ate sitting on a weathered pine table next to the wine cellar. Jack opened two cold beers, and they exchanged tales of what had been going on during the past two weeks. Zoya was fascinated with the Ted and Carrie Bitner gambit, but Jack was far more impressed that she had aced her exams and successfully challenged the research statistics course. She was sailing through the program and even Zoya admitted that she was impatient to finish the coursework and get to the dissertation. Only the comprehensive exams worried her. English was a second language, and she felt handicapped writing under time deadlines. Jack reassured her that, unless Stanford had changed dramatically, Ph.D. candidates took all day to complete a section of a comprehensive exam. He recalled writing for thirty-six hours over a five-day period. It was as much a physical ordeal as mental. Still, that was more than a year away, even at the pace she was going.

"Do you want to see the house now?" he asked, as they finished their second beer.

"Yes!"

"Follow me." Jack led the way. She was overwhelmed with the kitchen and dining room.

"It's just like in Russia when I was a girl. No one went to restaurants. They entertained at home. The food was far better."

The vaulted living room and huge fireplace made her anxious for winter to set in. Jack explained that there would be no snow, but they would burn plenty of firewood during December and January.

She marveled at the antiques, especially those in the master bedroom with its grand four-poster and marble topped-tables. Everything she grew up with was in St. Petersburg with no hope of extraction. When she viewed Jack's boyhood bedroom, she laughed at his tales of sneaking out over the roof at night. "Our flat was on the fourth floor," she said. "No chance of that for me."

The wine cellar commanded her greatest interest. The entire chemistry of winemaking fascinated her, and Jack was hard put to answer her pointed questions. She loved the feel of the large French oak barrels and marveled at the dusty, dated stacks of wine-filled bottles. "We'll take a couple with us to the beach tonight. Felipe has set up a bonfire in the pit for us. We can roast kielbasa and bake potatoes in the hot coals. As I recall, that's a good Russian outdoor feast."

Sunset found them walking the path to the beach. They sat in the sand and enjoyed the early chill of a fall evening. The dry grape wood in the fire pit sent flames and sparks high into the darkness. They sat at one of the picnic tables, talking and laughing, sipping wine and dipping Marta's bread into olive oil and vinegar. When the fire finally reduced to a mass of glowing coals, Jack tossed in the wrapped potatoes and they waited for the right time to suspend the kielbasa on a long metal skewer over the glowing pit. The sausages spewed as they turned. Soon they were eating and drinking good wine like country peasants. The rest of the world had ceased to exist.

"How shall we find our way back?" Zoya was clinging to Jack's arm with both hands. He had cast sand on the few remaining coals, and the blackness of a country night and its creature noises now encircled them.

"Like so." A beam of light shot forward, carving a path through the darkness. "I brought this for your sake. Otherwise, we always preferred the night."

As they walked, Zoya pressed as close to him as possible. "What are those sounds?"

"Crickets, owls, muskrat, raccoon, and in the distance, dogs barking. Then, of course, there's your imagination." He chuckled and put his arm around her. "Don't worry. None of them are interested in us. This is their time, and we are making the disturbance."

"I suppose you know how not to make a disturbance."

"I once did, but that was a long time ago. We'll save that story for the next time we sit by a fire." They were coming up on the house now, and the porch light cast a yellow halo on the grass. Jack flicked off the flashlight. He opened the screen door and as they entered he dropped the knapsack onto the kitchen counter.

"I'll bet you'd like a shower and some warm towels."

"Oh yes!"

"Your stuff is in the master bedroom. Use the large bathroom there. That's yours. There are robes there if you want one. I'm going to shower down here and then make some tea." He smiled at her. "You were very brave." She punched him on the arm and ran for the stairwell.

Jack was sitting low on the big leather couch facing the fireplace when Zoya finally came down. Flames from a small fire were crackling, casting flickering shadows about the floor.

"Where are you?" Zoya was at the foot of the stairs peering into the darkened room.

"Here, babe," he called over his shoulder. She made her way in the direction of his voice and the firelight. He was sitting slouched down with his bare feet resting on the edge of the stone hearth. He looked up at her as she sat next to him. She was wearing shorts and a t-shirt under a big white terrycloth robe. Her head was wrapped in a towel. "Sorry to take so long, but I decided to wash my hair."

"There's no clock when we're here, Zoyechka." He reached for the teapot and filled two cups as she snuggled closer to him. "It's a bit chilly in the house. I thought you'd like the fire after your shower."

"I love it." She took the cup that he handed her.

"Umm, just the way I like it. Not too strong with fresh lemon. How did you know?"

"I guessed."

They sat quietly, staring into the fire and sipping tea.

"I was admiring the bed upstairs. It's so big and the carvings on the headboard are beautiful."

"The clusters of grapes, you mean?"

"Yes. And the four posts look covered in ..."

"Vines. I know."

"I've never seen anything like it."

"Dad had it made for my mother. He got the idea from a picture of a sixteenth century royal bedchamber. They never let anyone wander into that room. For one thing, the bed, as you saw, is really huge.... more common these days, but not then. The story goes that I was a breach birth and it was touch and go for Angelique. He knelt by her bed all night holding her hand and praying. When she was still with him at dawn, he promised to build that bed. Did you sit on it?"

"No." Her eyes were moist. She raised the sleeve of her robe to her cheek. "The quilt is so beautiful, I didn't want to ..."

"Well, you're going to love it," he interrupted. "The mattress is goose down, eighteen inches thick. You'll disappear from sight." He seemed amused at the thought. "Mom and my grandmother made the quilt. It tells the story of the family from when they arrived in America in 1898." Jack waved his arm toward the library as they reached the base of the stairwell. "There's a journal somewhere in there that belongs with the quilt."

Zoya was very quiet.

Jack pulled her closer. "You're thinking of home, aren't you, and all the ones you loved who are gone and the things you grew up with and had to leave." He kissed her softly on the cheek. She leaned into him and pulled her legs up onto the couch. The towel had fallen from her head and her long auburn hair fell about his chest. He simply held her, stroking her forehead with his fingertips. The fire burned steadily lower. He looked down at her. "We both know too much of being alone," he whispered. She was fast asleep.

Morning sunlight was streaming into the bedroom when she stirred and opened her eyes. Jack was breathing deeply, still asleep. They were buried in the goose down mattress, with an ivory comforter pulled partially over them. She was still in her silk shorts and t-shirt. Moving her head slightly she looked about the room. The carved posts at the foot of the great bed reached toward the arched beam ceiling. Textured, pastel wallpaper covered the far wall by the entrance to the master bath. Matching cut glass lamps sat on two cherry, marble-topped bedside tables. A 19th-century love seat upholstered in green cut velvet sat by the bay window. Her robe lay tossed over one of the arms. A tapestry covered platform rocker occupied the far corner of the room next to what appeared to be a small walnut writing desk with a folding shelf. A spindle back chair was tucked between the desk's tall graceful legs. Suddenly, a cool draft of morning air fluttered the bathroom curtains, and she shivered and drew the comforter up, moving closer to Jack.

"*Dobroe utra,* (good morning)" he whispered, turning slightly and facing her.

Zoya blinked at him and smiled. "And how did I get up here?"

"You were asleep. I carried you."

"That's never happened before." She ran her index finger along the cleft of his chin. "At least not after I was five years old."

Jack turned and stretched his arms above his head. "Well, we better get used to it. I think you like falling asleep on the couch."

She smiled and rubbed her hand in a circular motion on his bare chest. "Are you ..?"

"No, I wore pajama bottoms last night, just for you."

"So, what you're saying is that you usually sleep in the…"

"Correct," he said, sliding his arm under her neck and shoulder and pulling her into him.

"Well that's going to change, I hope?"

"*Bozhe moi,*" he exclaimed, "already it starts!"

She whacked him on the chest, and slipped out of bed. "I'm going to take a quick wake up shower. What's for breakfast? I'm hungry."

He kicked the comforter off as she headed into the shower. "Oh, thank God," she called over her shoulder. "You really were wearing them." He heard the knobs turn and the rush of water against the tile.

"Country breakfast," Jack announced, as she entered the kitchen. Thick slices of bacon were sizzling slowly in an iron skillet. Buckwheat pancakes were stacked in the warming oven, and he was dishing out scrambled eggs and chives onto warm plates.

"Wow." She sat and poured hot tea into a mug.

"You'd maybe rather have *kasha* (porridge)? I thought you said you were hungry?"

She was already pouring syrup on her pancakes with one hand and taking a bite from a slice of bacon held delicately in the other. "This is fantastic bacon. It's peppery, and so lean."

Jack took a bite of pancakes. "Felipe still makes it. You should have seen the things he and my father used to do. God, those days are gone forever."

She took a sip of tea and looked up from her plate. "We'll see. What are we going to do today?"

"Well, it looks like it's going to be warm enough. What do you say to a canoe trip down the river? Maybe stop for lunch at some little place on the water."

"You can paddle a canoe?"

"Are you Russian? My God, Zoya, I grew up on these rivers."

"Sounds good. Will you teach me?"

"Oh yeah, count on it." He chuckled to himself and reached for another piece of bacon.

The canoe excursion down river proved to be a magical experience. As they paddled steadily or floated with the current the river curved and wandered through the countryside. At some points they encountered children swinging out on ropes hung from tall trees and dropping into the water. At others, the river would be hardly moving and overhung with towering oaks and vines. They exchanged friendly waves with ranch families picnicking on the shore. The sun was high in the sky when Jack pointed to a widening in the river in the distance.

"There it is, Catfish Charlie's." A large ramshackle building, built partially on shore and partially on tall wooden pilings, hung suspended over the water. Jack, steering from behind, maneuvered the canoe to a gentle stop alongside the floating dock, stepped out quickly, and secured a line to an iron davit. Holding his hand out to Zoya, he hoisted her onto the platform. She was wearing deck shoes, cut off faded jean shorts, and a tank top. Her hair was pulled up high atop her head and secured by large silver clip. Charlie's going to love this, Jack thought as he followed Zoya up the wooden steps to the diner. Pushing open the screen door, He could see that the place was nearly deserted. Tables were scattered randomly about, some with chairs stacked on them seat down. A couple of regulars were perched on bar stools eating hamburgers and drinking beer from long neck bottles. They glanced up, their eyes following Zoya as Jack led her across the room and out a screened door which opened onto a graveled parking area near a narrow asphalt road. In the distance you could see fields of feed corn, their stalks broken and crumpled after the harvest. A few scattered farm houses surrounded by clusters of trees dotted the landscape. Half a dozen milk cows were grazing lazily in the noonday sun.

"Jack Stark?" A grizzled old man in clean overhauls and a baseball cap was walking towards them.

"Charlie," Jack answered. "It's me, alright." He grasped the old fellow's outstretched hand. "It's been a long while. You look good, Charlie."

"So do you, son. Haven't seen you since Angie's funeral. You doin' all right?"

"I'm fine, Charlie, as you can see. Zoya Chalkin, meet an old family friend, Charles Lester Pruitt. Don't let the coveralls fool you. He owns damn near everything as far as the eye can see."

Charlie gave Zoya an appraising glance. "I don't see no car, so the two of you must have come down the river. Nice day for it. First time for you, Miss?"

"Yes," Zoya answered, stepping forward and shaking his hand. It was softer than she expected, not the hand of a farmer. She smiled. "Jack's been boasting the whole trip down about your famous chili and hamburgers."

"Sounds like a girl with an appetite." He turned and waved them into the diner. "Things are quiet now…getting a bit late in the season. Up to a few weeks ago the crowds near drove us crazy. We even had a banjo player and a singer. Are you hungry?"

He wasn't waiting for an answer, tossing two huge ground beef patties on the grill and busying himself behind the counter. Zoya noted that, despite the rustic nature of the place, the open kitchen was state of the art and spotless. Charlie had rolled up his sleeves, put on an apron, scrubbed his hands, and was now busy chopping onions.

"How's that taste, young lady?" Charlie leaned over the counter obviously enjoying the way Zoya was reacting to the first bite of his culinary pride. He totally ignored Jack.

"Umm," she responded nodding and chewing. "Worth the trip." She took another bite as Charlie slid a tall wine cooler in front of her.

She looked at Jack. "What's this?"

"Taste it."

She took a sip and then a long drink. "I like it. Very refreshing."

"Just cheap white wine and 7-Up with a squeeze of lemon." Charlie looked pleased with himself and gave Jack an approving nod. Turning, he peered out the window down at the dock. "Nice canoe."

"Don't you recognize it? It's one of yours. Been sitting at the ranch since last year."

"By God, Jack, is that the one that got stove up? Had a couple of cracked ribs and a hole in the side, as I recall."

"Yep, Felipe repaired it over the winter and it's been waiting for me to float it down to you."

Charlie looked at Zoya, who had pushed her glass back in his direction. "Did you paddle down, Missy, or let him do all the work?"

"He helped," Zoya answered with a smile.

Charlie laughed. "Jack, I think you finally met your match." He walked from behind the counter, shut the front door, and flipped the closed sign which hung from a string on the window. "C'mon, give me a hand dragging it up the slope and I'll haul you all back to home in the pickup. The burgers are on the house."

"But it's your canoe, Charlie."

"It was, 'til it got busted. Now it belongs to you." He winked at Zoya. "Why don't you name it after your lady friend, here?"

When Charlie dropped them off at the Stark ranch, he and Jack carried the canoe into the barn and set it upside down on two sawhorses. Jack covered it with a canvas.

As Charlie moved to climb into the truck, Zoya stepped toward him and held out her hand. "You are a very sweet man, Charlie Pruitt. I hope we meet again."

The old man took her hand and held it briefly. Jack could see he was touched. "You're welcome, young lady, anytime." He slammed the door on the pickup, started the engine, and looked at Jack. "It's damn good to see you back on the ranch, Jack." He nodded at Zoya. "I better see her name on that canoe next time, or I'll take it back." He disappeared around the curve of the driveway, waving his arm from the open window.

Jack and Zoya walked slowly towards the great house, holding hands. It was late afternoon and the shadows from the buildings and trees were growing longer.

"It's Saturday night out there," he said as they moved through the eucalyptus trees. "The rest of the world is getting ready to party."

She stopped walking. "Listen."

He stood next to her for a moment. "What is it?"

"Nothing, that's the point," she sighed, "It's so quiet you can almost hear the silence."

As they drew near the house, she pulled him down the grassy slope toward the wine cellar. "Let me choose a bottle for tonight."

Jack swung open the great doors and they stepped into the cool dimness of the cellar. He pulled a string hanging from the ceiling and a light came on. "Take your pick."

She strolled past the racks, studying the dates and notes tacked to each section. "This is your father's handwriting?" Jack nodded his head.

"Very strong character." She observed, finally pausing at a bottle labeled 'zinfandel', 1970. "This one...the year I was born."

Jack smiled. "He'd be pleased with your choice. Lift it out gently. There's sediment at the bottom of the bottle."

As they walked back toward the open doors and daylight, Jack plucked a long slender bottle from a high shelf. "Muscat De Oro," he said. "Not ours, but pure gold like the name, and fruity."

Once in the house, she set her bottle down carefully. "Let's hurry," Zoya dashed upstairs to the master bathroom shower. "I don't want to miss a minute of the sunset."

Jack decanted the zinfandel, slipped the bottle of Muscat into the freezer ice to chill, and made for the back porch shower. Ten minutes later he stepped into a pair of faded jeans, pulled on an old football jersey, grabbed the Muscat, two glasses, and headed barefoot for the deck. Zoya was already standing at the rail dressed in light green cargo pants and a black knit pullover and sheepskin slippers.

"Oh, you look so cute, Jack, in your old high school clothes." She held up one foot. "I found these in the closet. I hope it's okay."

"Nothing is off limits here for you." He put his arm around her neck and kissed her. "Please remember that, and no more 'cute' comments, please."

"I meant it! You look absolutely sexy in those old jeans."

"Sexy is okay. You look sixteen years old in that outfit, so I guess that makes us even and me a little nervous."

She laughed as they sat back on the swing couch. The sun was a golden late-harvest orb, hanging over the horizon. Streaks of red and gold cut through the trees and crossed the fields below. Jack opened the bottle of Golden Muscat and poured two glasses. "Hold it up to the sun, Zoya."

She held up her glass for a moment and then turned to him. "*Za nas, na vsegda* (To us, forever)." They drank the toast, kissed again, and bundled together, talking and sipping the elegant vintage while the sun sank slowly out of sight.

As twilight grew into darkness, they moved into the great room and Jack touched a match to a fire he had laid earlier. As the flames rose, crackling and spreading their warmth to the couch, she pulled her legs up and lay back into his arms. Looking up at his chiseled, handsome face, she traced the line of his jaw with her finger.

"Jack," she whispered softly.

He looked down at her.

"I won't fall asleep tonight."

SIXTEEN

On the day that Jack received his B.A. in Economics his proud grandfather sent him a 19th-Century edition of Machiavelli's *The Prince*. On the frontispiece of the book the old man, then ninety, had written in Italian, "To help navigate the journey." Four years later, upon completing his Ph.D. at Stanford, his doctoral advisor and mentor handed him a copy of Sun Tzu's *The Art of War*. "I know the classroom can never hold you, Jack. You will need this where you are headed. Good luck.'

The November elections swept Duke Butrum into the Governor's office. He immediately summoned Jack to a private meeting at his Lake Tahoe lodge where, as governor-elect, he had gathered a group of the state's high-rollers.

"My administration is going to focus, like none before, on economic development. Those California high techs are going to get a taste of Nevada hospitality." He placed his hand on Jack's shoulder. "And this guy knows how to bring 'em to the table."

ROBERT M. BERSI

Later, he took Jack aside. Did you hear that applause, Chancellor? They're on board with this."

"I agree with your ambitions, Duke, but remember, I still work for the Board of Trustees… and I didn't see a single one here today."

"That's because they weren't invited. You've got a talent, Jack, and it's wasted on those assholes. Just cool your jets 'til after I'm sworn in."

A more celebratory event took place at the home of Ted and Congresswoman-elect Carrie Bitner. Jack found himself included in a dinner party for family and a few select friends. As he was departing, Carrie and Ted walked him to his car. Carrie took both of his hands into hers and held them. There were tears in her eyes.

Jack smiled and straightened her lapel pin. "Give 'em hell back there, Congresswoman."

The weekends at the ranch with Zoya had become soul-saving respites. She scoffed at his concerns that their age difference could in some way be to her detriment. Marta chided him for questioning the blessing God had brought them.

During Thanksgiving dinner the old woman looked across the table at the two of them sitting close together. "I have seen much of life," she advised them that evening. "And I can see that you both have what your sainted parents and grandparents had… a love made in heaven." She held up a thin kitchen knife. "You could not slip this blade between them. Could you, Jack; could you, Zoya?" There were tears in her eyes as she reached out and covered their hands with hers. Felipe had placed his arm about her as she continued to speak. "It goes beyond love, to a place few come to in this life." She sat back with a smile, glanced at Felipe, and crossed herself. "So there, I have said it."

Felipe kissed her on the cheek. "So, mama, can we have the apple pie now?"

Later that evening, seated together on the couch in front of the fire, Zoya turned to Jack with a wry smile on her face. "You know, I think Marta sort of married us over dinner."

"Yeah, I felt that." Jack chuckled. "She probably feels better now about us living in sin."

"No, I didn't hear that at all. She loves us, Jack."

"I know." He pulled her close and gave her a kiss on the cheek. "So, what would you like to do?"

"As long as we're together..." She shrugged her shoulders.

"I want more."

"Really?"

"Yes, absolutely. What we have should be dignified by marriage. You say when."

"Umm." She was smiling broadly. "How about spring break, in April?"

"Okay, but let's keep it to ourselves. It's precious and it belongs to us."

She was nodding her head emphatically. Zoya was even more private about her life than Jack who was fiercely protective of his own personal life.

"So." She looked at him with an impish smile. "You just proposed?"

"And you said yes!" Jack swept her up from the couch and proceeded to carry her upstairs.

"I need to take a shower!" She protested.

"Tomorrow morning."

The scheduled committee meetings of the Board of Trustees took place in Las Vegas. Jack had not seen Paddy O'Banion since the fateful October meeting of the Board in Reno. Judi Chang, with Jack seated to her right, conducted business in a flawless and businesslike manner. It wasn't until they adjourned for the day that Jack and Paddy had occasion to cross paths.

"Surprised to see me here, Chancellor?"

"Not at all, Paddy," Jack responded. "I wasn't one of those who expected you to resign in a huff. You bought your seat on the Board fair and square. Why would you give it up?"

O'Banion laughed, but his eyes were slits. "Always got the needle out for me, huh, Stark? Be careful."

"Even you're too smart to cross that line, Paddy. And the guys who could, work for people who like me. So why don't we just call it a push and walk away from the play."

"Not on your life, asshole. You'll fuck up sooner or later, Stark. You'll make a mistake, and I'll be waiting to drop the hammer."

They both looked over to see Chris Paladanos' three hundred pound frame headed in their direction. He was carrying a plate piled high with buffalo wings. "What the hell is this? Don't tell me you two guys are gonna kiss and make up?"

"Only if he kisses my ass," Paddy growled, and walked away.

Back in his office the next afternoon, Jack was on the phone with Zoya. "Sorry about the weekend, kid, but when the Trustees get together it's always unpredictable."

"No, it worked out fine for me. I've got finals and papers coming up. I need every minute I can get. Are you okay? You sound tired."

"I'm all right, babe. I'm off to the gym as soon as we finish. I'm just tired of the bullshit, Zoya. More importantly, how are you doing?"

"What do you call it? Burning up the road. I challenged my last course. They won't let me do any more. Actually I had to get a waiver to take this exam."

"Oh hell, you've got those guys eating out of your hand. They'd damn near do anything for you. Don't deny it. Newman keeps me up to date."

"It's the grant money, Jack, and you know it. They really want to get their hands on it."

"Well, we can talk about how to play that to your advantage on the flight out to New York and Connecticut. Did you call June? Can she meet you for dinner on the twenty-second?"

"No. I'm so disappointed. She had another commitment. Maybe on the way back."

"Yeah, maybe. Well then, here's our schedule. We can leave from the ranch at the crack of dawn on the twenty-first, or we can drive down the day before and play around in San Francisco and stay at the Airport Hilton."

"Let's do the city and have dinner at the Carnelian Room."

"Why didn't I think of that?" Jack had already made reservations, but it was supposed to be a surprise.

"Our flight leaves at eight, and we arrive JFK at four-twenty. We'll stay in Manhattan for two nights. I know you want to do that. Then we'll limo up to Roy and Ginny's on the twenty-third. Sound okay?"

"I'm a little anxious about meeting them. They're such an important part of your life."

"Don't worry about that. We'll do some shopping there. That will distract you. Just think snow, sleigh rides, and Christmas in Connecticut. We can pick up gifts for them when we're in the City, but I'm damned if I know what to get. They already have everything."

"Oh, I'll find something."

"I'm sure you will. Okay, see you next weekend. I'm going to work out. *Tak lublu.* (Love you.)"

"*Ya tozhe.* (Me too.) Bye."

SEVENTEEN

The thermometer read thirty-three degrees as they hopped into a cab at Kennedy and headed for the Hilton in Manhattan. Zoya wanted to be close to 5th and 6th Avenue for shopping and she told him that there was a fantastic Russian restaurant only four blocks walking distance away.

"We'll freeze," Jack complained. They had unpacked quickly and were headed out.

"This is spring in St. Petersburg," she teased as she peered out from her hooded fur great coat.

Looking at that precious face framed in fur with her green eyes sparkling with excitement, Jack relented, "Sure, what the hell. I'll buy some ear muffs."

"I already have them for you." She pulled a parcel from her bag. "Here, my mother sent them."

"For me?"

"Yes."

"Then you've been talking?"

"Of course, I call her every week."

"So, she knows about us?"

"She knows that I'm happy for the first time in six years. I've been on my own halfway round the world for a long time now, Jack. My mom was only twenty when I was born. There's a sort of parity between us. We're mother and daughter, of course, but we're girlfriends as well. Don't be concerned. When you finally meet, the two of you will get on wonderfully. Walk faster, I'm hungry."

"You're always hungry."

After Zoya had ordered, Jack asked the waiter to bring them another vodka. "For the cold," he explained.

"So tell me," he asked. "Are things any better for your mom at the Academy?"

"Worse. The government is in chaos. No one was ready for this breakup of the old system. Nothing works anymore. She and the faculty have not received salaries for months. I'm worried about her."

Zoya's mother was Dean of the School of Economics and a distinguished professor of engineering/economic. In short, Zoya's mother was still well connected, even with all the changes.

Jack was shocked. "How does she live?"

"How do you think?"

"You?"

"Of course, who else?"

"How difficult that must be for her."

"She's not just sitting around, Jack. Life there is rather like Chicago was during your prohibition. Everything is up for grabs. There are unbelievable opportunities to make money, but it won't last forever. An old friend of my grandfather in Finland made her a business proposition, but we can't talk about it much on the phone. All I know from our last conversation is that she has entered some venture with him."

The waiter returned with the first course. "Oh boy," Jack exclaimed, "soup with pelmeni!" The rest of the evening they chatted about the next few days and Christmas in Connecticut.

The afternoon of the twenty-third found then in a limo loaded with packages. Zoya had carefully chosen something for everyone. She was especially thrilled with two Hermes pleated scarves from Paris that she found at Bloomingdale's for her mother and Ginny. They each came in elegant round boxes that Jack commented must surely be filled with gold. They had great fun clothes shopping for one another. As the limo cruised towards their destination, Jack gave Zoya a running commentary on the countryside. As they moved off Route 7 onto the road to Bridgewater, the rolling countryside became even more beautiful. Slowing, they rounded a sharp curve and Jack directed the limo into the driveway which wound its way upward towards the Adler house.

"There, that's where we will be staying." Jack pointed through the leafless cluster of trees which surrounded the picture-book farmhouse nestled next to a frozen pond. As the limo drew closer to the main house, Zoya checked her lipstick and gave her long hair a quick brush. She adjusted her grey tweed slacks and cashmere sweater, and giving her soft leather boots a tug, prepared to meet Ginny and Roy.

"Just a bit further," Jack told the driver. "Clear around the house and park in back by the garages." The limo came to a stop and Jack clasped Zoya's hand, opened the door himself, and stepped out. He helped her with her coat and pulled on his own sheepskin jacket. Ginny came rushing out to greet them.

"You guys… finally!" She gave Zoya a quick hug and hustled her off to the warmth of the house, leaving Jack to help the driver unload. By the time the luggage and parcels were safely inside, and Jack had dispatched the limo, Ginny and Zoya were sitting by the kitchen hearth having a cup of tea and talking.

"Hey, how about me?" Jack complained.

"Oh, you," Ginny laughed. "Who cares about you? She's the one we've all been waiting to meet." Zoya was smiling and already obviously at ease.

Jack poured himself a mug of tea and walked over to stand next to the fire. "Speaking of 'we', where's your other half?"

"Oh, he's out with Shannon and Jordan checking the upper pond to see if the ice is thick enough for skating. We're having a few friends over tomorrow for a party. They'd kill us if they found out you were visiting and didn't get to say hello. Actually, we thought you'd enjoy seeing the old gang." Turning to Zoya, she said with an impish smile, "You'll have to forgive us. We saved you for the big surprise."

Male voices could now be heard along with a bit of stomping and cursing coming from the mud porch. Roy, boots off and in his stocking feet, came crashing into the great kitchen, followed closely by nineteen-year-old Shannon and his brother, Jordan who was younger by two years. They were still disagreeing about the condition of the pond ice, when all three caught sight of Zoya, who was now standing next to Ginny.

"Boys," Ginny addressed the startled trio, "please pay your respects to our very special guest."

Roy stepped forward immediately. "Welcome to our home, Zoya." He took both of her hands in his and smiled broadly. "We've been so looking forward to meeting you and having you and Jack here for the holidays."

"Shannon, Jordan," Ginny ordered. "Stop gawking and come over and say hello." The boys moved forward, self-consciously extending their right hands.

"Boys, I would like to introduce Miss Zoya Alexandrovna Chalkin."

"Zoya, these are our two sons who, I assure you, when cleaned up well, make a much better presentation."

Roy had moved across the room to stand close to Jack who was leaning against the brick wall near the fire. "Christ," he hissed under his breath to Jack.

"Yeah, I know," Jack whispered back.

"We'll talk later." Roy moved towards the group.

"Ginny, why don't you take Zoya down and show her the guest house and let her get settled? I turned the furnace up a while ago, so it should be toasty with plenty of hot water. Boys, help your mother and Zoya with the luggage."

As soon as the house cleared, Roy went to the bar, poured two brandies and handed one to Jack. They stood for a moment in silence, then Roy began to chuckle.

"What's so funny?"

"Did you see the look on the boys' faces?" He was holding his sides. "They didn't know whether to shit or go blind."

Jack began to laugh. "I was too busy watching you."

Roy finally got control of himself and gripped Jack by both shoulders. "Are you sure about this, Jack? I mean don't get me wrong. I'm happy for you and all. I mean, Jesus, I can't think of anyone who deserves it more, but can she really be as great as she is looks?"

"Like I told you on the phone, you may think they broke the mold when your mother, Mary, passed on; God rest her soul. But there it is man, she's the real thing, with a heart of gold and Jewish to boot. And, yeah, she's smart enough to have an MBA with honors from Columbia, a Ph.D. soon from Stanford, and brave enough to love me."

Roy poured another drink. "So, you're going to get married?"

"Damn straight, so when Ginny tells you, act surprised."

"What about the date?"

"As soon as possible, probably no later than next spring. But we want to keep it close and personal. Of course we wanted you and Ginny to know how happy we are. This is real, man. I've been waiting for it all my life, and she, well, she feels that I'm the center of her world."

Roy looked out the window towards the guest cottage. "Well, there's smoke coming from the chimney, so they must be bonding down there. I better shower and set the table. It looks like the boys took off in the Range Rover. We won't be seeing them for hours. Just the four of us tonight."

Jack had moved into the living room and was standing, lost in thought, staring out the picture window at the valley below when he suddenly felt Ginny's arms around him. "Oh Jack, she's an angel."

"Thanks, I think so too." He turned and she gave him a big kiss on the cheek.

"I told you she'd appear someday, didn't I?"

"You did indeed, Gin, you did indeed."

"She loves you so much, Jack. It shows on both of you."

Roy came down the stairs in jeans and a Pendleton shirt. "Where's Zoya?"

"She stopped by my bathroom for moment. Oh, here she comes."

Zoya had changed into tartan pantaloons and a loose fitting long sleeve sweater. She was wearing a pair of fur mukluks.

"Where'd you get all that?" Jack asked.

"They're mine." Ginny sighed. "They look better on her."

"Not so," Roy objected. "I've been watching your figure for twenty years and you're still a size four. Tell me I'm wrong."

"You're wrong," Ginny answered. "I'm a six now, but you get points for lying. And, honey, now would be a great time to open a bottle of champagne."

Roy reached into the cooler. "What are we celebrating now?"

"Jack and Zoya. They're getting married."

Roy feigned surprise, popped the cork, and poured four crystal flutes.

"Is Clarence coming tomorrow?" she asked.

"Yeah, he's really looking forward to seeing you again, Jack. You probably didn't know, he lost Bette Ann last year and doesn't come out much anymore."

"Well," Ginny said. "I've a proposition for him that just might tickle his fancy."

Clarence Hughes was one of the first of the Connecticut bunch to befriend Jack when he and little Gus would weekend at Roy and Ginny's. Hughes was an intrepid hiker and he led Roy and Jack on regular treks along the old Mohawk Trail. They would fortify their outings with good brandy and great conversation. At seventy-six, Clare Hughes was the long-standing Chief Justice of the Connecticut Supreme Court. He held a reputation as one of the nation's sharpest legal minds as well as that of being an inveterate rake. He possessed a rapier wit and sense of humor to match. An evening with Clare was an experience to remember, especially if the party was peppered with attractive women of any age. He was the 20th-Century answer to Ben Franklin, charming his female admirers with a web of clever anecdotes and titillating flirtation.

"What shall I wear?" Zoya asked Ginny.

"Oh honey, like I said earlier, there'll only be a few of our closest friends. And they all know Jack. That red dress with the suede pumps will be perfect. It's Christmas."

Guests began arriving in the early afternoon for the Adler's Christmas Eve brunch. It was a bright, sunny, cold day without a trace of snow. Jack stood by the fireplace in the great room and graciously accepted greetings from acquaintances he had not seen for years. Ginny stayed close to Zoya, introducing her as Jack's fiancée. The hugs and smiles validated their warmth and regard for Jack. When Clarence Hughes arrived he went directly to Jack. The two men were obviously delighted to see one another again and were engaged in a lively conversation when Ginny brought Zoya over to meet Clare.

"My dear girl." His eyes twinkled with mischief as he took her hand and raised it to his lips. After a thorough appraisal of a slightly embarrassed Zoya, he turned and gazed at Jack. "My friend, I should caution you that you are probably in violation of some law of the State of Connecticut." Still holding her hand, he turned to Zoya. "My child, I'm compelled by curiosity and as an officer of the court, to inquire as to your age."

"Clare!" Ginny protested. "I thought we agreed that..."

"Tut, tut." The old jurist was holding up his forefinger.

"Twenty-six, your honor," Zoya responded in her rich Russian accent.

"Ah, then." Clare began to walk them away still holding her hand. "We must talk, my dear, about this rascal with whom you propose to spend your life." He cast a disdainful look at Jack and led a smiling Zoya away.

Ginny placed her hand on Jack's arm. "Let them be for a while. He's completely fascinated. I haven't seen him so animated in a long while. She'll be fine. Don't worry."

Jack chuckled. "I'm not worried about Zoya. She can handle herself. Look at her. She's having a great time. It's Clare that may have the heart attack if he doesn't stop staring at her bosom."

Roy came walking up. "Everyone wants to talk with you, Jack. Don't disappoint them."

Jack mingled with old friends through brunch. They were so delighted with Zoya and his engagement, and he graciously satisfied their curiosity about how they met and volunteered their plans to marry soon. He felt a tug on his arm.

Roy explained, "I've got to steal this guy away for a few moments."

"What's going on?" Jack asked as Roy led him from the crowd towards the library. As they entered, Jack saw Ginny, Clare, and Zoya sitting together. Jack sat next to Zoya. She smiled and took his hand.

"Jack," Clare began, "I must say, that today I met my match. Your Zoya listened graciously to my salty tales of your checkered past and countered with such enchanting revelations of the love you two have found together, that I must say, marry, by all means."

"Thank you, Clare. That means a great deal coming from you."

"I have only one heartfelt request."

"Anything, Clare. You mean the world to me and it's obvious that you've captured Zoya's affection."

"On the contrary, she has stolen my heart. Swear to God, Jack, if this were the 18ᵗʰ century I would have us at the dueling oak this moment, challenging you for her hand."

"Okay, Clare," Jack smiled indulgently. "I'm impressed. What's on your mind?"

"Jack, Zoya, would you allow me to marry you, here, on New Years' day?"

Jack sat stunned for a moment. The room was silent. He turned to Zoya. "*Tu hochish?*"

"*Da, ochen.*" She was smiling, gripping his arm tightly and nodding her assent.

The room erupted with shouts and laughter. Ginny and Zoya were hugging. Roy was pumping Jack's hand. Clare was beaming.

"What about the license?" Jack was shouting over the clamor.

"My dear boy," Clare admonished. "I am the Chief Justice of the Connecticut Supreme Court."

"We've been missing long enough," Roy said. "It's all settled but the details. Let's get back to our guests."

Roy quickly climbed halfway up the curving stairwell, pulling Ginny with him. Striking on a glass with a spoon, he finally got everyone's attention.

"Dear friends, today we celebrate not only the holidays but also the fact that our Jack finally fell in love, and what a love she is, Zoya." There was applause and someone whistled. Roy raised his hands for silence. "Now, it's my pleasure to invite you all to attend a wedding, here in our home, at ten a.m. on New Year's Day, Chief Justice Clarence Hughes presiding."

Gasps and a spattering of applause gave way to cheers. Someone shouted, "Great, that leaves the afternoon free for the bowl games!"

Later that evening at the cottage, Jack and Zoya sat sipping hot cider before a fire of red oak and hickory. When they finally climbed the stairs to the bedroom, Zoya, brushed aside the lace curtains and peered into the night. "Look, Jack. It's snowing."

At Christmas dinner, Roy leaned over to Jack. "Look at Ginny, she's beaming. You've given her the dream holiday gift. She gets to plan a whole wedding in only one week."

"Jack," Ginny said from across the table, "Zoya and I will be quite busy for the next few days. Maybe you can go into the office with Roy or something. Oh, and give your bride to be one of your credit cards. On second thought, better hand them all over."

"Keep one, buddy." Roy smiled at Jack. "You're going to need it."

As they turned onto Interstate 84 headed for Manhattan, Jack looked over at Roy. "I thought we were going into the office."

"We will, but right now we're headed to the diamond district in the City. The bride usually feels better about the wedding when the groom produces a ring at the proper moment."

Jack looked perplexed. "I don't know what her ring size is."

"She's a six."

"How the hell do you know?"

"Ginny told me."

"Of course."

"Don't worry, I know a guy. We'll find something great."

"No matter how great it is, she won't wear it for a time. We've decided to keep this to ourselves back there for at least six months."

"Take my word for it, Jack. She'll wear it to bed." He laughed and turned off the west side highway into the city.

"It's a beautiful blue-white." Roy's man was turning a stone with the tips of his tweezers.

"What size did you say it was?"

"260 points, a bit more than two and one half carats." He kept turning the stone so it would catch the light. He scribbled a number on a piece of paper and pushed towards Roy. "I can let you have it for that."

"Yasim," Roy responded, showing the number to Jack, "If your father were here, he would cover his face in shame. Do we look like the kind of people to whom you suggest such a number?"

"But he is not here today."

"Go back to your office. Look to see what he has sold to the Adler family over the past fifty years. We'll wait."

Ten minutes past as Jack and Roy browsed through the shop. They were going out the door for a cup of coffee when young Yasim returned and motioned to them. "My father called while I was going through the records. You must understand, Mr. Adler, I was not familiar with the long relationship between our families."

"Of course, Yasim, how could you be? So many years, so many transactions. How much?"

"For you, half."

"Mounted?"

"What did you have in mind, Mr. Adler?"

Jack spoke up. "Since it's a wedding ring, I think it should be mounted high on a wide gold band, size six."

"Too wide a band may not present the stone as well as one would like."

"As always," Roy responded. "My family defers to your judgement. And Yasim, we need it today. Is that possible?"

"No, no. The band must be cast. The setting for such an exposed stone should be six prongs. This time of year, the holidays, it will take at least two weeks."

"We'll be back Saturday morning before noon. The wedding is New Year's Day."

"I'll manage, sir. Someone else will have to wait a bit longer."

Roy looked about as he was driving out of the city in holiday traffic. "It would be just our luck to run into Ginny and Zoya somewhere in this jam."

"Are they in the city?"

"Christ, Jack, they left right after we did this morning. They're probably having lunch at Bloomingdale's right now."

"Do you know anyone at Bloomingdale's?"

Roy laughed and turned onto the west side highway ramp heading north.

New Year's Day arrived, sunny and cold, with a blanket of fresh snow covering the ground. Ice crystals glistened from the trees and shrubs. Earlier in the week, Ginny had prevailed on Jack and Zoya to move to the guest quarters in the main house so it would be easier to coordinate the preparations. Everything went like clockwork. Ginny considered herself a damn good tactician, but she made it clear to everyone within earshot that when her sons finally married, she wanted Zoya by her side. "Nothing," she emphasized, "absolutely nothing slips through the cracks with that girl around. And she's always cool as a cucumber. I love her!"

Clare Hughes arrived early with his judicial robes over his arm. He insisted on taking tea with Zoya privately in the library, so he could "give her one last chance to recant and escape." Actually they shared their philosophies of love and commitment and its generational ties to those long gone but not forgotten. He proclaimed his respect for the honorable and decent man she was marrying and opined that she was a diamond in a universe of pebbles. He thanked her for giving a used up old man a place of honor at the banquet of her special day. They were both wiping away tears and smiling when they exited the room.

Ginny bustled Zoya upstairs to the master suite and instructed Jack and Roy to greet the guests who were beginning to arrive. Clare donned his robes and made himself and the groom a stiff drink. "Don't worry, Jack, this will be brief and dignified and devoid of any maudlin commentary from the pulpit."

The grandfather clock in the great room began its Westminster chime. In seconds it would be striking ten. Everyone gathered and waited for the bride to appear at the top of the grand staircase. The string quartet began to play and Ginny escorted Zoya down to her place next to Jack. Zoya wore a fitted knee length white Brussels lace dress and white satin pumps. Ginny had seated a delicate diamond and pearl encrusted tiara onto the crest of Zoya's cascading auburn hair. "Something borrowed," she explained.

With everyone in place at the bottom of the staircase, Clare now moved a few steps above so he might oversee the bride and groom. Clearing his throat, he looked about the room and began. "We are gathered here on the first day of the New Year, privileged to witness the union in marriage of Jack Stark and Zoya Chalkin. Who stands to offer this woman's hand marriage?"

"I, Lara Chalkin, stand with my daughter, Zoya, and to offer her hand in marriage." The Russian accent was deep, but clearly spoken. From an alcove off the great room, strode an elegantly dressed woman with her gloved hands extended to a stunned Zoya who had moved from Jack's side to greet her mother. They embraced and clung together rocking gently from side to side whispering softly to one another. Ginny was in tears. Jack was beaming with self-satisfaction. Roy gave him a congratulatory slap on the back. Someone found a box of tissues and was passing them around the room.

Finally, Clare cleared his throat loudly, and Zoya, accompanied by her mother, moved back to stand beside Jack. True to his words, Clare whisked through the obligatory exchange of vows. All the while Zoya and her mother held hands. Finally, Clare called for the ring and Jack produced the breathtaking diamond and slipped the band on her finger.

"I now pronounce you husband and wife." Jack and Zoya kissed long and lovingly. She squeezed his forearm tightly to let him know how she felt. When she turned again to embrace her mother, Clare reached down and shook Jack's outstretched hand. "I hope I married you to the right lady, Jack. I've had a few brandies and the two of them were standing pretty close together."

The string quartet was playing vigorously. People were mingling, lifting flutes of champagne, and crowding Jack and Zoya to congratulate them. Lara embraced Jack and whispered in Russian, "Zoya has not yet noticed the diamond, but her mother has." She gave him a kiss on the cheek and a wink.

Zoya pulled Jack aside for a brief moment. "How did you...?"

"I've been planning this with your mother for weeks. Her visit here was supposed to be my holiday present to you. But then the wedding took off and, well, it all seemed to work out. We'll talk later when everyone's gone."

The guests finally left and the caterers were nearly finished. Clare Hughes, Roy, Ginny, Jack, Zoya, and Lara sat together near the west side of the great room, gazing out at the falling snow and talking amongst themselves. Roy complimented Lara on her English.

"Ah," she responded, "English is the language of commerce, and this is my life today."

"But weren't you with the university?"

"Yes, but times have changed as you must know. Now I am partner with Finland furniture and wood products conglomerate. They would not be familiar to you, but very well known in Europe."

Jack, sensing her reluctance to go into further detail, interrupted. "Lara's an expert on forestry economics and wood products. She also attended the most distinguished music academy in the Soviet, the Juilliard of Russia, established by Catherine the Great."

Zoya clasped her mother's hand. "Mom, please play. It's been so long."

Lara raised her hands to demur, but Jack spoke up. "It is her wedding day."

Roy pointed to the grand piano. "It's in tune."

Lara Maximovna rose slowly, rubbing her hands as she approached the piano. She sat on the bench for a moment, thinking. Slowly her hands moved to the keyboard. Pausing for a second, she closed her eyes, raised her head slightly, and filled the room with Rachmaninoff. One with the music now, she enthralled her audience with an unbroken stream of medleys from great Russian composers. Finishing with a flourish, she turned and smiled at her daughter. Zoya rushed to her side and they embraced and kissed one other on both cheeks.

"My God," Clare spoke reverently. "We've actually done something wonderful today."

When the last of the guests had departed, Ginny looked at Jack and he nodded. "It's been a long day for all of us," she proclaimed. "I'm for a nap. Roy?"

Jack rose. "Zoya, why don't you change quickly and the three of us can retire to the cottage for a cup of hot tea."

Roy motioned towards the window. "It's still snowing pretty hard. Clare, why don't you leave your car and take the Land Rover? Jack and I will drive over tomorrow and we can have lunch at the Inn."

"I accept." Clare gave the bride a kiss on the cheek. "Where's my overcoat?"

Zoya and her mother were in the cottage kitchen tending to the tea and talking as Jack touched a match to the tinder and wood he'd laid in the fireplace. He smiled to himself as he listened to them conversing in Russian. It had been nearly six years since they had seen one another. The words were flowing so rapidly that he could only make out half of what they were saying. Soon they came in from the kitchen with the tea and a plate of heated scones and butter. They sat together on the couch facing the fire and sipping their tea in silence.

Zoya raised her left hand, so the light from the flames illuminated the facets of her diamond. "*Ochen krasivoe, Jack. Spaciba, moi daragoi muzh.* (So beautiful. Thank you, my darling husband)." She kept admiring the ring, turning it from side to side.

"Ah, I almost forgot." Jack reached into his shirt pocket and extracted a small box, handing it to Lara. She held it for a moment, then carefully opened the cover revealing a beautiful diamond and pearl lapel pin in a floral design. She carefully removed it from the box, holding it out for Zoya to see.

"Jack, I never expected …"

"To remember the day, dearest Lara," he said in Russian.

Lara turned to her daughter, and again in Russian. "You chose the right man."

Zoya extended her long graceful neck and with regal distain glanced impishly at Jack, as if waiting for his response.

"*Pravda* (that is true), and I now have two beautiful women in my life."

"Okay," Lara responded with a bright smile, raising her eyebrows coyly to Zoya, who, in turn, was beaming at Jack.

Later that evening as they were sliding beneath the goose down comforter in their bedroom, Jack asked, "Do you think your mother will be comfortable in the small bedroom downstairs?"

"Are you kidding?" Zoya cuddled close to him and laughed. "You put her in the clouds tonight."

"What about you?"

"Soon," she whispered. "But let's try not to make too much noise."

The ringing phone woke Jack the next morning. He groped about from under the comforter and finally found the receiver. It was Roy. "Jack, sorry to disturb your honeymoon, pal, but I've got to shoot down to the factory. Ginny's left for the city to pick up some flowers. Can you guys manage until tonight?"

"Hell yes, Roy. Go tend to business. We're fine. Ginny stocked this place with enough food for the Red Army. We've a lot of family catching up to do anyhow."

"Great. We're going up to Litchfield tonight for dinner. Ginny thought Zoya's mother would like that."

"We all will. Thanks. See you tonight."

Zoya was still buried out of sight under the comforter, oblivious to what was going on. Jack slipped out of bed. His moved quietly in his bare feet across the chilly hardwood floor and onto the even colder tile of the bathroom. He carefully shut the door and emerged moments later in pajama bottoms, wool socks, and a bathrobe. Downstairs, he found Lara sitting near the kitchen stove, sipping tea and reading the *New York Times*.

"*Dobroe utra, Jack.*" She poured him a cup of tea and smiled. "She still sleeps, yes?"

"Of course, you know her, Lara. She will sleep on for hours if you let her."

"Well, we will let her then, yes? It will give us time to talk."

"Good. How are things in Russia for you, really? I never felt free to talk with you openly on the phone."

"That is always wise. Things are fine, Jack, but everything there has changed."

"You know, Lara, the three of us could live very well together here in the United States. I'm sure we could arrange permanent resident status for you as a political refugee."

"I understand, but for now let me explain why I feel I must stay in St. Petersburg. You are a man of the world and you will appreciate the situation. First, the transition to democracy in Russia will fail. At this moment the country is in free fall. There is economic and political chaos, and the government is partnered with hooligans in high positions who will soon be obscenely wealthy. The oil, the gold, the weapons are already on the carving block. How do you say it in America, 'the low fruit' is being picked as we speak. The Finnish conglomerate that I spoke of is comprised of a group who wish to gain access to the lower timber in the regions surrounding Arkhangelsk, Murmansk, and Karelia. My years as professor and as Dean placed me in close partnering relationships with those regions. For decades, my family and then I developed trusted relationships on behalf of the Soviet government with every local official in charge of the forestry resources in those regions. Now those same officials are without a government, without a paycheck or an infrastructure, and no knowledge of how to develop free economy trade relations. I am uniquely qualified to do this. The Finns as well as the former Soviet officials there knew and trusted my father as they do me. I am, therefore, offered an opportunity to be the architect and a principal shareholder in a legitimate venture. However, I have no illusions. In time, the gangsters in Moscow will take notice, but they will be feasting on richer fare for years. When they finally move in to extort our operation I will cease being a part of it. I should have made a great deal of money by then, and I have close friends in France. I may even look to you for assistance in relocating here. Meanwhile do not expect to hear much of the details. It will only worry Zoya."

"I understand, Lara. Meanwhile, we will see you from time to time and speak with you often. *Udachi!* (Good luck)."

"*Spaciba,* Jack. Oh, look who is up." Zoya had just walked downstairs, rubbing the sleep from her eyes. She gave Jack a pat on the head, kissed her mother on the cheek, and accepted a cup of hot tea.

"*Skolko vremya* (What time is it)?"

"Zoya, we've been waiting for you to wake up so we can make plans." Jack stood and opened the pantry door and took out a box of Bisquick. "But first, how about some waffles and scrambled eggs?"

"You are indeed a lucky bride," Lara declared to her daughter. "You have a husband who cooks."

As Jack poured maple syrup on Lara's waffle, he asked, "How long can you stay?"

"Three more days only. Then I must return to Helsinki."

Zoya began to protest, but Jack spoke up. "Your mother has no choice, Zoya, so let's make the most of the time you have together. We'll have a farewell dinner with Ginny and Roy this evening up in Litchfield. It's a beautiful town. Tomorrow let's take the early train to Manhattan and check into a suite at the Hilton. The two of you can play together for two days while I spend some time at the Feingold Foundation offices. We'll coordinate our departures from JFK as best we can."

On the flight back to San Francisco, Zoya was quiet, reading, or gazing out the window... occasionally toying with her wedding ring. Jack simply held her hand or reminisced about their time in Connecticut and New York. He knew she missed her mother and now he understood firsthand some of the reasons why. Lara was a remarkable woman, who with her daughter, constituted the sole survivors of an extraordinary family. There was good reason why Zoya deported herself beyond her twenty-six years. The acorn, as they say, does not fall far from the oak tree.

At one point, Jack leaned close and whispered, "Do you feel married?"

"It's beginning to sink in," she responded with a smile and held up her diamond. She had been pleased and surprised by some of the airline hostesses who had admired the ring during meal service.

"Marta and Felipe will be overjoyed, but other than those two, let's keep to our plan as long as we can." Zoya nodded her head in agreement and grasped his arm tightly.

"I think your mother is happy about it, don't you?"

"Oh, Jack, she adores you. And she knows now that I am no longer alone over here. That has always preyed on her mind. Remember also, there hasn't been a real man in the family since my grandfather died."

Russian women, by necessity and culture, are a courageous lot. History has dealt them a series of wars and disruptions which decimated the male population and the women of mother Russia shouldered much of the burden for carrying on. Indeed, the eighth of March, for generations, has been celebrated as 'Women's Day' in Russia, and for good reason.

As they drove from the airport onto the Bayshore Freeway, Jack asked if Zoya wanted to come up to the ranch for a few days since classes did not resume for a week.

"Oh, I want to very much, but I need the time on campus to get a head start on the quarter. You know I'm trying to finish classes and be into my dissertation by September."

"My God, girl, I hear you say it, but it's hard to believe. If you pull it off, you're going to set some kind of record. Okay, I'll drop you off in Palo Alto and drive on to Nevada. There's plenty of work waiting for me there. I'll phone you tonight. Do you need money or anything, meanwhile?"

Zoya gave him a curious look. "I like the sound of that, but no, I'm fine."

"Okay." Jack smiled. "It's just that as your husband, aren't I supposed to take care of you?"

She scrunched up her mouth and punched him playfully in the shoulder. "I can take care of myself." She sat in silence for a moment. "But, now that I think about it, I kind of like the idea."

EIGHTEEN

"You missed the fun," Bonnie dropped a bulky draft of the January Trustees meeting agenda on his desk and plopped down in the chair facing him.

"What fun? You're not supposed to have any fun around here when I'm away."

"I know. That's why you always leave Dan Feldman in charge." The system General Counsel had a reputation for discouraging frivolity among his own legal staff and his sober no-nonsense demeanor extended to the entire central office when Jack left him in command. That's why he did it, but Bonnie never missed a chance to comment on the dull hiatus.

Apparently, there had been a bit of a dust up in the headquarters office over the holidays. One of the office's more senior female custodians had inadvertently walked in on Vice Chancellor for Academic Affairs, Doyle Hennigan, and his attractive new assistant apparently utilizing the couch for other than sitting. In her panicked rush to escape the embarrassing scene, the elderly woman had tripped and fallen. All hell had broken loose as Hennigan pulled on his shirt and stumbled to her assistance. By the time

Dan Feldman and Bonnie reached the scene, someone had called 911, Hennigan was sitting on the hall floor next to an unconscious custodian, and his assistant had locked herself in his private bathroom and refused to come out.

Bonnie was laughing as she painted the scene for Jack who was definitely not amused. "You should have been here," she went on, ignoring his obvious displeasure. "They finally had to call security to get the bathroom door open."

"No, this is one time I'm happy I was away from this nut factory," Jack fumed. "It's lucky someone didn't call Eyewitness News to come over. Jesus Christ, Bonnie, exactly when did this happen?"

"Late afternoon, Christmas Eve. Feldman had sent the office staff home early, and we were closing down for the next week until after New Year's. So the whole thing sort of happened in a vacuum, boss."

"So where are we on this? Is General Counsel around? Get him down here."

A few moments later, Dan Feldman walked through the door with Bonnie. Jack started to motion them over to the corner couches. "No, on second thought, let's stay away from couches for a while." Instead, he moved to the conference table, sat, and waited for them to begin.

"Okay. Break it down for me, Dan."

"Well, Jack, it's a lot better than it could have been."

"Yeah, I know that. Nobody was around. But what about the parties?"

Feldman looked down at a yellow legal pad. "Well, I followed up on things over the holiday break. First, the custodian checked out all right at the E.R. and lucky for us she isn't exactly sure what she saw precisely, but she knows she walked in on something inappropriate. I have her signed statement here. It's pretty benign. She kept lamenting that in three months she would have been retired and living with her daughter and grandchildren in Bakersfield, California. I told her to take an extra two week vacation on the house. We've got plenty of days in the pool to cover it."

"Good for you. So she won't be back for another week?"

"Ten days, actually."

"What about Hennigan and the assistant, what's her name?"

Bonnie spoke up. "Kelly Branson. She's been here about six months."

"They were up to something when the custodian walked in?"

"It would appear so, but she and Hennigan must have gotten their heads together pretty fast. They claim they were merely working on the couch amidst a mass of papers and files with their jackets and shoes kicked off for comfort."

Jack gave a long sigh and looked out the window for a moment. "But you could crack them; couldn't you, Dan?"

"The girl, probably. I don't know about Hennigan. I simply listened to their stories separately, took notes, and didn't respond. That's it up to now."

"Dan, if you called the custodian, Mrs. Uh ..."

"Ortega, boss. You gave her a 30-year service pin last September.

"Oh yeah, Carlie Ortega. I remember. Always cheerful... a really sweet woman. Listen Dam, you call her and indicate that with sick leave and vacation hours from the pool, there would be no need for her to return in order to retire three months from now. Answer any questions she has, honestly and with her interests in mind, but offer to get human resources to handle it for her if she likes the idea."

Feldman tapped his pencil on his pad for a few seconds. "I think she deserves that. You'll have to sign off on it, however."

"No problem. Now, about Miss Branson?"

"Mrs." Bonnie corrected.

"Oh, that's just great," Jack groaned. "Okay, then, with Mrs. Branson we do nothing, not a word, nothing. How does that play with you, Dan?"

"Barring evidence or official complaints, we really have no choice."

"Fine, that's fine. Cut the woman some slack. But Hennigan, that son-of-a-bitch doesn't get off that easy with me. He's an officer in my office and her boss, for Christ's sake!"

"There's not much we can do without a formal complaint," Dan counseled.

"Bonnie, step out and see if Hennigan is in his office."

"I don't have to, I saw him come in this morning."

"Step out anyway."

Bonnie left the room, and Jack waited until she closed the door. "Dan, can you draft a document on plain bond, no letterhead, that cites statutes and regulations on the books which address supervisor-subordinate parameters of behavior in the workplace. List stipulated violations, consequences, and anything else you want to throw in that's appropriate? See if you can get it all on one page."

"Sure."

"Good. Then please draft a standard, not for cause, letter to Hennigan informing him that his service as Vice Chancellor is terminated as provided for in the management agreement. Also include that he will be granted a leave of absence this spring semester in order to prepare for his return to his teaching duties in the School of Liberal Arts. Put in all the usual bullshit and expressions of appreciation for his service to the central office."

"Sounds like you're going to fire him."

"I'd like to. But under the circumstances, I'm going to have to settle for scaring the shit out of him. If I'm not satisfied, I'll walk away and the next day hand him the termination letter in your presence. But I'll give you a heads up if it comes to that. There will be some fall out over it. Some of the Trustees like him."

Feldman stood. "I better go to work. When do you want this?"

"Early this afternoon, if possible. And Danny, be certain that there can be no link made between the two documents. You create them personally, originals only, no copies, and nothing on your computer, understand?"

"So it's a bluff?"

Jack looked hard at his General Counsel. "It's never a bluff, Dan, when you're telling the truth. We'll talk about it later. Go."

Bonnie stepped in. "Do you want some lunch?"

"No, I'm not hungry. You go get something for yourself, and Bonnie, sorry about throwing you out like that."

"I know the drill by now, boss. I don't have privilege with Counsel. What I hear I can be forced to disclose." She put her hands on her hips. "So, are you going to fire the bastard?"

He waved her out of the room. "Go shopping or something. I'm going to read through this crap you piled on my desk. Game time is around two this afternoon, if you must know."

Precisely at two p.m., Bonnie ushered Dan Feldman into Jack's office. Jack was at the conference table which was covered with papers, and he waved Dan over. He stood next to Jack and, without comment, placed the two documents they had discussed in his outstretched hand. Jack carefully read through each piece and looked up at Dan. "They look all right to you?"

"Yeah, depends what you intend to do with them, however."

"Well," Jack said as he rose to his feet and crossed to his desk, "This termination letter is going in my safe drawer. You can witness my locking up the only copy, yes?"

"Right, and the sheet with the workplace regulations?"

"That's going in my inside coat pocket." Jack slipped on his suit jacket and made for the door.

"By the way, Jack," Dan called after him, "Mrs. Ortega took the offer. She thinks you're an angel. So thrilled, she didn't even mention Christmas afternoon. The paperwork should be completed by next week."

"You did a nice thing for a sweet old lady, Dan. Now I have to take a walk with that ass, Doyle Hennigan."

"As they say, that's why you get paid the big bucks."

"Vice Chancellor." Jack walked unannounced into Hennigan's office, startling him. "It's a sunny day, let's get some air."

Hennigan didn't move from his chair. "It's pretty cold out there, Jack."

"Grab your coat. Let's go through the park. This won't take long. We need to talk." Jack's tone was more of a command than a request.

It was indeed sunny, but they walked briskly and their breath created small clouds in the cold January air. Jack slowed a bit as they entered the park, and took the folded sheet from his coat pocket and passed it to Hennigan. Neither spoke a word as they paused for a moment while Hennigan read.

"Why are you giving me this?"

"Are you familiar with all of those regulations and statutes Doyle? Because until a short while ago, I only had a cursory acquaintance with the mass of public law that has accumulated around this issue. During the last 48 hours I've put myself through a crash course on the literature. It's quite a minefield unless one knows how and where to tread."

"Look, Jack, if this is about what happened two weeks ago, that old lady has ..."

"...your professional balls in the palm of her hand." Jack finished Hennigan's sentence for him. "I didn't make up the rules, Doyle, but they are right in front of you on that piece of paper. Actually we wouldn't even be having this conversation a generation ago. People could pretty much bang each other on the office desktop and all one had to worry about was a little office gossip. Now Doyle, I'm not freezing my ass out here in order to accuse you of anything. You and your assistant know what went on that day. Mrs. Ortega may think she saw something she didn't want to see at her age. But goddamn it, unless you can manage to live by the rules on that sheet, your family and this university will someday surely suffer the pain of seeing your face plastered on the front page of every news rag in Nevada."

"You won't have to worry about that ever happening, Jack."

"I know I won't Doyle. Because there's a document locked in my office drawer as we speak which will, with certainty, relieve me of that burden by ending your career as an officer in this university."

"My God, Jack." Hennigan sat back on a bench and placed his face in his hands.

"You tell me what to do with that document, Doyle. You tell me, because I'm a little tired of following the parade with a shovel and cleaning up the horse shit."

Hennigan was wiping his eyes. "Can't you just … leave it where it is?"

"That depends. You've got the rules now, right in your hand."

"Okay. Okay, I get the message, Jack. Thanks."

"Fine, let's walk back. I appreciate you understanding my dilemma, Doyle."

Jack slammed the door to his office, tossed his overcoat on the floor, and slumped into his chair, swiveling it toward the frost-crusted window overlooking the parking lot. Doyle Hennigan was backing his car out and heading for home. He heard the door open behind him.

"Not now, Bonnie." The door closed quietly.

"This fucking job." His eyes followed Hennigan's car as it turned the corner and disappeared from sight.

NINETEEN

Immediately after Duke Butrum was sworn in as Governor of the State of Nevada, he and Jack hammered out a plan for a full court press to bring new industry into the state. Jack would spend nearly all of his time accelerating and closing deals he had been working on with out-of-state corporations.

"Jack, I talked big during the campaign. Now folks need to see a big spike in corporate investment in the State. And it has to happen early in this administration."

Butrum splashed some bourbon into a four-finger glass and held it up.

Jack shook his head.

"Goddamn it, Chancellor, it's after six and everybody's left the building. I crave a drink and I don't drink alone... at least not yet." Jack accepted the glass as Butrum poured a double for himself and slouched into an oversized leather armchair.

"That chair looks familiar, Duke."

"It's from my old office at the bank. You don't think I'm going to drop this big ass in any of those." He gestured at the Spartan prison-made furnishings of his office.

"So, tell me, Jack, what you got lined up?"

"Well, Duke, Right now I'm spread from Toronto and Detroit to the west coast. California is the fat hog, especially Silicon Valley. The state's taxing the shit out of them, but what's worse, they drive those young CEOs crazy with their fucking regulations."

Butrum took a sip of bourbon. "Remind me about Detroit."

"Burroughs Corporation. I've been working on it for nearly a year."

"That's a big time outfit, Jack. Why us?"

"Let's just say, I made them an offer they can't refuse."

Butrum laughed. "You been hanging around that Las Vegas crowd too much. So this is a southern Nevada deal?"

"Nope. It's statewide. And it's not a relocation. It's a partnership. And I'm talking directly with the Chair of the Board and their new CEO."

"How'd you get that far up the ladder with a fortune 500? And what do you mean by partnership. What the hell do we have to offer an outfit like that?"

"Salvation. They're in a bit of trouble, but they don't know I know."

"You got somebody on the inside?"

Jack rose out of his chair. "Goddamn it, Duke, I do my fucking research. I dig like hell into every published report. And, you know, I talk to folks... experts in the field Hell, I'm the Chancellor of a tier-one University System. People who wouldn't normally gossip with just anyone, enjoy talking to me."

"So like I said, then, you got to someone on the inside"

Jack sighed. "Better than that... someone who used to be on the inside. You see, Duke, that's how I do it sometimes.

It's more work because it's indirect. But such folks are prone to spill their guts and, most important, it's legal. Then, when you're prepared, you go topside to see the boss for a courtesy visit, hit him with a proposition that touches a nerve, and before you know it, he's got you sitting in a roomful of vice-presidents."

"You still haven't told me what's up with Burroughs."

"They're a main-frame computer giant, Duke. Their product centrally drives a building's desk tops... in a world that's about to flip to free-standing desk tops. They've got at least a hundred million invested in a system they are about to bring public. It's called 'Socrates.' It's designed for educational institutions. The point is, events are about to overtake them. They've got to capture the attention of the media and the entire country so they can sell like hell and recoup that hundred mil before everything goes to free-standing."

"Okay, if you say so. But what the hell do we have to offer?"

"The whole goddamn state of Nevada. Duke, we've got fifty-two school districts, plus two big universities, five community colleges, and a medical school. What if they were all hooked up to 'Aristotle' and could interact with one another?"

"What would it cost us?"

"That's the point... nothing. What do they get? Exactly what they need. The biggest marketing coup in the business: An entire state as a Beta for their roll-out, which would be unprecedented news. But wait, there's a cherry on top that would close the deal and only our Board of Trustees can deliver."

"What the hell would that be?"

"They would become the first corporation in the world chosen to have their computer, instead of a human being selected by a tier one university system to occupy a professorial chair... Aristotle."

Butrum sat for moment, thinking. "Yeah, I can see that could be a massive media coup for them"

"Right when the need it most, Governor."

"Where does the deal stand right now?"

"Burroughs top people are sold. The annual meeting of their board is this September. We can make our move in executive session at the August meeting of the Board of Trustees. But Duke, you and I are the only two, other than the top tier at Burroughs, who know about this. I don't have to tell you that deals at this level are fragile. If somebody on our end even farts, everything goes out the window."

"Well, shit. I like it." Butrum rose and stretched. "You wore me out, Chancellor." He looked at his watch. "I got to take a piss and get on the road. I take it the California corporations are a piece of cake compared to Detroit."

"They are, mainly because of how California takes them for granted. In the next few months I'll be bringing at least a dozen young CEOs through the kitchen door of the mansion for breakfast with the Governor."

Much of the routine operations of the university system now fell mainly to General Counsel Dan Feldman and Vice Chancellor for Administration and Finance, Marion Macoby. Macoby, a native Nevadan, and Feldman worked well together. Neither had ego problems and both commanded the respect of the system presidents and the Trustees. Butrum involved Judi Chang in the plan, and she concurred with Jack's judgment that his activities be kept low profile. The Governor and the Chair of the Board of Trustees, as elected officials, would occupy the public arena as "partners in progress."

The January Board of Trustees meeting celebrated a milestone when Chair Judi Chang announced Chancellor Stark's recommendation that as a result of the outstanding work of the presidential screening committee, he was pleased to present Dr. Bryna Nagourney for consideration as the next president of the College of Medicine. The vote was swift and unanimous and both statewide and national media reported Nevada's appointment of the first woman to occupy the post in the state's history. After spending a respectable period of time at the reception that evening, Jack slipped away and drove directly to the ranch. It was nearly eleven on Friday evening when he finally pulled his car to a stop next to the main house. Lights were blazing from every room. Zoya ran out to greet him and leaped into his arms.

"I was worried about you," she said, as they walked arm in arm toward the house. "I made some of that Russian cabbage soup you like and Marta helped me bake fresh bread."

Jack took a three-minute shower and was back downstairs by the time she began ladling the soup.

"I don't know how you do that, Jack."

"Do what?" He asked, tearing off a piece of warm bread and kissing her on the back of the neck.

"Shower so quickly. Are you sure you washed everything?"

He swatted her gently on her tight bottomed jeans. "It's a Marine thing. Too bad you can't do it. We'd save a fortune in hot water."

"Not so." She shook her head and sat next to him. "Since Felipe put up those solar panels, we're swimming in hot water. I think he overdid it."

"It's my fault," Jack confessed, blowing gently across his soup. "I shouldn't have mentioned your thirty minute showers."

She thrust her chin regally upward. "Well, you keep saying you like my hair long. It's a lot of time and work to maintain."

"And worth every bit of it. Can we turn a few lights off, though, now that I'm home?"

Her expression softened. "Say that again."

"What?"

"Home. Say that again."

"*Doma. Ya doma* (Home, I'm home)."

"*Ya tozhe, moi muzh.* (Me too, my husband). When we're in this house together, I feel truly married. Is that strange?"

"Not at all, Zoyechka, I feel the same. When I'm away from you I have to pinch myself and think, she's my wife… all mine. But here on the ranch when we're together, I'm in paradise." He placed his arm around her shoulder. "What shall we do this weekend?"

"If I tell you, you won't make fun of me?"

"Of course not. What?"

"Well, I've been here since last night and today I spent hours walking through the house."

"Good, go on."

"I came up with some ideas."

"I'm way ahead of you. The closets are too small. The kitchen needs a serious redo. Then there's the bathrooms. We need a second, more spacious one near the master bedroom just for you. We should get some magazines."

"I bought some today!" She started to get up but he caught her arm.

"Tomorrow honey. It's late and I'm beat. I promise, we'll cover the floor with pictures and sketches over the next few weekends. By then, the weather will have eased. Then we should really walk the property and begin to get a feel for what it will take to bring it all back: our new house, the cottage, the beach, the pond, the orchard ... everything that can't be seen from the main road. In fact, I've already talked to Felipe about planting more trees and thorn bushes along the road to make it even more difficult to see or get in."

Zoya was listening intently. "The house, will it cost a lot to remodel?"

"Don't worry about that right now. We'll have fun doing the grand plan together. You focus on making it the perfect refuge. Okay?"

She embraced him, pressing her face into his chest. "Let's go upstairs to bed. You must be exhausted."

They climbed into bed from opposite sides and came close together under the down comforter. As always, Jack turned onto his left side and she curled against his back with one arm cradling his head and the other over his chest.

By noon the next day, the living room floor was covered with magazine clippings and crumpled sketch pad sheets. Zoya had Scotch taped pictures she had clipped to areas of the house marked for change. It was the beginning of a much more complex task than she had anticipated. But Jack made regular trips to the wine cellar and they had a great time doing it together. On Sunday afternoon, Marta brought over a platter of tamales and when she saw the chaos, she threw up her hands and left muttering to herself in Spanish.

"Let's drive one car," Jack suggested the following morning. "I'll drop you off at Stanford and pick you up again on Friday, about noon. I've got round-the-clock meetings in San Jose all week."

"Okay. Can I drive the Mercedes?"

"Sure, why not."

By the March meeting of the Board, Governor Butrum and Board Chair, Judi Chang had jointly announced more than a dozen relocation agreements or intents to do so by California corporations. The media cited a "new Camelot" between the Governor's office and the Board of Trustees. One political cartoon depicted a pudgy Butrum as Santa Claus flying his sleigh over the state dispensing packages bearing dollar signs.

April proved to be a bonanza month led by Softech Corporation's announcement that it was relocating its two hundred million dollar per annum South American and Pacific Rim distribution operation from Toronto, Canada, to Las Vegas. Jack had not only been cultivating this deal for the better part of a year, but he had become good friends with the corporation's young genius president, Adrian Durnan. Durnan had made it clear that a primary component to the deal rested on the issue of freeway access adjacent to the proposed site. Abe Glassman and his associates had expedited its acquisition by deciding to bypass the banks and take back the paper on the site purchase themselves. Duke Butrum leaned on the Division of Highways to move a planned on/off ramp 500 yards north on Highway 15. Once that was done, the deal closed like a steel trap.

Jack was having lunch with Abe Glassman in Las Vegas the day of the announcement. "What if Softech goes belly up, Abe? You know how mercurial that industry can be."

"Frankly, Jack, I wish them well. It's good for the town to have such enterprises. But if, God forbid, they don't make it, we'll have a nice freeway ramp on the property. We could build another casino, or a hospital. You shouldn't concern yourself with such things. The people who count know you spend a hell of lot of your life schmoozing with these corporate guys."

"They're just business people, Abe. I'm a University Chancellor, not a competitor. So the door is open. We sit, we talk. They share their problems and I listen. Sometimes I offer to help. That's when I bring them to the Governor's kitchen table and to you."

"What folks don't understand, is why you keep such a low profile?"

"It works better that way. Besides, that's the deal I made with Butrum when he was running for governor. He'll cover me with the Board of Trustees if they ever have a problem with it."

"Don't count on that."

Jack looked surprised. "What do you mean by that?"

"Paddy O'Banion."

"O'Banion. He hates my guts, so what?"

"He's been stalking you for months, using some low-life private investigator. The only reason I picked up on it is most of these guys also work for friends of mine."

"So, what's going to happen? You know I run clean."

"Yeah, well, you can bet he's got some Trustees beginning to believe the shit he's pedaling. You better take some notes on this stuff."

Jack finally stopped writing and looked up. "None of this bullshit will hold water, Abe. I can counter every allegation."

"Jack, you surprise me. You know how it works. It's an ambush. It's over in the blink of an eye. You won't get the time to put together a defense. You've got to be ready that moment or it will be all over and you'll be reading about yourself in the papers."

"So, he got to some of the Trustees. I'm not surprised."

"Well, Jack, what do you expect? They're really just politicians, and that includes Duke Butrum. I wouldn't expect much help from anybody on this. You know the first rule of politics."

"Yeah, self-preservation… throw the other guy under the bus."

"I could talk to some people, maybe head this off?"

Jack sat silent for a long moment. "Abe, I think I'll meet this one straight on. Just give me whatever else you have on who and what, and I'll be grateful for that."

"You just got most of it. Give me time to dig a little deeper. Call me in a week."

"Thanks Abe. You're a good friend."

"Mazal Tov, Jack."

On the flight home, Jack didn't even notice the turbulence. When he landed in Reno he phoned Ted Bitner's office before leaving the airport.

"He's waiting for you, Dr. Stark. Go right in."

"Jack." Bitner held out both hands. "Where the hell have you been keeping yourself? Congresswoman Carrie and I have been meaning to invite you over."

"I appreciate that, Ted. I haven't been around much lately. Hustling corporate deals has me on the road."

"So I've heard. And thanks for the referrals, by the way. They're great clients. We figured you were behind that."

"They ask for the best firm in northern Nevada, so I'm really doing them the favor. And, yeah, I have been spending a lot of time out of state… California mostly."

Jack leaned forward. "Listen, Ted, I'm here on another matter. I have a serious situation brewing and I'd like to retain you as personal counsel. But before you say yes, you should hear the details of what you'd be getting into."

"Jack, I don't give a damn what it is. The answer is a definite yes. You've got yourself a lawyer, buddy."

"Well then, get ready to have some fun on June fourth. When will you have time for me?"

"Right now is fine." He crossed from behind his desk and sat next to Jack. "What's so special about the fourth of June?"

"The Board of Trustees meets that day in Reno, and they'll make a move to fire me for cause."

An hour later, Bitner tossed aside his yellow legal pad, now filled with scribbled notes. "That's everything you have at this time?"

"Yeah, pretty much. I'll get more as this thing moves ahead."

"This is heavy shit, Jack. I need to know your source. Remember, we are privileged here."

"Abe Glassman."

"I didn't know you two were that close."

"We are, and the information is 24-karat, Ted."

"With his juice, he could probably head this off for you."

"Maybe, if I asked. But I really want to take this on. I'm tired of the bullshit, Ted. You, of all people, can understand that."

"Absolutely, but we need reliable information. Our preparation has to be flawless, which means there's a hell of a lot to do in the next six weeks. We're going to have to step on the gas and it could get expensive."

"War always is," Jack declared.

"Well, that's what this is. I can already smell the gunpowder. Why do you think I'm so damned excited? After what I've heard today, I want a piece of somebody, a big piece. Hell, Jack, I'm sorry you have to go through this bullshit. But as an old litigator, I've got to admit to being a bit pumped up. Leave your notes. Meet with me here tomorrow at about six. In and out the back entrance. From today forward, all written materials will be kept in this office. I'll have a skirmish plan sketched out and a to-do list for you. We have to do our work in the graveyard 'til June. If this is an ambush, we can assume O'Banion will need to keep certain Board members in the dark, especially Judi Chang. There's no love lost between those two. Meanwhile, don't change a thing in your routine. O'Banion will have his eye on you, not me. Do just what I ask you to do and feed me everything that comes your way. I'm in charge now, understood?"

Jack took the elevator to the garage level and walked up the back vehicle ramp into the alley. He maneuvered past a couple of dumpsters and entered Sally Wu's Golden Wok Café through the kitchen door. Ten minutes later he walked innocently out the front entrance carrying a take-out order. The match was in play. In the next six weeks he would spend countless hours with Bitner preparing to checkmate his nemesis.

TWENTY

At 9:55 on the morning of June fourth the hall in which the Board of Trustees would meet was bustling with the usual crowd of faculty and staff representatives from each of the system campuses, the print and electronic media, and a menagerie of general onlookers. Most were still clustered about the bountiful continental breakfast table. The presidents had begun to take their seats adjacent to the long semi-circle table reserved for the Trustees. Judi Chang was already seated in the Chair's center position. Jack, as Chancellor, sat to her immediate right. Both were reading a memorandum which Paddy O'Banion had just handed her. Chang caught the eye of General Counsel, Dan Feldman, and waved him over.

"O'Banion just dropped this on me." She looked up at Feldman who was scanning the typewritten sheet. "Did he consult you about this, Dan?"

"First time I've seen it, "Feldman said, "but he's pretty much laid it out. He's declared here that as a member of the executive committee and as chair of the personnel committee of the Board he intends to move for an emergency executive session to consider a personnel matter of serious consequence to the conduct of university business. He plans to make his request as soon as you call the general Board meeting to order.

Chang looked over at Jack. "Do you have any idea what this is all about?

"Me, probably," Jack answered. Chang appeared surprised and turned to Feldman who had overheard Jack's response.

"You should have given us a head's up," Feldman said.

"About what," Jack responded, "that O'Banion has been gunning for me. That's not exactly breading news." He turned to Chang. "This is an ambush, Judi. Don't give Paddy the chance to open his can of worms in front of this crowd. It will be slanderous and highly consequential to everyone at this table."

Chang looked at Feldman. "Any suggestions?"

Feldman thought for a moment. "I'd play it safe. Simply don't convene the general session. Instead, take the entire board as a 'committee of the whole' into emergency executive session and find out what this is all about. Once inside, you can force him to justify his request to the entire Board. At that point, we can weigh the merits and vote to go forward or adjourn. All I can say as your General Counsel is that if you let him ring the bell out here, you can never un-ring it."

Chang turned to Jack. "Chancellor?"

Jack sighed. "Your first obligation is to the Board, Judi. You heard General Counsel. Don't worry about me. I've been expecting something like this. So, from this moment on, I'll be represented by my own counsel who is in attendance today."

Jack turned to face Feldman. "Sorry, Danny."

"Oh, God." Judi Chang looked around the room. The clock read 10:17. A few people were still standing and visiting.

Drawing a deep breath, she slammed the gavel down four or five times and leaned into the microphone. "Ladies and gentlemen, it appears necessary that at some point during the scheduled course of business the Board will be obliged go into executive session. So as not to disrupt the continuity and conduct of the regular agenda, the Board will retire as a committee of the whole into executive session immediately and convene its general session at one P.M." Chang looked quickly to her right and left, rapped her gavel, stood, and led the board members to a private conference room.

As Jack moved toward the Board conference room he spotted Ted Bitner headed in his direction. He was accompanied by a younger attorney pushing a cart laden with equipment and file folders.

"Here we go," Bitner winked. "Hang on, Jack, it's going to be an E-ride."

Judi Chang wasted no time convening the meeting. "Trustee O'Banion, as Chai of the Personnel Committee, formally requests to bring an urgent personnel matter to the attention of the Board." Dan Feldman, who was seated to her right, slid a note to her.

"General Counsel has brought to my attention and the Board should be aware that Chancellor Stark will be represented by independent counsel. Trustee O'Banion, you may now state the reason for your request." Judi Chang turned to where O'Banion was sitting, smiling at Jack Stark. "Paddy, now would be a good time to state your business."

O'Banion opened a large folder and cleared his throat. "Madam Chair, I wish to bring to the Board's attention certain actions and activities of Chancellor..."

"Excuse me." Jack interrupted. "I believe that according to the by-laws, I have the right to have my own counsel present at this time."

Judi Chang glanced at Dan Feldman who confirmed Jack's request with a nod. Rising, Jack opened the conference room door and beckoned Bitner and his aide.

"Most of us know attorney Bitner." Chang smiled politely. "Welcome, sir, and congratulations on your recent election to the presidency of the American Trial Lawyers Association. Please be seated." Turning quickly to O'Banion, she nodded. "You may now continue, Paddy. You were about to bring our attention to certain actions and activities of Chancellor Stark, I believe?"

"That's correct." Paddy stood and placed his hand on a stack of folders which lay on the conference table. "They involve the following: unlawful use of university property; misappropriation of university property for the use of non-university parties; abandonment of duties and responsibilities as the chief executive officer of the university system; and finally, personal behavior and acts of moral turpitude which render him unfit to occupy a position of trust and respect as required by this body for its Chancellor."

The room was stone quiet for a moment. Judi Chang looked to her right and left. "The members of the Board acting as a committee of the whole have now heard Trustee O'Banion. Is there a motion to proceed with the emergency executive session?"

From the far end of the table, Trustee Corabelle Lee raised her hand. "So moved, we might as well hear the rest of it."

"I'll second, Judi." Delona Davenport, from North Las Vegas, waved her kerchief.

"Is there any discussion?" Again, Judi Chang looked around the table.

O'Banion spoke up. "Call for the vote."

"The chair has only one comment before proceeding." Chang looked long and hard at O'Banion. "Paddy, I trust you have carefully considered the path down which you now propose to take this board and its members. Now, all in favor indicate your vote by a show of hands. The record will note the yea votes of Trustees O'Banion, Washington, Case, Lee, Doty, Baldwin, Paladanos, and Colvin. Opposing, none. Abstaining: Trustee Chang, Keeler, and Seeley. The motion carries. Trustee O'Banion now has the floor."

O'Banion began passing three ring binders to each member of the Board. "If you will note when you open your binder ..."

"Excuse me, Madam Chair." Ted Bitner had risen to his feet. "It should be formally entered in the record that I am attorney Ted J. Bitner, acting as counsel for Dr. Stark in this matter. With me as co-counsel is Mr. Jay Boyton." Bit smiled and acknowledged a number of the Board members with whom he was acquainted. "Would the Chair be so kind as to instruct Mr. O'Banion to supply me with a copy of this and any other documents he intends to introduce regarding this matter."

Chang nodded and Paddy slid a copy of the binder across the table to Bitner, who handed it back to his co-counsel. O'Banion then resumed speaking. "There are four tabulated sections which address my general allegations with greater specificity and accompanying probative material."

Paddy proceeded to take the Board through each section. The first tab was labeled "Mercedes Sedan, Nevada License JUK427." He proceeded to identify the vehicle as that assigned to Jack Stark in his capacity of Chancellor. He recited the University Code provisions for the use of said vehicle and listed more than a score of specific incidents of off-calendar state travel from mid-October of last year through May of this year which allegedly exceeded university guidelines.

The second tab was titled "BMW Coupe, Nevada License AKC826." O'Banion offered supporting documentation that the vehicle had been purchased and assigned to Chancellor Stark by the Board until replaced by the Mercedes Sedan cited in tab #1. O'Banion then directed the Board to written reports by a private investigator accompanied with photographs, that the BMW was in the possession of, and driven by a Miss Zoya Chalkin. He also directed the Board's attention to reports and photographs of Miss Chalkin driving the Mercedes Sedan, Nevada License JUK427.

The materials contained under Tab #3 were offered in support of O'Banion's charge or abandonment of administrative duties and responsibilities by the Chancellor. Over a six-month period, he cited Jack as absent from his office, usually out of state, for an average of 16 work days per month, constituting de facto abandonment of his duties and responsibilities as CEO of the university system.

The fourth section of O'Banion's report was the most bulky. Its contents were offered in support of the "moral turpitude" allegation, citing personal behavior which rendered Stark unsuitable to occupy the post of Chancellor. Shaking his finger in Jack's direction, O'Banion made an impassioned charge that Jack was maintaining an out of state "love nest" where he consorted on a regular basis with a female student from Stanford University. Moreover, said female student not only had possession of the BMW coupe as her personal vehicle and on numerous occasions had been allowed to drive the Chancellor's Mercedes. The allegations were supported by more than a dozen eight-by-ten, dated photographs attached to written reports.

"Based upon this evidence," O'Banion concluded, "I strongly suggest that the Board has no other course but to terminate Dr. Stark's contract immediately, and I hereby call for a motion to that effect."

Judi Chang spoke up. "Wait a moment, Paddy. With all due respect to what you have brought to our attention, I am still Chair of this body. Dr. Stark, you now have the opportunity to address the Board regarding the allegations Trustee O'Banion has presented."

Ted Bitner rose. "If you please, Madam Chair, by right of representation as Dr. Stark's counsel in this matter, I would like adequate time to speak on my client's behalf."

Judy Chang looked at Dan Feldman, who nodded. "Please, Mr. Bitner, proceed."

Bitner moved to the conference table so that he might stand closer to the seated Board members. "I will now present evidence which will satisfy the Board that Trustee O'Banion's allegations are not only without foundation, but motivated by a personal vendetta against Chancellor Stark. Why else would he pursue such an extensive and costly investigation without prior consultation with the Chair of this Board or with your own General Counsel, Mr. Feldman?"

As he spoke, Bitner's associate had quickly set up a projection unit and taken a seat next to where Bitner was standing.

"Before I begin, my client has requested that I convey his disappointment at the circumstances that have brought us to this point today. I can personally attest to Dr. Stark's respect for past and present members of this Board. Having declared this, it should also be clear to all present that the charges made by Trustee O'Banion place my client and this entire board in an unavoidable adversarial position."

Bitner glanced briefly at Jack, and turned again to the Trustees.

"First, as to the misappropriation of university property, to wit, the BMW coupe which was not owned, but rather leased to the University System by Craig BMW of Reno for the Chancellor's use. My colleague, Mr. Boyton has now projected on the far wall a purchase agreement dated October eleventh of last year between Craig BMW of Reno, and R. J. Pullen of Auto Court, Inc. Thus we have a legal sale of private property subsequently re-sold, as this second slide shows, to a Jack Stark for the *Blue Book* price of $11,950 and registered in the State of California."

"Next, if you will, Mr. Boyton. On the screen you see a marriage license issued on December 28, of last year in State of Connecticut as well as a certificate of marriage signed on January 1 of this year by none other than Connecticut State Supreme Court Chief Justice Clarence Hughes, one of the most respected jurists in the nation. Mr. Boyton, as you can see, is providing your General Counsel with certified copies of all documents as we progress."

Bitner paused for a moment. "So, to sum up thus far, it appears that Chancellor Stark purchased a used car from a California auto dealer and said vehicle is currently registered in that state. Moreover, the so-called 'love nest' referred to by Mr. O'Banion is in fact the Stark family ranch where Dr. Stark and his wife, allow me to repeat, his wife, spend occasional weekends together. Next, as to Chancellor Stark's current vehicle, no existing guidelines preclude such use of his personally assigned vehicle. A spouse is not excluded from driving said vehicle, especially I would submit, when in this case her husband is occupying the passenger seat as Trustee O'Banion's photographs show. At this point, I would hope that the Trustees might concur that the first two allegations made by Mr. O'Banion's shoddy investigations have been satisfactorily resolved. However, since we are on the subject of photographs and private investigations, I would like to raise the specter of invasion of privacy and trespass by an agent of this Board. Mr. O'Banion has only set before you a partial inventory of his malfeasance."

Bitner threw a stack of eight-by-ten photos on the table. "Please feel free to pass these among yourselves, and return them to your General Counsel for his records. They were taken, as were the photos contained in Mr. O'Banion's binder of accusations against Dr. Stark, by a private detective in Trustee O'Banion's employ and have come into our possession. You see there, in black and white, the private moments of a married couple in their own home. I also direct your attention the photograph of husband and wife seated together on the porch swing, enjoying the twilight with every expectation that they are not being illegally photographed. I have withheld more intimate scenes between man and wife for obvious reasons or in the event my client decides to pursue this matter in a court of law."

O'Banion leaped to his feet. "I've never seen these before in my life!" He threw a number of the photos back at Bitner. "I have nothing to do with these."

Bitner held up his hand for calm. "Mr. O'Banion, all these illegal and reprehensible photos were taken at your directive and you know it. However, we can take photos as well and legally since they were taken on Dr. and Mrs. Stark's property with their permission." He motioned to Boyton, who projected another photo on the wall. "Do you recognize this man?"

"Hell, no." O'Banion growled. "Who is he?"

"His name is Benjamin Brumefeld, known to his friends as 'Benny the Broom'. You should be acquainted. You chose to legally retain his services. He's shown here holding a camera and standing near the corner of a tool shed on the Stark family property, which by the way is posted. I have another photo in my hand of a van parked on Plumtree Road which abuts the Stark property. The Nevada license plate in this enlargement reads quite clearly. The vehicle is registered to a Benjamin Brumefeld. Here, let me expand the image of Mr. Brumefeld standing by the shed. Do you recognize him now, Mr. O'Banion?"

"I told you, I don't know the son-of-a-bitch."

"I would direct the Board's attention to Mr. Brumefeld's open jacket. What do you see there, Counsel Feldman, since Trustee O'Banion is having so much trouble with his eyesight this morning?"

"It appears to be a shoulder holster with a pistol of some sort."

"Precisely what our experts concluded. A Berretta 92, semi-automatic 9mm, for which Mr. Brumefeld holds a license to carry as a private detective in Nevada, not California."

Bitner gave a signal to Boyton who passed another document to Dan Feldman. General Counsel has just been handed a sworn statement from Mr. Brumefeld who is facing charges for illegally carrying a concealed firearm in the State of California. Attached to the statement, counsel will find a copy of a retainer check from Trustee O'Banion made out to B. Brumefeld as well as copies of numerous dated invoices, some stamped overdue, to one, Padrick O'Banion, for services rendered by B & C Brumefeld, Inc., a Nevada corporation. You know the law. Brumefeld was acting as an agent retained by the Chair of the Personnel Committee of this Board of Trustees in a matter involving a direct-report employee of this Board. Whether or not this body formally approved those actions is irrelevant. Trustee O'Banion is culpable and through his actions, so is this Board."

"That's arguable, Bit," Feldman responded.

"That's why they have courts of law, Dan. We feel pretty good about it, especially since we are prepared to prove in court that other members of this Board had prior knowledge of the material distributed by Trustee O'Banion today; which, by the way, raises the issue of conspiracy as well as the question of whether the Nevada open meeting law was violated. I believe the penalty for the latter transgression is removal from office and a monetary fine. Conspiracy to commit a felony is another matter, but all that will surely come out during discovery and sworn depositions which would be of interest to the State Attorney General's office."

Bitner pointed his finger at O'Banion. "Paddy, you still owe Benny a lot of money. We have both the physical evidence as well as Brumefeld's sworn statement that he was in your employ and under the clear impression that he was acting at your direction as chair of the personnel committee of this Board. The photos I displayed to the Board today are only a sample of what will be entered into evidence when we go before a jury. One usually gets exactly what one pays for, Mr. O'Banion. According to Mr. Brumefeld, you still owe him a great deal of money. And he is now in need of the best representation money can buy in California."

A number of Board members who had voted "yea" on Paddy's motion to proceed, were visibly agitated. Tuck Doty growled, "What the hell have you gotten us into here, Paddy?"

"Don't get on my ass, Tuck," Paddy spat back. "You were damned eager to see all the dirt on Stark."

Judi Chang rapped the gavel for order. "Mr. Bitner, if you could wrap up soon we would appreciate it."

"I'll move it along, Madam Chair." Bitner reached for a stack of stapled sheets. "As to the allegation of abandonment of assigned duties, if you read this codicil to Dr. Stark's contract signed by the Chair of the Board last October, you will see that his subsequent activities outside the state of Nevada were not only directed by the terms of this agreement, but are consistent with his appointment by the Governor as Nevada Ambassador for Economic Development. You will find that document therein, as well as Dr. Stark's record of ongoing contacts with Silicon Valley corporations, eleven of which have already declared various forms of relocation plans directly benefiting the state and the university system. Also I have included communications from numerous corporate CEOs written to the Governor and the Chair of this Board, all lauding Dr. Stark's efforts. I submit to you that the matter of Dr. Stark's fulfilling his duties as Chancellor is moot at this point."

Bitner turned to look at Jack who nodded his head. "Finally, and this is a most regrettable step, but I must protect the interests of my client. University Counsel is well aware that, despite our being in executive session, past history warrants that this committee's business will leak into the general population before the sun sets today."

Dan Feldman rose from his chair. "Ted, that's pure speculation and you know it."

"We won't argue that here, Dan." Bitner reached for a file folder. "However, we are in possession of evidence which proves that more than a few people at this table had prior knowledge of the accusations and physical materials that Trustee O'Banion formally presented this morning. Such constitutes publication under the laws of slander and defamation. I have assured my client that I must and will take steps to make him whole through either litigation or a significant compensatory settlement by this Board. In short, ladies and gentleman, you cannot get off lightly on what has taken place over the last several months and today. Dr. Stark's career has been compromised and his family's privacy invaded by an armed agent of a member of the executive committee of this Board. I assure you that the consequences of these reckless acts by Trustee O'Banion and other members of this Board will not be borne solely by Dr. Stark and his family."

"Nice speech, counselor," Dan Feldman responded calmly. "Be reminded, however, that you are not the only attorney in this room."

Bitner bowed his head for a moment, and drew a deep breath. "True. And I am relying on such and other rational heads to grasp the lengths to which we are prepared to go if we leave this meeting without an acceptable resolution. You all know me, some personally and some by reputation only. Be assured that once in public trial I will have no choice but to discredit this body before the court, the jury, the media, and inevitably before the voters of the State of Nevada. To that end we will first seek to establish an historical pattern of errant conduct by this elected body of which my client is only the most recent victim. In the spirit of early discovery I am willing to offer you a small sample of what we are reluctant to bring to bear in order to accomplish this."

"He's bluffing," Corabelle snapped. A number of others mumbled something about, "What the hell, let's hear it."

"Ten minutes, Mr. Bitner, not a minute more." Judi Chang was weary, but still in charge.

Bitner placed a small tape recorder on the table. "Last year, just after assuming the Chair of the Board, Mr. O'Banion met with Dr. Stark for lunch at an off strip hotel in Las Vegas to go over the Board Agenda. Chairman O'Banion has just requested the loan of Chancellor Stark's hotel room." Bitner pressed the 'play' button. O'Banion's voice came on first. "I only need it for an hour or so. Your room will do fine." Jack's voice follows, objecting to O'Banion's request. O'Banion persists. "Don't you like being Chancellor? Maybe I should just fire you and ..."

"You taped me, you son-of-a-bitch!" O'Banion was half out of his chair, glaring at Jack Stark.

Bitner placed a restraining hand on Jack's shoulder. "Oh please, Paddy, the fact is, you taped that meeting between yourself and Dr. Stark. The strip we just played came into our possession only recently. Besides, we would argue that a meeting between the Chancellor and you as the new Chair of the Board to review the agenda was official university business and arguably in the public venue. This is offered to the Board only to clear any doubts about Trustee O'Banion's motives. This obsession, of course, is what got us into this mess."

"This is bullshit," O'Banion growled and sat back in his chair. Bitner extracted the tape and passed it across the table to Dan Feldman.

"This tape I'm giving to General Counsel is a copy of official meetings of this Board. They are, as such, public property under the open meeting laws of the Stat of Nevada.

The recording contains numerous examples of Board members' comments to one another made during officially convened public meetings. The nature of these exchanges clearly indicates that they were not intended for the ears of the general public in attendance. Ladies and gentleman, a hand cupped over a microphone or stepping a bit out of range no longer offers us any assurance of privacy. With modern sound enhancement technology, voices are identifiable and what is said is captured for the public record. Taken individually, such covert exchanges during a legally convened meeting can prove embarrassing at best. Viewed collectively over the years, they may suggest a pattern of arrogant disrespect of the public trust."

The room was silent. Judi Chang glanced at her watch. "Mr. Bitner, you have three more minutes."

Bitner nodded, accepted some materials Boyton had extracted from the black file cabinet, and proceeded to rapidly project a series of documents on the conference room screen. "Ah, here's a good one: an invoice to a campus charitable foundation: $19,500 for a Lear Jet rental flight to the Final Four playoffs. The flight manifest includes two individuals sitting here with us today."

Boyton was in the process of passing additional sheets to Bitner who instead shook his head and turned to address Judi Change. "Madam Chair, members of the Board, you have been generous with your time. In return, I endeavored to honestly present the jeopardous position which we find ourselves in as a result of Trustee O'Banion's reckless actions." Bitner paused and reaching back, patted the bulky, black metal cabinet sitting on a four wheel cart. "By the way, if you have never heard of a 'doomsday file', well, this is what one looks like."

Dan Feldman leaned forward and pointing at the metal cabinet addressed the members of the Board. "Don't be intimidated by this show. Mr. Bitner knows as well as I that he will never be allowed to bring all this irrelevant trash before a court of law."

"Well, Dan, for purposes of today's discussion only, let's just stipulate to that." Bitner's voice took on an icy tone. "Frankly, I would never risk exhausting a jury by trying to get it all admitted. A selective fraction will be ample for my purposes." Bitner again placed his hand on the metal file cabinet. "All this trash, as you so aptly call it, is the refuse of past and recent activities and what is not admitted at trial is still grist for the court of public opinion." Bitner paused, as if to emphasize a point. "You know my record, Dan, and so do the members of this Board. I do not bluff. Please be aware that I am not only prepared, but eager to litigate this matter with the utmost vigor."

Bitner nodded to Boyton who rose and placed a sealed envelope directly into the hand of Dan Feldman, and quickly distributed similar envelopes into the hands of each Trustee.

"What's happening now?" Judi Chang leaned close to Feldman.

"We're being served. It's a clear message that they are prepared to go to court."

Judi Chang pointed the unopened envelope at Ted Bitner. "Are you indicating that your client is determined to go public with this?"

"With all due respect, Madam Chair, you and I both know that the moment this meeting adjourns everything that has been discussed in here will be blabbed by certain members of this Board… unless there are serious consequences."

"Jesus Christ, I'm being sued for five million dollars!" Members of the Board were each reading the letter of intent and service documents they had been handed.

"So am I, and I voted to abstain!"

Judi Chang rapped her gavel over and over until the din had subsided. "Is that it, Mr. Bitner?"

"Madam Chair, if we are to harbor any hope for a discreet resolution of this matter, the Board and its individual members must be confronted with the judgment we intend to seek upon departing this room today."

"I would say, Mr. Bitner," Chang had opened her envelope, "that a thirty-five million dollar claim against the university system and five million against each of us individually is patently unreasonable."

"Unfortunately, not so, Madam Chair," Bitner responded. "A review of recent awards in such cases indicates otherwise." He handed a file folder to Dan Feldman. "I agree that a full scale battle in Nevada Superior Court would be pyric, but my client at this point has nothing to lose. The Board, on the other hand, stands to lose not just treasure and reputation, but face impeachment from office as well."

Judi Chang looked about the room now filled with agitated discussions between individual Board members. "Mr. Bitner, I think we've heard more than enough. If General Counsel has no objections, I will ask you and Dr. Stark to leave the room, but remain in the building, while we discuss this among ourselves."

"May I remind the Chair of the concerns expressed regarding…"

"You were quite explicit, Mr. Bitner. General Counsel is nodding his head as well. But right now, we need to talk!"

Once outside, they stood quietly for a moment. Boyton volunteered to fetch some coffee and walked away. Jack turned to Bitner. "You really scared the shit out of them."

"I'll be honest with you Jack. I want to take them to court so badly I can taste it. I can't remember the last time my blood was up like this."

The door opened suddenly, surprising them. Dan Feldman stepped out and walked over to Jack and Ted Bitner. "They think you have a settlement offer already in mind. They want to hear it. Come in reasonable and it'll be over." He turned and re-entered the conference room.

Jack looked at Bitner. "Time to make a deal, Bit."

"Okay, Jack, but you're giving up a lot."

TWENTY ONE

Late afternoon shadows blanketed the landscape by the time Jack pulled into the gravel driveway. Marta, Felipe, and Zoya were still working in the garden. He came to a slow stop and stepped out of the Mercedes. Zoya handed her hoe to Felipe and ran toward his car. Her cheek was smudged with soil and she had a red bandana tied about her head. She pulled off her gloves and stuffed them in the pocket of her jeans.

"I'm all dirty," she protested, as Jack lifted her from the ground and swung her in a circle. They kissed. "Your beautiful blue suit... be careful."

"What are you doing over there?" Jack waved at Marta and Felipe.

"Weeding the peppers. Planting a new row of saffron. But Jack, you didn't call. I'm bursting to know what happened. You tried to play things down, but I knew that today was, what do they call it... the shoot-out at the OK Corral?"

"You smell good." Jack buried his face in her neck.

She helped him off with his coat and vest. "And you smell like a man."

After a few words with Marta and Felipe, they walked, arms entwined, toward the main house. Once inside, he ducked into the side porch and stripped.

"Don't change," he shouted. "Just wash your face and grab some bread, cheese, and salami." He came out wearing battered jeans and a denim shirt not yet buttoned. "Let's walk down to the beach and sit in the sand with our feet in the river. I'll tell you the entire story, blow by blow."

The sun was setting as Jack uncorked the second zinfandel. Unable to locate his glass, he drank from the bottle.

Zoya shook her head at his offer of a refill. "So, it sounds like Ted Bitner has them by the throat. Are we off to court, then?"

"We could be, but I decided to go another way."

She smiled and cocked her head. "Too many friendships?"

"No, God no. This was all business. There's more than one way to skin a cat, Zoya."

She made a face. "Another one of your barbarous Yankee sayings?"

"Just let me finish."

"Sorry." She settled back in the sand.

"First rule of battle, Zoya: know your adversary. High profile political entities, like the Board of Trustees, abhor the embarrassing prospect of large lump sum public settlements. Instead I offered to let them kick the can down the road, so to speak, and they jumped at it."

She nodded, waiting for him to go on.

"So, here's the deal. As of today, I'm on paid sabbatical. We've earned a rest and we can use the time to remodel the house. At the fall meeting of the Board I will present an eight-figure endowment gift that I've kept on ice for months. When the applause subsides I will publicly announce my decision to retire. The Board will reluctantly accept and move to bestow upon me the lifetime title of Chancellor Emeritus. I will thank them. One hour earlier that same day, in Executive Session, they will have settled upon me a lifetime retirement stipend of my current salary with full benefits, adjusted 7% annually for inflation. For this, I will not thank them."

"I want to be there!"

Jack laughed. "At the open session, absolutely. I'd love to see their faces when Judi Chang introduces you to the crowd. But wait, there's more. A life insurance funded trust is now being drafted by Biter's law firm that guarantees a $10,000,000 payout to our estate upon my death."

Zoya frowned. "I will never speak of this, Jack."

"If course not, Zoyechka." He cupped her face in his hands and kissed her forehead. "But that day will come."

She turned away.

"That's about it, babe. Bitner's legal fees and all costs will be paid by the Board. And there's an all-parties non-disclosure agreement which heavily favors us financially if ever breached."

"Then it's over, yes? I thought your attorney was determined to drag them through court."

"He was, and after a few years of litigation we probably would have ended up with a lot more, but I want us out now, Zoya, and this does it."

She embraced him. "And we'll have all summer together."

"Oh yeah, and there's this." Jack pulled a folded envelope from his pocket and placed it in her hand. It was addressed to Mrs. Zoya Chalkin Stark. Zoya gave Jack a puzzled glance and proceeded to extract what appeared to be an official bank draft. She studied it for a moment in the dying light. "*Bozhe moi!*" She leapt to her feet. "So much! Jack, how...?"

"You wouldn't think it's too much if you'd seen the pictures that private detective took of you. Thank Ted Bitner. He made it clear to the Board that settling with me did not relieve them from liability for eight separate violations against your privacy. And it would be a public relations nightmare for them. They were eager to settle. You have to sign a release, of course, and the money is yours." Jack paused and smiled. "Unless you don't think it's enough?"

"My God, Jack." She ran to the crest of the levy and waved her arm in a sweeping arc. "We can..."

"...restore the entire ranch, Zoya. You can remodel your house and the old cottage from top to bottom; even build a lavish bungalow near the beach for your mother. We can do anything we want and, speaking of that, I've been thinking..."

"About what?"

"Well, I've been getting job offers from all over the country. Frankly, I haven't wanted to bother you with any of it."

"You don't sound very enthusiastic."

"I'm not. I don't want us harnessed to another organization with a bundle of problems. When you and I are together we enjoy a deep, abiding sense of bliss. That other world is always there for us, Zoya, but it can't be allowed to intrude on this thing we have."

Zoya sat quietly for a moment. "Shangri-La."

They began walking hand in hand through the vineyard in the moonlight.

"I still have my doctoral work to complete."

"And I'm on the Feingold Foundation Board." Jack laughed. "Wait 'til they meet you."

"Well, you like Stanford, and I love New York." She tightened her grip on his hand. "It shouldn't be a problem. In fact it could be fun."

"Yeah, the more that I think about it... you with that high powered doctorate, plus our contacts, and combined language skills. Hell, we could be a high profile team, even global. That can add up to serious money for small pieces of our time."

"Uh huh." Zoya responded, as they climbed the porch stairs to the balcony.

"And this," Jack swept his arm in an arc, "will always be our home, our refuge."

Zoya gently placed a finger to his lips. "You're still such a boy, so excited about winning one fight, that you can hardly wait for the next." She leaned forward and kissed him on the cheek. "*Moi geroy* (My hero). It all sounds very exciting, but the night is upon us. I think we should go up."

A full moon hung outside the bay window, illuminating the great bed and the two figures lying quietly amidst the rumpled sheets. Zoya was cradled in Jack's arms.

"So, Zoyechka, what do you think about our plan?"

"I think it's brilliant." She whispered, her hand slowly stroking his chest. "We'll talk more about it in the morning. Turn over now so I can hug you."

Thus entwined, they fell fast asleep, together in the moonlight.

www.ingramcontent.com/pod-product-compliance
Lightning Source LLC
Chambersburg PA
CBHW031110030726
47496CB00002BA/480